REALITY BLURRED

AVEN ELLIS

Reality Blurred

Copyright © 2018 Aven Ellis

Cover Design by Becky Monson

Formatting by AB Formatting

BOOKS BY AVEN ELLIS

If you enjoyed this book, you might enjoy my other romantic comedies:

Connectivity

Surviving The Rachel

Chronicles of a Lincoln Park Fashionista

Waiting For Prince Harry (Dallas Demons #1)

The Definition of Icing (Dallas Demons #2)

Breakout (Dallas Demons #3)

On Thin Ice (Dallas Demons #4)

Playing Defense (Dallas Demons #5)

The Aubrey Rules (Chicago on Ice #1)

Trivial Pursuits (Chicago on Ice #2)

Save the Date (Chicago on Ice #3)

Hold the Lift (Rinkside in the Rockies Novella)

Sugar and Ice (Rinkside in the Rockies #1)

Squeeze Play (Washington DC Soaring Eagles #1)

CONNECT WITH AVEN

Amazon Author Page
Website
Facebook Page
Twitter
Facebook Reader Group

ACKNOWLEDGMENTS

Thank you to CeCe Carroll, you once again did a brilliant job copy editing this book. Thank you for your dedication and guidance in taking my work to the next level.

Thank you to Paula and Joanne for proofreading and polishing my work.

To Alexandra, my assistant. Thank you for being you on a daily basis and always being my calming center.

To the SJFC-thank you for reading, debating, and supporting every step I take. I love you girls to pieces!

Thank you to my Beta Baes. Thank you for always giving me what I need, and not just with the writing process. Thank you for reassurance, for reading, for being a part of my life every day. None of these books happen without you.

Amanda and Claudia-Your love, friendship and support is always a given. I love you so much!

Alexa Aston, thank you for always providing your thoughts and your feedback. You are the best.

To my Twinnie, Holly Martin- Thank you for always reading my work, offering suggestions, helping me be a better author. But it is your friendship I value about all else. I love you.

Thank you to Jennifer and Mary, who run the Aven Ellis reader group on Facebook (Kate, Skates, and Coffee Cakes.) You both are such amazing women with such a passion for books. I love you ladies so much!

The Aven Ellis ARC Team-thank you for wanting to read my words and review my books. I'm so lucky to have such an amazing group of readers with me, no matter what adventure we take!

A big huge thank you to Maryline Van Puymbrouck, my Belgian native, for all your help with creating Maxime. You brought him to life.

Kayla, thank you for the insightful read and for helping me find solutions to problems. You are the best!

I'm also grateful to Janel Amador for Maxime's translations. Thank you for all the back and forth to get it just right!

Finally, thank you to all my readers. None of this happens without your support. I'm truly blessed.

PROLOGUE

Brussels, Belgium
The previous July

I ABSENTLY GLANCE AROUND THE CAFÉ, WORKING MY long, honey-blonde locks into a single braid. It's a habit of mine, something I do when I'm anxious. I work the strands in a rhythmic motion—up, over, underneath—as I sit on a terrace surrounded by leafy green trees and vibrant blooming flowers. It's a beautiful summer evening in Brussels, and the surrounding tables are filled with people talking, reading, working on laptops, or typing on phones.

Nobody has noticed me. Not one cell phone has been aimed in my direction.

I've never been so grateful for anonymity in my entire life.

"*Votre café au lait,*" the server says, interrupting my thoughts as she places a white ceramic mug in front of me.

"*Merci beaucoup,*" I murmur, grateful that my photographic memory can still recall greeting lessons from my high school French class.

If only it could forget everything else.

She smiles and leaves me alone.

I glance down at my latte and see the foam has been artfully designed into a beautiful heart.

My throat grows thick at the sight of it. If this latte art were to reflect my life right now, that heart wouldn't be perfect.

It would be in fragments all over the cup.

A chill runs through me even though the evening is warm. I wrap my hands around the mug, trying to regain some warmth.

If you had told me last March that I'd be sitting alone in a café in Brussels, regretting every decision I made over the past six months, I would have laughed. I, Skye Reeve, would have smiled and said, "Impossible." Fate had led me in the right direction. Okay, maybe fate with the help of my agent, Charlotte, but I was meant to go on *Is It Love?* and meet Tom Broaden on a reality dating show. The plan was to get onto the show, appear for a few episodes as the fresh-faced California girl who wanted to open a cupcake shop—

I cringe. Anxiety rushes through me, and I begin unbraiding my hair. I should have refused that idea the second Charlotte suggested it. I have no interest in owning a cupcake shop. I can't even bake. The idea was to portray me as sweet and memorable, and it would help me land a lifestyle-reporting job, which is my dream. Cupcakes were hot, Charlotte assured me, and who wouldn't love a sweet cupcake shop owner? After all, hadn't a million chick lit books been written about heroines like that? We'd get the audience behind me, and when all was said and done, I'd move to my TV career and say I was putting the cupcake shop on hold while I pursued "new opportunities."

So, to increase my odds of being cast for the show, I had lied.

I work the hair faster, my fingers shaking as embarrassment and regret roar back to the surface. I remember parts of me dying every time I talked about cupcakes on the show. But after week one on *Is It Love?*, I didn't have to talk about them anymore, because Tom took an interest in me and that became my story.

Silly me. I didn't realize I was playing a part in Tom's *fictional* love story.

I blink back tears. I'm not in love with Tom anymore. It didn't take me long after I was dumped on a beach in Seychelles to realize what I'd thought was love wasn't. But my life has shattered into tiny pieces because of how I handled everything.

Make that *mishandled.*

I comb my fingers through my hair, letting the waves fall past my shoulders. I take a quick glance around because I swear I can feel someone watching me. There's a young couple to my right, holding hands and kissing across the table. I turn to my left, and there's a group of teenage girls laughing and showing each other their phones.

My gaze lands on the table diagonally across from me.

There is a man with a baseball cap, reading a vintage book. I can tell it's an antique copy from the cover. I peer closer. It's *The Fellowship of the Ring* by J.R.R. Tolkien. He reaches for his coffee, his eyes not leaving the pages of the fantasy world he's in. He begins to lift his head, and I quickly look away, not wanting him to catch me staring.

I'm losing my mind.

Ha. I'd have to have a mind to lose it, and apparently that went out the window as soon as Tom started telling me I was different from all the other girls he was dating on the show.

Ugh.

Little did I know he was telling the same thing to the other finalist, something I discovered while painfully watching the show back this summer.

But no, I'd fallen in love. I was special.

We were special.

I close my eyes and relive a magical date we had sailing on a yacht in Monaco. We sipped the finest champagne, dipped into the gorgeous blue waters of the Mediterranean Sea, and shared salty sea kisses as the cameras rolled around us.

I studied for a career in broadcasting at UCLA, so I was used to cameras. They never bothered me on dates, which allowed me to quickly become lost in Tom. So lost that on a picnic in Napa Valley, I told him he was my first love and I wanted nothing more than to love him forever.

Oh, how America has mocked me on social media for being such an idiot.

As they should.

I reach for my coffee cup again, simply using it for a hand warmer as my stomach is too jittery to drink anything. I fell for all his lines, every damn one of them. He told me he admired my intelligence and sweet nature. He said nobody made him laugh like I did and he saw forever when he looked into my blue eyes. He even promised we could celebrate our anniversaries in all the exotic spots around the world where we had started our journey.

I'm going to throw up.

I push the latte cup away, and as I do, the heart in the foam sloshes and breaks apart.

Perfect.

I bring my fingers to my mouth, trying to hold back my retching stomach. My face flames as I remember the way I've been lit up on social media for how I kiss. People said I used too much tongue and I was too eager to shove it down Tom's throat.

And that's just the tip of the iceberg as far as my public humiliation goes. People have judged my eyebrow shape and the way my body looks in a bikini. They said I was there for the wrong reasons. And while some were "Team Skye," others thought I was an immature idiot.

Those who chose "immature idiot" won the office pool.

Ugh.

I'll never get another date for the rest of my life.

After the finale, I was slammed with interview requests and plastered on tabloid covers. I abided by the contract I signed and said nothing negative about the show or the producers who'd fueled my love for Tom by telling me "he's only into you" and insisting if I "shared all my feelings" it would let Tom know how much I cared and only strengthen his feelings.

I start to section my hair again. Oh, I fell for all that crap. His crap, the show's crap, all of it. I got sucked into a vortex of romance and Tom and, being the stupid fool that I am, fell in love.

I don't know what love is.

My hands shake as I work my hair back into a braid. Watching it back on TV was torture. Why didn't I see I was being swept up by the production, not the man? Exotic locations with Tom, doing utterly romantic things? It was a dream, but it was fluff. Despite spending hours on dates together, Tom hadn't shared much with me.

I glance back at the guy reading the book. Does Tom even like to read? I have no idea. Would he read fantasy like this guy in the baseball hat?

I close my eyes, swallowing hard.

I'm so lost.

I slowly open them, shifting my gaze down to the tabletop in front of me. My agent has some TV offers she wants me to consider, but I can't discuss them now, not when I'm a mess like this. All the opportunities involve discussing the show.

Or talking about falling in love.

You know, the one topic I obviously know nothing about.

I've said no to everything. Charlotte is furious, but I don't care. I can't do it again. It was too painful to hear from my friends, their voices full of excitement as the show started to air, and have to smile and play dumb. I was contractually obligated to lie. As the episodes aired, their excitement shifted to horror as Tom was shown saying duplicate things to the other finalist. My family was confused by my newfound passion for cupcakes and mortified by the things coming out of my mouth. Oh, God, where do I go from here?

I feel awful about how I let down my family. My parents both work in the entertainment industry, and Mom, who is a reporter, was so mad she insisted on writing a reality dating show exposé until I begged her not to out of embarrassment and fear of a lawsuit. Dad is a TV sports executive, and while he supported me going on the show, I know he's taken crap for it. I know people are talking about their daughter behind their backs, and that hurts, too.

But the worst is the example I set for my sisters. Lizzie is a sophomore at Berkeley, and Ashlee is a senior in high school. What example have I set? That it's okay to lie to get in the front door for a career? To throw caution to the wind and brazenly fall in love with a man you've just met, without even knowing what types of books he reads?

And instead of staying strong in the face of adversity, I couldn't cope. I drained my savings account and took off for Europe, wanting to disappear. I closed my eyes and tapped a finger on a map of Europe. I figured if I made crap decisions with my eyes open, making one with my eyes shut couldn't be any worse. I'm spending the next few days in Brussels as I try to figure out who Skye Reeve really is. What do I want? How do I rebuild my life after making such a mess of it?

Yet, while everything else in my life is in chaos, there is the one thing I know with certainty.

I thought fate led me to that show for a once-in-a-lifetime career opportunity. Then, after my first solo date with Tom in New York City, I believed fate put me there to find my soul mate.

I was all wrong. And now I know:

Fate cannot be blindly trusted.

CHAPTER ONE

Celebrate Life With Sprinkles—The Blog
New City, New Life, New Start

I PULL OPEN THE DOOR TO THE DONUT SHOP, EAGER TO get out of the snow. Okay, so only a few wet snowflakes have fallen from the gray sky, but I'm a Southern California girl. Anything below fifty is brutally cold.

Correction. I *was* a Southern California girl.

I tug off my gloves, and a sense of amazement fills me. As of yesterday, I'm a resident of Boulder, Colorado.

I stuff my gloves into the pockets of my puffy black parka and pause in wonder over two things. The first is the endless array of gorgeous donuts in cases before me, their magical, wonderfully sweet scent filling the air and making me want *all the donuts.*

The second is that I've landed a position as a new lifestyle correspondent for *Boulder Live,* my first official TV job.

AVEN ELLIS

A blush fills my cheeks as a third thought hits me.

No. That's a lie. The last thought didn't *hit* me but has been with me since I interviewed for my new job.

I'm living in the same town as Maxime Laurent.

I get in line, my thoughts shifting from donuts, rich with vanilla icing and a spectacular dose of sprinkles, to the Belgian hockey player that came into my life in the most unusual of ways.

I met Maxime a few months ago through my friend JoJo Rossi. He is a teammate of her fiancé, Cade Callahan. When Maxime said he knew me, I was mortified. Of course he did, from my disastrous showing on *Is It Love?* But I was wrong.

He was in the café in Brussels.

I move up in the line, wrapped up in thoughts of Maxime. How could I have not noticed the gorgeous man with brown hair and golden highlights, and the most intense blue-green eyes I have ever seen? I couldn't believe he'd remembered me. I was stunned, but when he brought up how I wrapped my hands around my latte cup and kept braiding my hair, I knew he indeed had been there.

Against what must be astronomical odds, we met again in Denver.

Some would call this fate.

But after what happened with Tom, I don't believe in fate.

I study the donuts in the case, my gaze falling on those made to celebrate the upcoming holiday.

Valentine's Day.

I wonder if Maxime will be celebrating with someone special.

I chew thoughtfully on my lower lip. Maxime and I talked that night in Denver, and I can't deny I found him intriguing. He was intelligent. Quiet, but I could tell that was because he was really listening to those around him. He recalled everything I did in that café, so I knew he was extremely observant.

He also happens to be the most gorgeous man I've ever seen and has an oh-so-sexy French accent.

We connected on social media, but Maxime rarely, if ever, posts anything. He always "likes" my stuff, so I know he's actively following me, but that's the extent of our communication.

I wonder if he reads my blog.

"May I help the next customer?" a woman behind the counter calls out.

I move up, and there are now only two people ahead of me.

I launched my blog last year with a specific purpose in mind. My life was broadcast on TV for the entire world to see, but that was a blurred reality, produced and manipulated. I wanted to show the world another side of me and share my real life. Today's post was about celebrating a new beginning by moving to Boulder and starting on *Boulder Live*.

As part of my branding, I celebrate everything with sprinkles. Therefore, I'm here to get heart-shaped donuts lavished with sprinkles. I'll record a video for my Instagram story, and it's something I can talk about when I'm introduced on *Boulder Live* next week.

"Next, please."

I move up again, my thoughts drifting back to

Maxime and wondering what he would do for a Valentine's Day date. I picture something quiet and private.

I shake my head. I'm thinking about him way too much.

I actively pursued TV work in Denver after my friend JoJo sold me on the idea. I did a feature with her for *Bake It!* magazine, and she encouraged me to give Colorado a try, saying that a change of scenery might be what I needed. After spending time here, the idea of moving to Colorado felt right. I like the rugged beauty of Colorado and the change in the seasons. I felt I needed to escape the fishbowl of LA. The fact that I had JoJo and Sierra Crawford—JoJo's friend and now my friend—here made it even more appealing.

It doesn't hurt that Maxime is here, too.

Though he can like my Instagram photos whether I'm living in California or across town.

There was a tiny part of me that hoped he would reach out and say he could show me around Boulder when he saw I was moving here, but instead he simply said "Congratulations," on my social media post about it.

Since I know crap about love and dating—the one solid thing I learned from *Is It Love?*—I should be grateful. I'd no doubt screw it up if he did ask me out.

I retrieve my phone from my Louis Vuitton bag, my pick-me-up splurge for the hell that I endured after the show aired—which, as some people gleefully pointed out, I should have expected when I signed up for a dating show—and prepare to record the donuts in the case.

Enough about Maxime. Time to celebrate my new beginning.

Starting with a latte and heart-shaped donuts.

————

THE SNOW PICKS UP AS I EXIT THE DONUT SHOP WITH A steaming coffee in one hand and a bag of two chocolate-ganache filled, heart-shaped, pink-frosted donuts covered with sprinkles. My celebration is officially ready to begin.

I wander back up Pearl Street, which is lovely. An eclectic blend of shops, bars, and restaurants, all one block from my apartment in the historic Whittier neighborhood of Boulder. I have a wonderful view of the Rockies from my patio on the third floor of my modern loft building, and I love the neighborhood that I will call home. With Victorian-style homes and tree-lined streets, I find the area a charming mix of old and new.

I haven't had much time to explore the area, but I'll get to do that as part of my job, which will be a blast. That's what I love about TV. Being on camera and bringing unique stories to people energizes me like nothing else. Meeting people and sharing their stories is something I feel I was born to do.

A chalkboard sign outside a shop catches my eye, written in pink and white chalk with hearts drawn all over it:

BE MY PURRFECT VALENTINE—Adopt-A-Cat event today!

I stop. Oh, this would be great for a lifestyle feature. I take some pictures of the sign and the pet food store that is hosting the event. Then I decide to head inside to find out more information.

Maybe they'll have another one next year, and I can be here live to promote it, I think.

I move my donut bag to the hand with the coffee and push open the door. It's a few minutes past nine, and since the shop is filled with cats and cages and loads of volunteers but zero customers, they must have just opened.

"Hello, may I help you?" a woman says from behind the counter. She pulls leashes out of a shipping box as she greets me.

"Hi, I was wondering if I could get some information about your Adopt-A-Cat event today?" I ask, smiling at her.

"Oh, Greg can help you; he's with the rescue group," she says. "Greg? Can you help this woman, please?"

A tall, lanky young man in a knit cap walks toward me. "Hi, I'm Greg. Are you interested in a cat?" he asks hopefully.

"Oh, no, I just want to know more about your program," I say, shaking my head. "I'm Skye Reeve, with *Boulder Live,* and I thought this might be a great organization to feature on the show at some point."

"Oh my God, you're Skye Reeve!" a young woman

squeals, rushing up toward me. I notice she is wearing a sweatshirt with Greek sorority letters on it, and my guess is she probably attends the University of Colorado. "I totally watched you on *Is It Love?* Tom never should have picked Miley. Our whole house watched you every Wednesday, and we couldn't believe he didn't pick you!"

I smile the practiced smile I have when people talk about the show. Inside, I want to run from this part of my past.

A Usain Bolt kind of run.

"That's so kind of you, thank you," I say. "But things work out for a reason."

Even if I'm still searching for that reason.

"Can I get your picture?" she asks, nodding excitedly at me.

Crap. I ran out this morning in my puffy black parka and ripped up jeans. I have a cream blanket scarf covering my neck, a matching knit hat on my head, and my braid peeking out the side. I'm wearing my black cat-eye glasses and have no makeup on.

I look like the Michelin Man, with rubber snow boots as an accessory.

Yet, this is reality, so I need to say yes.

"Sure," I say, continuing to smile.

The girl runs around next to me and snaps my picture.

"Thank you. Oh, you have to see the kittens. They're so cute," she exclaims.

"You're on TV?" Greg asks.

"Yes, *Boulder Live,*" I say.

"No, she was on that dating show *Is It Love?*" the girl

15

says knowingly. "Skye is famous! Cara is going to *die*. She was *obsessed* with your wardrobe. Let me go get her; she's in the back."

Greg smiles. "Sorority volunteer project. Come on, let me show you the cats and what we do."

Greg escorts me to the cages as more people begin trickling into the shop. I see cats with info cards explaining their histories. Greg tells me how they rescue cats from different situations and foster them until they can find forever homes.

"Kittens are obviously easier to place, but even then, we get some special ones that need certain homes," Greg explains.

"Like what?" I ask.

"Well, take these two," Greg says, walking over to a cage with two tiny gray kittens. "These kittens are very, very shy. We have people who have returned cats after a day because they weren't *affectionate enough*."

My mouth pops open. "After a day?"

Greg sighs. "Yeah. It's frustrating. It can take time to adjust. Think about it. They're scared. Not all cats are confident going into a new home. It can take a long time to adjust. They might hide under the bed or sofa and only come out at night or when people are gone. It takes time to build confidence and trust with some animals."

I look at the two tiny kittens in the cage. They are backed up in the corner, eyes wide in fear as I look at them.

I know how they feel.

This is how I felt when *Is It Love?* started airing. I was scared every morning to log onto social media. I knew going on TV would cause people to talk about me, and in theory, I understood that I would need a thick skin.

Knowing it and living it are two different things, however.

With the media crush after the show, I wanted to hide. While some of my friends on the show ran with the media spotlight and built their public personality brands, I hid and questioned every decision I had made.

It took me a long time, but with the help of my new friend JoJo, I began to find my confidence again.

I know I can do that for these kittens.

"I think I'm interested in these two," I say to Greg.

"Really?"

"Yes. I just moved here, and I want to give them a home."

"They are a bonded pair," Greg says, "meaning they go together."

"I wouldn't have it any other way."

"Want to hold one?"

I nod and set my coffee and the bag of donuts on the table. "Yes."

"These are Russian Blue mixes," Greg explains. "I think there might be some Maine Coon in them because of the long coat and the hair on the ears and between the toes on the paws."

Greg is speaking Latin to me now, but I nod as if I understand.

He opens the door to the cage. "Come here, Natasha," he says, picking up one by the scruff. "Don't worry; this doesn't hurt her. It's the same way the momma cat would pick them up."

I nod as he shows me how to hold the kitten. The warm ball of gray fluff is placed in my arms, and I know she's petrified.

"It's okay, little one," I murmur to her.

I become aware of more eyes on me. People are now taking pictures with their cameras, but I go into shut-down mode and continue to stroke Natasha's tiny head.

"She's four months, already spayed. Her brother is named Boris, and he's been neutered. They are microchipped and have all their shots, too."

"This is all included in the adoption?" I ask.

"Yes."

"It's Skye with a kitten!" someone shouts.

More people begin to come around, and I feel Natasha grow tenser in my arms.

The sorority girl comes back with her friend, and her friend looks at me in amazement.

"Holy shit, it's really you!" she gasps.

I hand the kitten back to Greg. "Um, I suppose I can get all the supplies here for them?"

"Absolutely," he says, putting Natasha back in the cage. "Why don't you do that while I get the paperwork ready for adoption?"

"You're getting the kittens!" the first girl cries.

"Yes, after I get supplies," I say.

"Oh, I'll help you," the counter woman says, moving around. "I'm sorry I didn't know who you were earlier."

"That's okay," I say, grateful that she didn't.

"Follow me," she says, "I can show you everything you'll need to be a kitten mom."

Before I know it, she's heaping stuff into my arms. I

have a bag of organic kitten kibble in one hand and a litter box in the other. She hands me cans of wet kitten food, and I shove them into the pockets of my coat because I can't hold anything else.

I look like I'm shoplifting cat food.

"You'll need a good scratching post," she continues, walking down an aisle and oblivious to the fact I can't hold anymore. "And a carrier."

As I follow behind her, a can of cat food falls out of my coat pocket and rolls across the tiled floor. I bend over to pick it up, and more go flying out, hitting the floor and rolling in different directions.

Shit!

Cans are rolling all over the place, and I'm scrambling to pick them up in my puffy coat, which makes it hard to move. In the process, I drop the bag of dry food, which explodes onto the floor, sending kibble everywhere. The brown bits are stuck in the fringe of my huge blanket scarf.

And oh crap, is it stuck in my braid?

I'm wearing kitten kibble.

Tuna flavor, apparently, if the scent is any indication.

"Oh dear, I should have grabbed a cart. I guess I'm excited being around a TV personality," the sales woman says, laughing nervously. "Let me get a broom."

As I put the litter box down and begin flicking kibble out of my hair, I become aware of people laughing. I look up from my crouched position, and of course, I'm being recorded.

Super.

With as much dignity as I can, I stop cleaning up the

kibble and opt to gather up the canned cat food instead. The time it takes to walk to the front of the store and ring up my purchases feels like an eternity. I summon all of my strength and try to remain as poised as my humiliation will allow.

After my items are bagged up, Greg goes over the adoption agreement, my responsibilities as a pet owner, their medical files, and tips for socializing Boris and Natasha. I make arrangements to get the kittens and the items I've purchased tomorrow, so I have a chance to kitten-proof the apartment before they come home.

By the time I'm ready to go, my coffee is cold, so I ditch it. I say goodbye to my fur babies-to-be and take my donuts. I realize I haven't checked my phone since I've been here, so I pull it out as I exit the store and glance down.

My phone is lit up with notifications.

I furrow my brow as I step out onto the sidewalk.

I see an urgent text from JoJo:

IGNORE SOCIAL MEDIA TODAY

A sinking feeling hits my stomach. I wish I could ignore it, but I can't. I go to Twitter and enter "#skyereeve" and boom! My phone is filled with tweets about me. The first one is from the tabloid that has made my life hell with false stories this past year. They have posted photos of me on the floor of the pet store, glasses falling down my nose and kibble in my hair with the headline:

WILL SAD SKYE CELEBRATE VALENTINE'S DAY ALONE?

Finally seen in public again, with kittens and bingeing on donuts, apparently Skye isn't over Tom

What? Bingeing on donuts? I haven't even eaten one yet. What fresh hell is this?

I scroll down, and there's a picture of me getting donuts. Then the worst ones are of me in the pet store, with cat food cans falling out of my stupid Michelin Man coat and then a close up of me with kibble in my hair.

I'm mad at myself. Once again, I can't just be the new reporter in town, or a normal woman who is picking up donuts and cat food.

Thanks to the dumb-ass decisions I made last year, I will never be "just Skye."

I remember how Cade and his teammate, Jude, tried to help me deal with the negative media last fall, and I know they are right when they say I know the truth. I know myself and the efforts I put forth; the rest of it doesn't matter.

But I resent this. I resent not being able to eat donuts without it being a sad binge over a man I no longer love. I don't appreciate the fact that I can't be alone on Valentine's Day without making me out as desperate for Tom. In the back of my mind, though, I'm not surprised. The station has been sending out press releases announcing my hire. It's my first time back in the TV limelight since *Is it Love?* ended. The tabloids will be interested for a while, and specifically when I get a new love interest that isn't Tom, and then the furor should die off again.

An icy freezing wind whisks across my face, and snowflakes catch in my eyelashes. I blink them away as my phone continues to go off in my hand. I'm done with this. JoJo is right. I'm not reading any more about pathetic Skye who still loves Tom and is parading around Boulder with cat food stuck in her braid while eating a dozen heart-shaped donuts on a broken-hearted sugar bender. I put my phone on silent as I can practically count the seconds until my agent will call to remind me to keep up my image, even when taking out the trash, and continue walking home.

Where I'll enjoy my donuts and pick kibble out of my hair in complete, ignorant-of-social-media, bliss.

————

OKAY. I'VE PROBABLY GONE A WEE BIT OVERBOARD regarding Project Kitten-Proof.

As I get ready for bed, I think of all the things I've done today to prepare. I've put protective covers over my cords and moved the cleaning supplies to an upper cabinet. I've stored away any plastic bags, and I've vacuumed twice. I even read the sheet of tips Greg gave me and now know to keep closet doors shut and toilet lids down.

In addition to creating a safe home for Boris and Natasha, I've unpacked my kitchen supplies and organized my wardrobe. I went to the DMV and got my Colorado license, and then I researched some potential doctors that are on my insurance plan. I desperately need to get a few décor items, like art and some cozy throws and baskets, but that will have to wait for now.

I finish flossing my teeth and reach for my brush. I need to go grocery shopping, too, but I've been so tired from the move out here that the idea of going up and down each aisle of a new grocery store trying to learn the layout seems exhausting.

Although if I got dressed up and put a smile on my face, maybe I could convince fans of *Is It Love?* that I would rather be grocery shopping alone than with stupid Tom. That might be a good enough motivator for grocery shopping.

Best of all, I remained unplugged the rest of the day. I find days when I do this to be more productive. I've gotten better about letting comments roll off my back. I knew reading hate messages and accusations that I am drowning myself in donuts, going to become a cat lady, and shoplifting cat food would probably suck up half my day. Once you fall down the rabbit hole of reading comments, it's hard to stop. And after you binge on social media, you end up feeling gross about yourself and remorseful for giving in.

So, it was nice to have a day not hearing from my agent or the trolls. I got a lot accomplished, and I feel good about myself.

I flip off the light, shivering as I walk across the hardwood floor in my bedroom. I'm grateful for these thermal pajamas and my down comforter, but I think I'll add an electric blanket to my shopping list. It's freezing here, and once again, I wonder if I'll ever get used to it.

I crawl under the covers and reach for my phone on the nightstand, taking it off the charger. All right, my disconnect from the world is over. I won't check email or Twitter, just my texts and private messages. That should be harmless enough. I have a public account for myself on Connectivity, but a private one, too, reserved for friends only.

I sink back into the pillows, the business of the day hitting me and exhaustion seeping into my bones. I yawn as I swipe open to my notifications.

As soon as I do, one immediately jumps out at me, one that jolts me wide-awake and causes me to sit upright in bed. My heart stops. I can't breathe as I read the notification over again, to make sure I'm not imagining it. But it's there. And it says:

You have a Connectivity Private Message from Maxime Laurent.

CHAPTER TWO

I HAVE A MESSAGE FROM MAXIME.

He has *never* sent me a message.

My heart is in my throat as I dare to click it open:

**Skye, I promised myself if I ever thought
you needed me, I would not make the
same mistake I made in Brussels. I won't
sit by and merely watch. So here I am. I
saw the pictures in that online tabloid
after the game tonight, and after so long
of not seeing them cover you, I wanted to
make sure you were okay. I know you're
not sad—your eyes tell me that—but
invasive photos like that must be
upsetting. Are you okay?**

Maxime is reaching out to me. He wants to make sure I'm
okay.

I read his sweet words over and over, thinking no

man has ever done anything so wonderful for me. It shows genuine concern.

I study it, transfixed by his words. Maxime seems haunted by our missed connection in Brussels. He remembers my despair in the café that night; he saw the look of sadness in my eyes. Something about these photos with their false headline compelled him to action.

This is how a real man acts.

I begin to type a response:

Maxime, nice to hear from you. I

Wait, does that sound like a business reply? I delete it and start over:

Maxime, thank you for reaching out. I

Thank you for reaching out? Is that how I reply to an interesting, sexy, mysterious, European man that I wish I had the opportunity to know better?

I bite my lip. Do I want to know him better? After all, my judgment doesn't have a stellar record. I thought Tom was wonderful. Bleurgh. He turned out to be a colossal wanker, as Sierra's British boyfriend, Jude, would say. I type what I really need to ask Maxime:

Maxime, you aren't a wanker, are you? Because I really don't think my self-esteem could take it if I was wrong again regarding men.

I laugh as I type. Now that would be an interesting reply. I'm about to hit delete when I go on autopilot and hit a different button instead.

The send button.

GAH! SHIT! I JUST HIT SEND BY MISTAKE! NOOOOOOOOOOOOOOOOOO!

In a panic, I think of how to fix this, but what can I say? I typed out the answer as a joke to myself?

I shouldn't be allowed to have a phone.

Ding!

A new message from Maxime drops in:

I can assure you I'm not a wanker.

My face is raging like an inferno, and I want to throw up. How on earth do I recover from this? What do I say? I was joking? I was hacked?

Maxime will never talk to me again.

I toss the phone aside and pull my blanket over my head like the child I apparently am.

I must reply.

HOW DO I REPLY?

I throw the covers off and pick up the phone, dying inside as I read Maxime's reply.

I stare down at the message.

What must Maxime be thinking? I asked him if he was a wanker.

I cringe.

I don't want to know what he's thinking.

Okay. I need to be an adult and respond and wish Maxime the best in life because I'll never see him again.

Wait. We live in the same town. I could see him all the time. Like at Whole Foods or Trader Joe's or on Pearl Street.

I need to apply for a new job.

Preferably in Tokyo.

I force down the nausea rising in my throat and begin to type, which is hard to do with such shaky hands. Before I know it, the words are flowing from my fingertips:

I feel better now that you have confirmed you're not a wanker. I felt like I needed to hear that even though I know there's NO WAY you could be a wanker. Your sweet message tells me you're not. And you're right. I went to get some confetti donuts and coffee. For the record, I bought two. That's not a binge. Who can eat just one donut, anyway? There's something fundamentally wrong with that. But I should have skipped the latte; my coffee at home was better than that water they tried to pass off as coffee. I also ended up adopting two terrified kittens, and I dropped cat food in the pet store, and a bag of kibble exploded in my face. This does not mean I'm mourning Tom, because trust me, he is a FOR REAL wanker and I'm beyond over him. As in that was an infinity ago. It's hard to go out with people constantly labeling each

**experience of my life. I know I went on
the show. I know I "should have known"
this would happen, but that's like saying
you "should have known" you could fall
off a bike before getting on it. Does that
mean you never ride a bike? NO. I took a
chance going on the show, but I didn't
think, this many months later, people
would still be obsessed with everything I
do and attribute my actions to feelings
that I don't have. By the way, I'm posting
this at the end of a long day, so I'm sorry
I just verbally threw up on you and wrote
you a message the size of *War and Peace*.
Don't feel like you have to message me
back because I'm obviously crazy.**

I hit send, deciding to let reality happen. I told him
exactly what I'm thinking. This is my reality, not blurred.
I addressed everything and gracefully gave Maxime an
out, which he will no doubt take me up on because he is
a normal man who doesn't want a bag full of crazy in
his life. I lay back against my pillows.

Ding!

Maxime has replied.

I click it open, my heart pounding as I wait for his
message to pop up. As soon as it does, I read it:

**What kind of coffee do you drink at
home?**

I gasp in shock. He's not fazed by my message! I feel a smile spread across my face, and I message him back:

Café de Cuba Nespresso. Dark roast and very tasty. Do you drink coffee?

I hit send and wait.
Maxime is typing …

Nespresso is good. I can't stand American coffee. It's horrible. What did you think of the coffee in Brussels?

Now I'm grinning like an idiot. I reply:

Brussels had AMAZING coffee. I couldn't get enough of it.

I hit send, eager to see how this conversation develops.

I don't have to wait long for Maxime to continue:

Have you ever had 't Molentje?

I text him back:

Will you hold it against me if I've never even heard of it?

He replies:

You're from California, so no, I won't. That wouldn't be fair. That's something a wanker would do, and we both agree I'm not a wanker.

Oh, I like this cute side of him. It's the first glimpse I've seen of it. I grin and message him back:

That's very generous of you. I promise the next time I'm in Belgium, I will look for it.

Maxime Laurent is typing …

Well, because I'm so generous, and not a wanker, I should fix this for you.

Oh! I hold my breath as I wait for his response: *Maxime Laurent is typing …*

I have 't Molentje in my kitchen. I import it.

I swear I can't breathe as he continues to type. I'm dying as I wait for his next response to drop in, and finally, it does:

If you are inclined, you could come over and have a cup of Belgian coffee with a Belgian.

31

I think my heart is going to burst inside my chest. I type back:

When are you thinking this cup of Belgian coffee with a Belgian should happen?

His reply is instant:

Tomorrow.

CHAPTER THREE

I STARE AT MY PHONE IN SHOCK.

Maxime asked me over for a cup of coffee.

My hands begin shaking with excitement as I reply:

I would like that. I do have to pick up my kittens tomorrow, but I'd love to have coffee with you first.

Maxime Laurent is typing …

I have practice tomorrow morning. I'll eat lunch there before driving back. Let's say 2 p.m.?

I'm grinning as I happily type back my response:

That sounds perfect.

Maxime shoots back his address and closes with one last message:

Goodnight, Skye. Sweet dreams.

I wish him the same and then fall back onto my pillow, holding the phone out so I can read his words over and over.

For once, I'm grateful for the awfully invasive pictures that people snapped of me today. Yes, the world thinks I'm bingeing donuts, buying cat food, and preparing to celebrate Valentine's Day with tissues and sugar, but I don't care.

I know what matters is my reality.

I'm having coffee with Maxime.

I stare at his last words to me before placing the phone back on the charger.

Sweet dreams indeed, I think happily.

———

Celebrate Life with Sprinkles—The Blog Opportunities

I WORK ON MY BLOG IN AN ATTEMPT TO FOCUS ON something other than my coffee date.

Of course, it is a big fat fail because it took me all morning to write a post that should have taken an hour, if I could have concentrated without drifting off to think of a certain sexy Belgian hockey player, with luscious brown hair streaked with gold and intense blue-green eyes.

I decided to use my coffee date with Maxime as inspiration for my post. I read it one more time before I schedule it to run later this afternoon:

If you read my blog on a regular basis, you know I'm a big believer in opportunities presenting themselves if you are open to receiving them. I often think about the things I want in life. What do I aspire to be? How do I want to continue to grow? When I run in the mornings, I think about my life vision. I prepare myself to take chances on opportunities, like the one to come out to Colorado to follow my career dream.

Maybe you are looking to establish new relationships. Are you open and receptive to meeting new people? Do you put yourself in places for these opportunities to happen?

Sometimes, they can be completely out of the blue, like an invitation to coffee. The opportunity to get to know someone who intrigues you. It's a simple opportunity that could lead to making a connection with someone. And isn't that a beautiful thing, when you find someone you can truly connect with in this world?

Be open. Think about what you want, what you need, and what your goals and dreams are.

Then be brave and take the opportunities when presented. XO Skye

I smooth my hands over the ends of my hair, re-reading my words and hoping someone out there might read them and be inspired to seize new opportunities, whether they are big, like a new job, or small, like a cup of coffee.

Except I know this cup of coffee is not a small opportunity.

I schedule the time for my blog to go live. Then I go to my bathroom to check myself before heading over to Maxime's house. I study my appearance in the mirror, seeing the truth reflected in my blue eyes.

This is a huge opportunity to get to know a man who interests me.

I haven't felt this way in ages; I'm full of excitement to meet a man and get to know him. This time, it will be different. There will be no cameras or fancy dates. No producers playing with my head to get the responses they want for sound bites.

This will be real. In the world we exist in, not one created for a TV audience.

And I'm not the same woman I was the last time I dated.

I will be *cautious*. I will get to know Maxime over time. I will not go trusting fate and tumbling head over heels into Stupidland like I did for Tom. Getting my passport stamped in the country once was more than enough.

I fluff my hair with my fingers, watching the waves tumble past my shoulders. I've done the makeup I wear when I'm not on camera: a champagne-colored crème eye shadow, a pop of bronzer across my cheeks, a bit of mascara, and my beloved Charlotte Tilbury nude lipstick in Hepburn Honey, a shade that looks beautiful and soft against my fair skin. I also give myself a nice spritz of J'adore by Dior on my wrists and neck, and I breathe deep as the beautiful floral scent mists over my skin.

I walk down the hall, pick up my winter boots, and review my approach for this opportunity to get to know Maxime as I sit down on the sofa.

It's okay to be excited by the prospect of getting to know him, but after a romantic crash and burn on national TV, and knowing my past judgment of men is crap, the last thing I need is to dive headfirst into anything other than a cup of coffee.

I mean, not that Maxime is interested in anything other than coffee. I can't assume he is, right?

We're two people who live in the same town, simply hanging out and having a conversation over ceramic mugs and getting better acquainted.

That's it.

But if it's not …

I will be smart. My brain will rule instead of my flighty heart. I finish changing into my winter gear, complete with a hat, scarf, and gloves, and head downstairs to my car.

My teeth chatter as the underground parking garage wraps me in bone-chilling cold. Surely this gets better with time, right? I have to adjust to my new environment without thinking I'm going to die of frostbite whenever I head outside. For a brief second, I long for the palm trees and ocean of Laguna Beach, where I grew up. I want to feel the warmth of the sun on my skin and the salty air drift over me as I take a morning walk along the shore.

My old home.

I still can't believe I up and moved to Colorado. I grew up in California, and the bulk of *Is It Love?* was shot in Los Angeles.

It's all I've ever known.

Now my life is full of unknowns, from living in a new state to starting my first professional job as a lifestyle reporter, but this is exactly what I need. A fresh start, away from the person I was on *Is It Love?*, as the person I am now.

I'm stronger. Braver.

More careful.

I hit the key fob and unlock my hunter green Acura MDX. I slip behind the wheel, desperate to crank up the heat and get warm. I was grateful my SUV made the drive out here without dying. It's the car my parents gifted me when I turned sixteen. It's been through high school, college, and internships at TV networks that had me driving for errands all over Los Angeles.

Now it has taken me to Boulder.

Fingers crossed it can hold on until I have enough in the bank for a down payment for a new car.

I turn the key, and the car slowly comes to life. I exhale, seeing my breath escape from my lips in frozen puffs. As I think about money, an offer from a publisher in New York flashes through my head. They want a book chronicling my experience on *Is It Love?* It's tempting. I turn on the heat, thinking of how easy it would be to share my story. I could explain how naïve I was and how I existed in the show's bubble, swept up by the most romantic dates a girl could ever imagine. I could describe the crushing blow of rejection, the public humiliation as the show aired, and the pressure of being cast as America's Sweetheart. I think I have a lot to share about my experience, and some of it could help women.

But I don't know if now is the time to do it. I'm starting over. The new career that I'm building is based on truth, not the fabricated image of sweet, cupcake-loving Skye. While the book would be my truth, it would also bring back to life *Is It Love?* Skye and not Skye Reeve.

The woman I so desperately want to be now.

I clear my throat, putting the book idea away for the moment. I put Maxime's address into my phone, as I need GPS help to find anything in Boulder, and head out. I turn up Jessie James Decker's "All Filled Up" and get lost in her words as I drive. The windshield wipers brush away the snow that falls in huge flakes from the purplish-gray sky.

Excitement rushes through me. I'm seeing Maxime. Even though we will only be sharing a cup of coffee, I wonder what it will be like to get to know him. Questions roll around in my head. Will we pick up where our Connectivity messages left off? Will I see more of his clever side, the one I got a glimpse of last night? What's his house like? Unlike his teammates, why did he choose to live so far from Denver?

I grin. The broadcast journalist in me is coming out in spades.

I enter his community at the base of the mountains. The homes are bigger here, with lots of land in between.

I glance up through the leafy trees, dusted with a layer of snow, to the mountains capped in white.

Beautiful.

My GPS guides me down Maxime's street, and when it announces my destination is on the right, my heart flutters nervously inside my chest. I pull up the drive and park my car behind a Jaguar SUV. I take in the home in front of me, which looks nothing like where a single, professional athlete would live. At least in my mind, it's not. It's an older, split-level home, easily built in the seventies, if not the sixties, nestled amongst the pines.

I turn off the engine and slip outside. I walk across the freshly fallen snow, and the crunching of my boots is the only sound I hear. This place suits the pieces of Maxime I know. He's quiet and private. Not flashy.

His choice of where to live becomes clearer in my mind.

I make my way up the steps, noticing some fresh footprints and paw prints in the snow. I smile. If these tracks are any indication, he's recently taken his dogs out for a walk.

I put my fingertip on the doorbell, hesitating before ringing it to give myself some reminders.

This is coffee. A cup of coffee with a neighbor, so to speak. No different from a cup with JoJo and Sierra. Perhaps we'll become friends. That would be nice. If there is more between us, I will take the time to get to know him.

No six-week fast track to the love of my life this time.

With fresh confidence, I ring the doorbell.

Within seconds, I hear dogs barking at the door. I reach up and fiddle with the end of my braid as I wait.

"Coming," I hear him call out.

Then I hear him tell his dogs to be quiet—*in French.*

The second I hear him speak French, I freeze.

Good Lord, that is one incredibly sexy language for a man to speak.

The dogs fall silent as soon as Maxime issues his command. The lock turns on the other side of the door, and all my bravado begins to crumble. My fingers work faster on the end of my hair as my heart accelerates in response. Nerves fill me, despite my badass self proclaiming this is "just coffee."

The door creaks open, and my remaining bravado vanishes.

Maxime stands before me, more handsome than I remember. I look up to take in his full six-foot frame. His hair is thick and wavy, a gorgeous combination of blond and brown. He's wearing a plaid flannel shirt in a rich camel and chocolate brown color, layered over a white T-shirt and paired with dark jeans and suede boots.

I swallow hard.

He's easily the most gorgeous man I've ever laid eyes on.

My gaze meets his. Maxime's piercing blue-green eyes, the ones that studied me so intensely in a café in Brussels, are on me once again, this time studying me up close through the fringe of his long, thick, dark eyelashes.

"Bonjour," he says softly. *"Bienvenue chez moi, Skye."*

Then the most beautiful smile I've ever seen lights up his face.

Butterflies appear out of nowhere, dancing furiously in my stomach. I can't breathe.

In this moment, I know I'm in trouble.

Because suddenly this is so much more than coffee.

And I don't know if I can even try to fight it.

CHAPTER FOUR

I FIND MYSELF UNABLE TO LOOK AWAY FROM HIS sparkling eyes and beautiful smile

I never considered a cup of coffee to be a perilous situation until now.

If Maxime is even a tenth as charming in person as he was in his messages, I don't know how I will be able leave here without developing a full-blown crush on him.

"I'm sorry," he says in his heavily accented English, "I should have greeted you in English."

"Je parle un peu de français," I reply, telling him I speak a little bit of French.

"Very good," Maxime says, his smile widening at my French. "Please, come in."

"Thank you," I say, stepping into his foyer. As I move past him, I get a hint of a scent lingering on his skin. I detect vanilla and bourbon and a hint of smoke. It's one of those colognes you know would be amazing up close.

While I have never smelled anything like it, and I don't know what it is, there's absolutely one thing I can confirm.

It's super sexy.

The sound of the door closing behind me jars me from my thoughts.

"Please, let me take your coat," Maxime says, moving behind me.

The butterflies go crazy. I'm aware of his masculine presence, his height, his scent, everything about this mysterious man who has re-entered my life.

I place my purse on his sleek black entry table, which I notice is immaculate. I tug off my gloves and place them on top of my bag, nervous energy coursing through every inch of me. I reach under my blanket scarf and unzip my puffy coat, and Maxime helps me slip out of it as his big, black, furry dogs circle around us.

"Merci bien," I say.

I turn around, and Maxime smiles at me, a smile so genuine my heart leaps.

"You're welcome," he says, opening his hall closet and retrieving a hanger.

As Maxime hangs up my coat, I glance down at the dogs, who are sniffing my jeans.

"What are their names?" I ask.

"Amè and Henri," he says, closing the door. "Siblings from the same litter."

"Just like my kittens," I say, thinking of Boris and Natasha.

"They are friendly; you can pet them if you like,"

Maxime says, bending down and ruffling the fur of one of them. "Aren't you, Henri? You're a good boy."

I let Amè sniff my hand, and then I bend down and affectionately stroke her between the ears, which sends her tail swishing happily.

"They are loves," I say as I continue to stroke Amè's luxurious fur.

"Thank you," Maxime says. "Are you a dog lover? Or a cat person?"

I stand up. "I'm an animal person. I've loved them since I was little. I had no intention of adopting kittens yesterday, but when I saw them, I knew they were meant to be mine."

"That's how I felt about Amè and Henri," he says, patting Henri before standing back upright. "I knew they were going to be my family here in America. Isn't that right, Henri?"

Henri barks, and I smile.

"He agrees," I say.

"No, he wants treats," Maxime says, smiling back at me. "Come on, let's have some good coffee."

"As an American, I feel compelled to defend our coffee," I say as I follow him into the living room. I'm about to finish my thought, but I'm distracted by what I see. The home has been updated inside and features an open floor plan. The living room is huge, with vaulted ceilings and pale gray walls. A large stone fireplace dominates one wall. I step across the grayish hardwood floors and stare out the back windows, which show a postcard picture of a lake surrounded by towering trees dusted with snow.

"Are you trying to figure out a way to defend American coffee?"

I blink. I was so distracted by his house that I forgot to finish my thought.

"I do love my American coffee," I say slowly, "but I have to admit the coffee in Brussels was fantastic."

"I'll win you over," Maxime says.

I don't think I can breathe.

I think you're already in the process of doing that, Maxime Laurent.

"As you can see, the kitchen is here," Maxime says, leading me into the open space, which has also been updated with beautiful gray cabinets and white marble countertops. A glossy white, subway-tile backsplash pulls it all together, along with stunning pendant drop lighting and stainless-steel appliances.

I watch as Maxime reaches for a canister on the counter, and both dogs begin barking excitedly.

"I take it that's not the coffee container?" I tease.

Maxime grins. "No, it's not, but my coffee is worth getting that excited for," he says, feeding a treat to both dogs. He speaks to them in French. Of course, he would; that is his native language after all.

"Would you like something to eat with your coffee?" Maxime asks as he washes his hands. "Do you like sweets?"

I can't help but notice how huge his hands are as he dries them on a towel, but I force myself to stay on point with the conversation. "I love anything with sugar. Sprinkles are *everything.*"

Maxime places the towel down and moves over to

his coffee machine. I notice it's not a one-cup machine like mine but something that an upscale coffeehouse would have. It can make espresso and drip coffee, and I think new tires for my car would be cheaper than this luxury coffee maker.

"That is a serious machine you have there, Maxime," I say.

"I take my coffee very seriously," he says, "as I do with all the things I'm passionate about."

His eyes meet mine for a brief moment, and pure electricity shoots down my spine.

Do I want to be something he's passionate about, too?

I reach for my hair and run my fingers over the ends, anxious about how easily, *way too easily*, that thought entered my head.

"Would you like a latte?" Maxime asks.

"Oh, that would be lovely, thank you," I say.

Maxime nods and reaches for a ceramic container. "I need to go back to what you said a moment ago. Why are sprinkles everything?"

I watch as he works like a barista, freshly grinding the beans for brewing. I wait until he's finished, and then I answer his question.

"I have loved sprinkles since I was a little girl," I explain. "To me, they are a magical topping. You can't help but smile when you see them. They are sweet, colorful, and whimsical. Tiny rays of sunshine. I *adore* them, and I think they make everything infinitely better."

Maxime nods and moves to his stainless-steel refrigerator. I can't help but peek as he opens it, searching for another glimpse into his personality. The shelves are neat and organized. I can tell everything has a place, and he likes it that way. I spy bottles of water, food in glass containers, plain yogurts, and loads of produce.

He likes order, I think as he shuts the door. He's health conscious, too.

"I bet you don't like sprinkles," I say.

Maxime sets a gallon of organic milk on the countertop, a questioning look passing over his handsome face. "Why do you say that?"

"The reporter in me noticed your refrigerator contents. You're extremely healthy. I'm thinking sprinkled foods are not a part of your rotation."

"You underestimate me."

"Oh, so my reporter deduction is all wrong?" I ask. "You like sprinkles?"

"I have the best sprinkles in my pantry."

He has sprinkles.

My heart skips at this news.

Then my brain reminds me my heart is stupid.

I watch as Maxime moves to his pantry and opens the door to step inside. I bet that is organized as well. In my head, I see rows of healthy food stored in air-tight glass containers.

As opposed to my cabinet, where boxes of confetti cake mix are thrown haphazardly in with oatmeal and canned soup, squeezed around a pyramid of canned frostings that I eat with a spoon by myself.

Because, you know, frosting with Funfetti is *everything*.

Maxime returns, holding something in his hand.

Instead of a shaker of sprinkles like I was expecting, it's a box.

"These are Dutch chocolate sprinkles from Holland," Maxime says, handing the box to me. "I promise you they are the best sprinkles you'll ever have."

I give him an odd look. "A chocolate sprinkle is a chocolate sprinkle, and they aren't nearly as fun as colored sprinkles."

Maxime studies me. "I'll have you rethinking this," he says seriously. "I'm going to introduce them to you the way they were introduced to me: on buttered bread for breakfast."

"You're going somewhere if you are endorsing sprinkles for breakfast," I tease.

"Let me finish the coffee first," Maxime says, going back to his expensive machine and frothing the milk.

I watch as Maxime serves me a latte in a large white mug.

"Sorry, I can't do the art," he says, smiling at me.

Skip, skip, skip goes my heart at the sight of that smile.

"I didn't come here for the art," I say. "I came here for coffee with a Belgian."

"I hope the coffee, and the company, doesn't disappoint you."

Now my heart is racing.

"I'm not too worried about that," I say.

Maxime studies me for a moment. "I hope not," he says softly. "Sometimes I'm not what people expect, once they get to know me."

The conversation has turned serious. What does that

49

comment mean? I'm about to follow up when Maxime turns away, busying himself with a loaf of bread.

"The team nutritionist wouldn't like this," Maxime says, switching the subject as he opens a cabinet and retrieves a loaf of bread. "But I eat this every day with my coffee as part of my morning. We'll enjoy it as an afternoon snack today."

"Is this a Belgian thing?" I ask, letting the serious comment go for now. I pause and take a sip of my coffee, and the rich, bold flavor practically slaps me upside the head. "Maxime! This is just like that café in Brussels! It's so good!"

"That is because your coffee might as well be water," Maxime says as he slices the bread. "You need to drink six cups of your stuff to get any kind of caffeine hit."

"Okay, I'm a believer," I say.

Maxime smiles. "You'll be a believer about the sprinkles on bread, too. I grew up eating this."

I watch as he butters a slice of bread for me. He adds a thick layer of chocolate sprinkles and passes me a plate.

"Let's sit at the kitchen table," he says. "I'll join you in a minute."

I nod and take my plate to the table at the other end of the kitchen. His dogs drop down near my feet, and I smile, thinking they must be Maxime's companions when he's home.

Maxime joins me and slips into the chair across the table.

"Go ahead," he encourages.

I stare at the bread, hardly believing this is breakfast

food. I guess compared to all the sugar-loaded cereals out there, it's not that unusual.

I lift my bread and take a bite of the buttery brioche. The taste of milk chocolate is rich and decadent and completely different from any chocolate sprinkle I have ever eaten. Combined with the rich butter and wonderful bread—oh my, I'm a believer.

I put my slice down and wipe my lips with a napkin.

"Maxime, this is a game-changer!"

A smile lights up his face. "It's good, isn't it?"

"Life-changingly good! I could eat this every day."

"I do when I'm home," Maxime says, pausing to take a bite.

"These sprinkles are like eating little bits of high-quality chocolate," I say, picking up my bread and taking another bite.

"They are completely different."

"Mmm, in the best way," I say, going in for another bite.

Maxime clears his throat.

"So, congratulations on the new job," Maxime says, putting down his bread and picking up his coffee.

"Thank you," I say. "It's my first TV job. I'm nervous but excited."

"Why are you nervous? You've been on TV before."

I freeze. He's talking about *Is It Love?*, and that's the last thing I want Maxime to think of when he sees me. I put down my bread and reach for my hair and absently begin braiding it.

"I'm sorry," Maxime says quickly.

"What? What for?"

"Your expression changed when I brought up the show. I didn't mean it like that. I mean that you have experience being on camera."

"You're insightful, aren't you?" I ask.

"Like you are?"

"Trust me, I'm not insightful. If I were, I wouldn't have been in the mess I was on that stupid show."

Maxime's gaze holds steady, but I don't see judgment in his eyes. What I do see, however, is interest.

"I wouldn't say that. Circumstances can cloud your decisions. I know I've been guilty of that."

"You seem way too even-keeled to make mistakes like the ones I did."

"What mistakes have you made that are so unforgivable?" he asks, a perplexed look crossing his face. "Take the TV show out of the equation. You dated a guy, and it didn't work out. How does that make you different from most human beings?"

I swallow hard and find every inch of bravery I have to ask my next question.

"Have you seen the show? It's okay to be honest."

Maxime shakes his head no, and inside, I breathe a huge sigh of relief.

I reach for my hair again. "Maxime, I'm glad you haven't. I made many mistakes. Editing made me look worse. If I could do it all over again, I would never have put myself in such a vulnerable position. Nor would I want anyone to see it."

"Do you want to tell me your version of what happened?"

I cringe, ashamed to tell him the reality of the

52

situation, but before I can answer, Maxime's expression shifts to one of regret, and I don't understand why.

"I'm sorry, you don't have to answer that," Maxime says, shaking his head. "You just told me you were glad I didn't see it. Please forgive me for asking, Skye."

"No, no, it's okay," I say.

"It's not," Maxime says firmly, running his hand through his thick, two-toned hair. "I shouldn't have asked you that."

"It's a fair question," I say, wanting to reassure him.

"It's none of my business. I'm sorry."

I hold still for a moment. "I promise I'm okay with you asking."

Maxime begins drumming his fingers on the tabletop.

"It's not a first coffee question," he says.

"What is a 'first coffee question?' There are no rules here. I don't mind answering if it's something you want to know."

Maxime stops drumming his fingers. "I have a habit of being too serious."

"Liar."

Maxime's eyebrows shoot straight up in surprise. "Excuse me?"

"You own *sprinkles*. You can't be too serious."

Maxime's expression relaxes, and I get a laugh out of him. I clear my throat before addressing him.

"It's not that I mind you asking," I say gently, "but I'm embarrassed as to what you will think when I'm done with my story. I don't want you to think badly of me. I have a lot of regrets, Maxime. Too many."

53

I feel heat fan across my neck as the shame of my past rises to the surface. I lower my gaze to my latte cup, running my finger around the rim, preparing to tell him the whole story if he wants to hear it.

"I have regrets, too."

I lift my eyes to find him staring intently at me.

"One of the biggest ones I'm correcting today," he says.

"What is that?" I manage to ask.

"I should have talked to you in Brussels. I watched you. I saw how upset you were, and I wanted to know what could make you so sad. But it was more than that, Skye. If you were happy, I still would have wanted to know you and find out what was making you smile. I let that opportunity slip through my fingers."

Oh!

"When I saw you were moving to Boulder, I knew I had another chance," he continues, "to have the coffee with you I should have had in Brussels. Now is that time. I want to know about your time on the show because it's a part of who you are. But only in your words, if you want to tell me."

I stare at him in shock. Maxime has been thinking about me in the same way I have been thinking about him.

We have another chance, I realize, *to have the moment we should have had in Brussels.*

While I never imagined coming here and sharing this part of my life, looking at Maxime's genuine concern for me, I know what I'm going to do.

"I think this is another chance, too," I say quietly over the pounding of my heart.

"You do?"

"I do. And Maxime?"

"Yes?"

"I will tell you everything."

CHAPTER FIVE

MAXIME'S BLUE-GREEN EYES STAY LOCKED ON MINE. "You don't have to. I understand the need to keep something like that to yourself."

As I stare back at him, I see sincerity in his expression. I also see a man who guards his own privacy fiercely. How will he ever understand? How can I begin to tell him this story without him losing respect for me?

I sit up straighter as a realization hits me. This story is a part of my life. Whatever happens between Maxime and me, either as friends or something more, he has to accept it if he's going to accept me.

"I went on *Is It Love?* because of my agent," I say, wrapping my hands around the large ceramic mug and feeling immediate warmth. "My goal has always been to be on TV, not in a reality capacity but as a lifestyle TV host. I planned to start out as a correspondent. My parents work in the industry out in Los Angeles, and they helped me get some great internships. I worked my ass off, doing internships year-round while juggling my classes at UCLA. Thanks to my dad, I got agent meetings. I landed one: Charlotte. She's the one who had contacts at *Is It Love?* and said she could get me cast."

Maxime wrinkles his brow in thought. "So you didn't want to be on the show?"

"No. I was appalled at the idea. I didn't want to springboard because I was on a dating show. I wanted to land a job due to my skills and hard work and the enthusiasm I put into my features. Charlotte told me there were millions of girls like me trying to land one of the extremely limited jobs available in TV. She said I would need more than a good demo to make it, unless I wanted to toil for years in small markets and move all across America to get what I wanted. Which I was willing to do."

"Why didn't you?" Maxime asks.

I pause to take a sip of my latte. I place the cup back down and sigh. "She gave me the statistics for girls that appeared on *Is It Love?*, and it was hard to negate them. A lot of them come away with huge social media followings and become influencers on Connectivity and Instagram. They host podcasts and write books," I say, thinking of the proposal that is in my Inbox. "Some are doing what I want to do. She said I would be wasting a tremendous opportunity, and it was hard to argue with her after thinking about it."

I study Maxime's face to see if he disapproves. His expression remains one of interest, not disapproval.

Yet.

I pause for a moment. "I let her handle everything,

and that's when things started to get out of control. Charlotte made up my backstory by saying that my life's dream was to open a cupcake shop."

I see nothing but confusion on Maxime's face. "What? That was made up?"

My face grows hot as shame surges through me. "I'm done presenting an alternate reality. Yes. It was completely made up. I *like* cupcakes, but I'm a horrible baker. I don't know *how* to bake. It's a crapshoot if I can get a box mix to come out right. When I found out that was my casting description, I was livid. Charlotte told me to quit being overly dramatic. She said everyone embellishes to get ahead, and since I like cupcakes, it's not a total lie, just a tweak. I'm not proud to say I went along with it. I regret it, but Charlotte represents a lot of successful TV personalities, and I was right out of college. What did I know? I didn't trust my gut enough to say no to someone who was known to make dreams come true."

"So you became Skye the cupcake baker," Maxime says.

"More like Skye the cupcake faker," I blurt out.

Maxime begins laughing, and I can't help but join him.

"How does one be a cupcake faker?" Maxime asks.

I smile, relieved he's taking my past so well. "Well, I talked about the joy cupcakes bring."

"And?"

"How they have to have the perfect ratio of frosting —not too much—and of course, a generous amount of sprinkles. Because sprinkles make everything better."

Maxime is smiling at me, and I feel the weight of my past fall away.

"Sprinkles are everything, I once heard," Maxime teases.

I laugh. "Anyway, I go on the show," I say, taking another sip of my coffee and setting the cup back down, "and they asked me what I needed to make cupcakes in the house kitchen for all the girls. That was written into the script. Luckily, I was able to talk them out of that idea, which would have been a disaster."

"Script? I thought it was reality, outside of the cupcake fakery," he says.

Then he winks at me.

"Silly Maxime, there is no such thing as reality TV," I say, winking back at him for good measure.

A smile lights up his face.

Oh, he's *gorgeous*.

I continue. "In fact, I'd say it's a blurred reality."

"You talked about that on your blog."

My heart holds still. "You've read my blog?"

"Yes."

Ooh!

"Well, thank you for reading it," I say.

"You're a good writer. You have an ability to draw a person into your world."

"Really?" I ask.

Maxime nods. "Yes. I read a lot. Not only do you have that ability, but you do it with every post. That's a gift."

"Thank you," I say, flattered by his compliment.

"Sorry, I drew you offsides," Maxime says. "Go back to the show."

"Right. Well, it's not like you are given a script per se, but producers suggest things to you," I say. "You are prompted in your ITMs—in the moment interviews—which, by the way, are not in the moment but often re-created later. They make you wear the same clothing and re-style your hair the same way to re-create the moment. Then they suggest things to you. They might say, 'Tom should hear how you feel. You don't want him to doubt that.' So I would think, oh, I need to tell Tom how I feel so he's confident in us. All prompted by the script they wanted us to act out."

Maxime's face turns to one of disgust. "Is anything real?"

"My actions, outside of being a cupcake faker, were," I declare. "I'm a happy, upbeat person. That is why I want to be a lifestyle correspondent or host. I like bringing good stories to the forefront, things that entertain people or brighten their day. That is who I am. That part of me on the show—interacting with the other girls in the house and having fun on the group dates—was real."

Maxime is silent for a moment. "Were your feelings for Tom real?"

"Yes. I never went on the show thinking I would find love, but I did. Tom was charming and very romantic. I found myself having feelings I never felt before. He was my first love, but I was just a game to him. I went on magical dates: a romantic dinner on a pink sand beach in Seychelles and a yacht trip off the coast of Monaco. I fell hard and fast, and the things he said to me, well, I believed all of them. I had no idea he was saying the same beautiful words to Miley."

Maxime flinches. "I'm so sorry."

"At that point, all that mattered was Tom," I say, continuing. "I lost sight of everything else. I envisioned having my career and Tom at the end. I needed him. I couldn't imagine a life without him. In private, in the time we had when the cameras were off, he told me his feelings were the same. So we shot the finale, and I'm standing there before him in my designer gown, thinking my future is about to begin and all Tom had to say was, 'Skye, this is love,' but he didn't. That's when everything fell apart."

Maxime is studying me, and I see empathy in his eyes as if he understands the feeling.

"I knew what I was getting into when I went on the show," I say slowly. "I was opening myself up for heartache. To be criticized on social media. To have photographers follow me. To have to watch the show back and see what really happened between Tom and the other girls. It destroyed a part of me," I admit, something I have never said to another person. "I lost weight. My hair started falling out from stress. People criticized my weight, my hair, my cupcake dream. They said I was fake and that I was using the show to build a career. That one cut to my core because they were right. So I fled. I bought a book on traveling through Europe, flipped open to the map, shut my eyes and picked a spot. That's how I ended up in Brussels. I needed to be alone, to figure myself out, to learn how to cope with the insanity that I brought on myself.

"You really don't know what you are going to be in for until it all ends," I say, continuing. "I don't think I deserved death threats for being on a dating show."

"What? People wished you would *die?*"

I nod. "Yes."

"That's an absolute rubbish thing to wish on anyone. Social media can bring out the worst in humanity."

"It can, but I also have met a lot of lovely people because of it, people who were Team Skye and who want to see me happy and moving on with my life. Moving to Boulder is a start. While *Is It Love?* will always be a part of me, I won't let it define me anymore."

"What about your feelings for Tom?" Maxime asks softly. "Have you moved on from him, too?"

I smile. "My feelings ended after the show did. I realized I didn't know him. I thought I did, but I didn't. I didn't even know how he took his coffee."

"Did you know if he liked sprinkles?" Maxime asks, a smile tugging at the corner of his mouth.

Swoon.

"No, I never asked him about sprinkles. Obviously, it wasn't meant to be."

"Obviously," Maxime says.

Maxime rises and so do his dogs, their tails eagerly swishing.

"You are going to get your kittens this afternoon, right?" he says, picking up his cup and going over to his coffee machine.

"Yes," I say. "It was a complete surprise that I found

them, but I'm finding out surprises can be exactly what you need."

Like your invitation to come here, I think as I watch him.

"Would you like some help?" Maxime asks, pouring himself another cup of coffee and, this time, putting it into a portable tumbler. "I could drive you over, help you get your supplies and the kittens, and help you get them acclimated if you want."

Excitement surges through me. There is nothing I want more than to spend more time with Maxime, and now I have it.

"I would love that," I say, rising and bringing my plate and mug to the sink.

"Do you want me to make you a latte to go?"

"Please, that would be wonderful," I say. "I'll go get my coat on while you do that."

Maxime nods, and I cut through the living room on my way to the hall closet. A book laying out on his sofa catches my eye.

I stop dead in my tracks.

I've seen that book before.

My memory quickly flashes to Brussels. The café. The antique *Lord of the Rings* book and the man with the baseball hat sitting at the table in front of me …

I go over to the book and pick it up, holding it with a shaking hand.

The guy with the antique book was Maxime.

A huge smile lights up my face.

I remember him.

I remember our beginning.

CHAPTER SIX

"DO YOU LIKE TOLKIEN?"

I turn around, and Maxime is holding two tumblers of coffee as he cuts through the living room.

I'm shaking as I hold the book. "I remember you."

Maxime shoots me a smile as he stops in front of me. "I should hope that would be the reason you came over for coffee this morning."

"No, Maxime, I remember you. *In Brussels,*" I say, my words coming out in an excited rush. "You were wearing a baseball cap and reading this book. I can see you now. I can see the table you were sitting at, never lifting your eyes from the pages of your book."

"You're wrong."

"What?" I say, confused. "I know this was your book; I remember that it was an antique copy. It had to be you."

"No, it was me, but I lifted my eyes from the book, more than you know."

He extends the tumbler toward me, and I hold his

book to my chest as my free hand meets his. His fingertips lightly graze mine, the brief touch of his skin sending a shiver down my spine.

"Thank you," I say, taking the cup from him. "What do you mean by that?"

Maxime stares down at me. "I didn't read a word. I couldn't stop watching you. I wondered what was making you sad and what your story was. You seemed so alone, and for reasons I can't explain, I didn't want you to be."

My heart pounds at his words. Maxime knew, without any words being exchanged between us, the depths of my sadness. The isolation and loneliness.

He wanted to help me.

"I looked down whenever you turned my way," Maxime says, continuing. "I didn't want you to catch me staring at you. After you left, I wished I had asked if you were okay. I didn't want you to be alone, feeling that way."

I feel tears well up. Maxime cared more about me as a complete stranger than Tom ever did while dating me.

"I can't believe you read me so well," I say. "You saw all the things I was feeling inside."

"I'm sorry I didn't talk to you. I still regret that."

I shake my head. "Please stop apologizing for that. I was a *stranger.* Why would you have talked to me?"

"I knew I should have. I can't explain it," Maxime says. "My instinct was to go to you. I talked myself out of it because I thought you would think I was making a move on you. Or that I was some creepy guy stalking you." He pauses for a moment. "I also have a history of very bad judgment when it comes to women. I thought there could be a chance I was reading you wrong, like I have in the past with other women, so I shoved it aside. But when you left, my gut knew I had been right. I felt awful that you went through whatever was bothering you alone."

My head is sorting through his words, touched by his kindness.

I consider his telling comment about his judgment regarding women.

Has Maxime been hurt by misjudging someone, too?

"I think you've more than made up for that by reaching out to me today," I say gently.

"I hope I have, Skye," he says in his heavily accented voice.

I don't know what is happening here, but I feel a connection to Maxime unlike anything I've known before. I thought I knew what fate had in store for me when I met Tom, but I was wrong. I feel like fate is at work again now, but this time, it is different.

It makes zero sense, but I know, without a doubt, I'm meant to be here. With Maxime, in his house, sharing my story with him. I feel this magnetic *pull* toward him. I know I promised never to blindly trust fate again, but I can't deny we were seated on that patio in Brussels for a reason.

Now might be the time to find out what that reason is.

I clear my throat. "Are you ready to help me with some kittens?"

Maxime flashes me a beautiful smile. "Let's go."

I place the book down on the sofa and park my tumbler on the coffee table. We slip into winter gear, and when Maxime tugs on a gray knit cap, a lock of his wavy blond-brown hair escapes and sweeps across his forehead. I have to resist the urge to touch it, to brush my fingertips along his forehead and see what his wavy locks feel like against my fingertips.

"I can drive if you want," Maxime offers, interrupting my thoughts.

Heat sears my cheeks. I hope he can't read what is going on in my head and see that I'm daydreaming about touching him.

"Yes, if you don't mind, that would be great. I can get my car when we get back."

"Why don't you wait here for a few minutes?" Maxime says as he tugs on his black leather gloves. "I'll go start the car and get the heat running so you won't be cold."

I nod, amazed at his thoughtfulness.

"This Southern California girl is very grateful to you for doing that," I say, smiling at him. "Thank you."

Maxime grins. "My pleasure."

He heads out the front door, and I retrieve our coffee tumblers. I walk back across his living room and watch through the large back windows the snow fall onto his deck and pond. I can't get over the peaceful feeling I have standing here. Compared to the noise of living with the girls in the *Is It Love?* house, or living in an apartment with friends at UCLA, this feels grounded. Real. Grown up.

This is a house for a mature man, I think. And

judging by his home, I would guess he appreciates his solitude and values quiet and peace.

I can't help but smile. Nice of me to play pretend analyst and determine all of this from his choice of home like I'm some kind of psychology expert.

Yet my instincts tell me I know Maxime.

The door opens, and Maxime steps back inside.

"I think I have the temperature of Los Angeles inside my vehicle if that suits you," he says, flashing me a smile.

I think you might suit me, Maxime Laurent.

"Perfect," I say, heading toward him with the coffee in my hands. Maxime takes his, and I regret that we both have gloves on so I can't feel his fingertips against my skin. He opens the door for me to step outside first.

The snow is cascading faster from the sky, and I stop to take in the magical sight. Maxime's home is nestled between snow-capped mountains and towering pines, and there's nothing but stillness in the air.

"It's beautiful here," I think aloud.

Maxime moves next to me, and I'm aware of the scent of his cologne mingling with the frosty air.

"Better than California?" he asks, his voice breaking through the quiet that has blanketed us.

"There's nothing like the Rockies," I say, using all my willpower not to steal another glance at Maxime. "It's breathtaking here."

"I agree," Maxime says. "I've been all across Europe to play hockey, and I had no idea what Colorado would be like when I was drafted by the Mountain Lions. I had only been to the United States a few times, and it was so vast and different everywhere I went. But when I stepped off the plane here, it felt like a new start."

This time, I turn to look up at him. Maxime views Colorado the same way I do.

As a place to start over.

But what is Maxime starting over from?

I study him as he drinks in the view, the snow dusting his cap and the top of his luxurious cashmere overcoat, and I long to ask him what he left behind in Europe.

I want to know your story, Maxime, I think as I study his handsome profile. *I want to know you.*

"Come on, let's go," Maxime says, moving toward his car.

I stand still, watching him walk. My reporter skills tell me Maxime's life is not an open book like mine is. I shared my intimate moments with millions of people on TV and my thoughts with thousands across social media channels. Maxime is quiet. While I've revealed everything, Maxime keeps his thoughts guarded.

Maybe, with time, he won't with me.

I follow him to the car and slip into the passenger seat, the warm air enveloping me.

"Ah," I say, sinking into the heated seat. "This feels nice. While the snow is beautiful, I can't say I'm a fan of how cold I feel all the time."

Maxime puts his coffee into the drink holder and reaches back for his seat belt. "Try going to Russia in the winter. I played some hockey tournaments there. That's brutally cold."

"You've been all over the world," I say as he begins to drive.

I watch as a smile passes over his handsome face. "So have you. I've never taken a girl to Monaco or Seychelles for a date. You've had the more glamorous world travel."

"Oh, please. That wanker didn't take me there on his own accord," I blurt out. "He was paid to date a bunch of women and declare his love for one at the end. The show planned and paid for all those trips. Tom would probably take a girl to a posh restaurant with tiny portions and beautiful people as waitstaff. He's all about being seen with the famous people and eating chic food that leaves me starving."

Maxime laughs, and I join him.

"So what's your perfect date night food?" Maxime asks as he drives out of his neighborhood.

"I love good Mexican food, but if I'm being candid, I love New Mexican food."

"As opposed to old Mexican food?"

I giggle. "No, New Mexico, as in the state of New Mexico. The food is ridiculously good. To me, the perfect date meal is not at some posh restaurant, but at some hole-in-the-wall place, where the people are nice and unpretentious. The kind of place where you can wear jeans and kick back over a plate of good chips and red-hot salsa. I want to be able to dig into a plate of stacked enchiladas—that's where the enchiladas are flat and topped with red sauce and cheese—and eat until I've scooped up every bit of delicious chile sauce and cheese on my plate. Chased down with a margarita, of course. That is my idea of a great date."

I steal a look at Maxime, who is driving down the winding roads, his windshield wipers rhythmically wiping the snow away. He's smiling, ear to ear.

"You're not what I expected," Maxime says.

"How so?"

"You look—and I apologize in advance for the stereotyping—so chic and glamorous. I expected you to want more of the dates you had on *Is It Love?* Champagne at some trendy bar, then dinner at some see-and-be-seen kind of restaurant in Denver, followed by cocktails at a nightclub before Ubering home."

"I'll forgive you this one time for being so off-base," I tease.

"I appreciate your graciousness in not making me a wanker for that."

I laugh. "No, that doesn't make you a wanker. It makes you off-base, but not a wanker. Anyway, that girl you described? Not me. Did I think having a date on a yacht was amazing? Of course, anyone would. But that's a once-in-a-lifetime experience. What I want are real experiences. I want Friday night traditions. I want conversation and chips and enchiladas. I want to watch *Law & Order* reruns on my couch with the guy I'm seeing. I want him to be okay with me wearing no makeup and changing into my cozy pajamas the second we settle in for the night. I want to play Monopoly and place bets on who will win, or share a pint of ice cream on the couch with two spoons. I've had a lot of time to think about what I want after Tom. You can keep a

AVEN ELLIS

picnic in Napa Valley or candlelit dinners on a beach. I want real."

Maxime pulls up toward a red light. "I think both can be real."

"You think going on a yacht date in Monaco is reality?"

He turns his attention to me, and for the millionth time, I'm caught off guard by just how beautiful Maxime is in person.

"If you are with the right man, it's real. It's not the location that matters. It's the *feeling* you get when you are with that person. If it's genuine, it's real."

My breath catches in my throat.

Tom never spoke words from his heart like this to me. Yes, he said pretty things, but they were never sincere.

I've been with Maxime for only an hour, and already he's more of a man than Tom ever was on our dates.

This isn't a date, I remind myself.

I comb my fingers through my hair as the light turns, and Maxime continues toward the Pearl Street Mall.

I know my judgment with men is crap.

I know I should be working on rebuilding myself.

I know I shouldn't have butterflies.

But I do.

Maxime's sincerity during today's conversation tells me that if he were to ask me out, it wouldn't be a case of reality blurred.

It would be real.

CHAPTER SEVEN

I OPEN THE DOOR TO THE APARTMENT, CARRYING BORIS and Natasha inside the soft-sided carrier I bought for them.

"We're home," I say, not only to them but to Maxime, who is following behind me with the cat supplies gathered in his massive arms. "I've only been here a few days, so I haven't unpacked, let alone decorated. Don't judge me by the empty spaces and mess."

Maxime places the load of supplies on the countertop while I gently set the cat carrier on the floor and sit down beside it.

"I think you'll find I'm a pretty non-judgmental person," he says.

I have found that to be the truth. If he had any cause to judge me, it would be for making out with a man for millions of people to watch on TV, and that hasn't bothered him so far.

Neither did walking down Pearl Street with me and

having people stop and want me to take a picture with them. It's funny; I assumed people would ask *him* for pictures, too, as he's the alternate captain for the Mountain Lions, but he only had one request while I had five people ask for selfies. Maxime joked that it was because I'm obviously more famous than he is. Tom loved the spotlight, but Maxime seemed to prefer the fact that the attention wasn't on him for a change.

I think if he could play hockey in front of no one and make a living at it, he'd be absolutely happy.

"Where do you want to set up the litter box?" Maxime asks, interrupting my thoughts.

Crap. I hadn't thought about that.

"Restroom?" Maxime suggests when I don't answer.

Boris and Natasha begin mewing inside their carrier.

"Yes, but I'll do that," I say, shaking my head. "You've done enough by carrying all their stuff up. I'm going to take them out first. According to what the rescue guy told me, I'm supposed to sit with them in a small room and let them get used to me before moving them to a bigger room."

"Not that I'm the Cat Man of Belgium by any means, but I say let them get a lay of the land here. They'll get brave and explore. We can show them where the litter box is."

"Cat Man of Belgium," I repeat, grinning up at him.

"I had cats growing up," he says. "Do you have a pair of scissors so I can cut open this litter bag?"

I carefully unzip the side of the carrier. Boris and

Natasha are backed up against the other end, looking at me with sheer terror in their eyes.

"It's okay, babies," I say softly, but they remain frozen in the carrier. "Maxime, they're petrified."

Maxime stops what he's doing and moves over to me, dropping down on the floor beside me. We're both still in our winter gear, too focused on the kittens to have changed.

"Let's back up and give them space. Start talking to them," Maxime says. "They need to hear your voice."

I nod, and we both scoot back across my hardwood floor, giving them room to come out.

"Boris, Natasha, it's okay," I say soothingly. "This is going to be your home. You're safe and accepted here."

Boris—at least I think it's Boris, as he's meant to be a bit bigger—peeks his head out.

"Look, Maxime, he's coming out," I whisper excitedly.

Maxime is smiling. "He's so cute."

Boris creeps out, his body slunk low to the ground in a protective position. He then takes off, dodging boxes, and flies under the sofa for refuge.

Natasha follows next, a gray blur of fluff as she dives under the sofa to reach safety away from Maxime and me.

"Why do I have a feeling they are going to live there?" I ask.

Maxime laughs. "Only until you go to bed. Then it will be safe to come out and eat."

We stand up and begin peeling off our winter layers.

"That's why I had to adopt them. I didn't plan on

having cats, but I saw them and how scared they were, being in a cage where everyone could watch them, and I had to rescue them. I had to."

Maxime tugs off his gloves and tosses them onto my countertop, next to his phone and keys.

"Because you know how they feel," he says gently. "You know what it's like to be scared and trapped and have everyone watching you with no escape."

I don't say anything for a moment. I swallow down the swell of emotion that has appeared in my throat.

"Yes," I manage to get out. "That's when I knew I was meant to help these kittens. I know how they feel. I will do everything I can to build their trust in me."

I glance at Maxime, who is staring at me with a softness in his eyes.

I realize Maxime is rebuilding my trust in men, too.

"You have a huge heart," Maxime says.

"Thank you," I say, touched that he recognizes that in me.

"That's important. I've learned that from my past with women."

He moves back to the litter box, and as I unzip my parka, I decide he's opened the door for me to get to know him better.

"What is your past with women, Maxime?"

"You didn't waste time with that follow up. You are a journalist, aren't you?"

"I'd like to think my journalism skills are equal to my skills as a cupcake faker."

Maxime laughs. "I'll answer if you bring me a pair

of scissors so I can get this litter box set up for the babies."

My heart does a little flip.

He called my kittens *babies*.

Is there anything sexier than that?

I scan the boxes stacked in the living area, as I was using the scissors to cut them open earlier. I spot them amongst the clutter and hand them to Maxime.

"Scissors have been provided. Now women. Tell me all."

"Oh, no, you don't get all at one time. That would remove the journalistic challenge."

He winks at me.

I find myself feeling giddy. I love seeing this new side of Maxime. He's very serious, but there's a teasing side that comes out unexpectedly.

I like it.

I might like it too much.

"Where's the restroom? I'll get this set up for them."

"You realize running off with the litter box won't deter my line of questioning."

Maxime's eyes light up, and I feel my heart respond in the same way.

"Understood."

"Okay," I say, retrieving bowls for the kittens. I take a moment to peel a sticker off the side of one of them. "Down the hall to the left. Rather impossible for you to get lost, despite my cavernous digs."

"You're saying I won't need a GPS."

"Um, that's exactly what I'm saying."

Maxime picks up the litter box and flashes me a sexy smile. "I'll be right back."

My heart skips along as I wash the food and water bowls. How is Maxime not taken? He's sexy as hell. Thoughtful. Sensitive.

Unless he's been as burned by love as I have, I muse as I reach for the bag of kitten food and pour some into the bowl. Then I understand why he's content to live a quiet life in Boulder with the mountains and his dogs for company.

I fill the bowl with kitten chow and set it on the kitchen floor, along with water. I'll put out some moist food before I go to bed, and perhaps that will entice them to come out.

Along with my going to bed, I muse.

Maxime returns to the living room. "Okay, reporter. Fire away."

"Have you been in love?"

He laughs. "Okay, going for the tough one first. I thought you were a lifestyle reporter, not an investigative one."

"I think love is a lifestyle topic."

"Okay. Yes. I've been in love. Once." He pauses and gives me an adorable side-eye glance. "Remember, you said you are a lifestyle reporter. You need to go easy on me. You are supposed to bring good stories to the world, not pathetic tales of failure."

"I'll go easy on you, I promise," I say good-naturedly. "Who were you in love with?"

"Her name is Juliette," Maxime says. "I think it's fair to say I turned out to be far from her idea of Romeo."

And that's all he says.

I'm about to ask more when he clears his throat. "Let's try something with the cat treats."

Maxime picks up the packet and tears it open. He moves back toward the sofa, taking a moment to nudge some of my boxes aside, and to my surprise, he gets down on the floor, lying on his stomach.

"Oh, Skye, come here," he says. "Look at them."

I drop down to the floor and lie next to his huge frame, which seems to span much of the hardwood. I'm aware of his masculine presence, from his powerful muscular arms and long length to the intoxicating vanilla-bourbon scent lingering on his skin.

"They're so tiny and cute," Maxime says, breaking through my thoughts.

I shift my attention to Boris and Natasha, who are cuddled together against the wall.

"They're bonded," I say softly. "They have to be together to feel safe."

"I'm going to try something," Maxime says.

He reaches for the packet of treats and shakes some out onto the floor. Then he takes one and places it under the sofa, and using one finger, slides it toward the kittens.

"Here you go, babies, a treat for you," he says gently.

I watch as he takes his hand back, and Natasha goes for the treat, eating it.

"That's a good girl," Maxime says. "Want another one?"

Maxime places another one in front of her, moving it a bit closer to us.

She moves closer and eats it.

"Food," I say, grinning. "It's the great equalizer."

"This is how you'll build their trust, with food."

"I know it's a way to build mine," I tease. I reach for a treat and place it near Boris, who presses his back against the wall in fear while Natasha eats her way closer to where Maxime is.

"He's going to take more work," Maxime says, thinking aloud. "You're going to have to earn his trust."

"I'm up for that challenge. I have patience."

I push another treat in front of poor little Boris, who is still staring at me with deep fear in his eyes.

Maxime continues to feed Natasha, who is coming closer to the edge of the sofa.

"Are you going to try to touch her?" I ask.

"No," Maxime says. "I'm going to let her eat these and feel safe first."

Maxime and I continue to lie side by side, content to watch the kittens.

"Thank you for helping me with them," I say.

"It's my pleasure. They'll be out and about, tearing up your apartment before you know it."

I giggle. "It's a good thing I bought the scratching post."

"Yes, that will be needed."

"I want to give them a good home. I want them to be happy here."

Maxime is quiet for a moment. "I know they will, Skye. They were meant to be yours."

I turn to face him.

"If you had told me yesterday I'd be lying on my floor with you, staring at kittens under my couch, I would have told you that you were insane," I say.

Maxime stares at me. "I would have said the very same thing."

I like having you here, I think as I stare back at him.

"When do you start your new job?" Maxime asks.

"Next Monday," I say. "I can't wait. It's the break I've been waiting for."

"Didn't you get a lot of offers after *Is It Love?* aired?"

"None that I wanted. I received some offers for entertainment reporting in L.A., but that's not what I went to school to do. My agent was furious I turned them down, but I had to stay true to myself. More so after what happened on *Is It Love?*"

"I admire that about you."

"Thank you. Charlotte set up some initial discussions to do a cookbook for the *Bake It!* magazine people, but after a lot of thought, I turned it down. I don't know how to bake, and that's trading on the storyline the show created for me. I did the cupcake article for them this month, but that was more about my flavor preferences. I'm drawing the line there. I know JoJo was hoping to collaborate on the cookbook, but luckily she understood where I was coming from."

"JoJo is a great girl," Maxime says. "She's good for Cade."

I nod. Cade Callahan is Maxime's teammate and the love of JoJo's life. They were the reason Maxime and I reconnected in the first place.

"They got engaged fast, but with them, it seems right," I say. They began dating this past fall and got engaged last month during the Mountain Lions' break in January.

"What they have is real," Maxime concedes. "Cade is one of my best friends. He loves her, and once he knew it, he wanted to marry her. For him, love is very straightforward."

"And it's not for you?"

"You don't miss anything, do you?"

I'm about to answer when my stomach unleashes a hideous sound that practically bounces off the walls of my living room. It's the kind of sound that says I haven't eaten in days, despite having had bread with sprinkles a short while ago. I feel my face grow hot in embarrassment. Shit. There's no way he didn't hear that.

It was so loud that I'm pretty sure the guy living *across the hall* heard it.

Maxime bursts out laughing. "What was *that?* Was that your *stomach?*"

Oh my God. My stomach has a history of releasing hideous sounds at the most inopportune times, like in a classroom when it's dead silent, or when the audio guy is putting a mic on me.

Or apparently when I'm in front of a sexy Belgian hockey player, who is now staring at me in disbelief that my body can produce such amazing sounds.

"Okay. I know it sounds like the Abominable Snowman from *Rudolph the Red-Nosed Reindeer,* but *yes,* that was my stomach."

Maxime looks completely lost now.

"I have no idea what you just said. What are you talking about?"

"You mean the movie? Have you never seen it? It's stop-motion animation, and it's a holiday classic."

"A holiday movie with an Abominable Snowman? Sounds very cheerful," Maxime teases.

"No, it's about misfits fitting in. I can't believe you don't know about the Island of Misfit Toys! You *have* to see it, Maxime."

"I never realized my American holiday experience was lacking until now."

"It's messed up. I feel sad for you."

As soon as our eyes meet, we both crack up.

"Are you hungry?" Maxime asks.

"I guess I lost track of time," I say. "But, yes, I could use a snack."

"Me, too. But I should get going."

My heart drops as Maxime sits up. I quickly think of a way to spend more time with him. I could offer to make him a snack as a thank you.

Except all I have is oatmeal and a can of Funfetti frosting.

While I think oatmeal topped with a dab of Funfetti frosting is an amazing snack, I doubt Maxime would.

Kicking myself for not fully stocking my kitchen, I sit up, too.

Maxime rises, and I reluctantly do the same, knowing it's time for him to take me back to his place to get my car.

So I can leave.

AVEN ELLIS

Ugh. I don't want to leave him, not when I'm just starting to get to know him.

There are no plans on the horizon to see him again, either.

"I should take you back to get your car," he says.

I nod, although my instinct is to shake my head no.

Which is ridiculous.

Isn't it?

"Can you wait that long to eat? Do we need to stop and get something first?"

"No, I think I can survive the trip to your house and back."

"You're sure?"

"Well, I could bring my can of Funfetti frosting and a spoon, but I'll refrain."

"I've seen that on your blog," Maxime says.

"I know you must be dying to try it."

He begins to laugh. "Yes. I'm waiting for the right moment to break out the Funfetti." Maxime slips into his cashmere overcoat once again, and I love how sophisticated it looks on him. He takes a moment to tug on his gloves, and then he pauses before picking up his keys. "Give me a few moments to warm up the car for you."

"Maxime, you don't have to do that," I say, shaking my head.

"I want to. You shouldn't be cold. Come down in a few minutes," he says.

Then he heads out the door.

As soon as it's shut behind him, I exhale, my breath shaky. I like him.

I like him, I like him, I like him.

But isn't this how it always starts? With Tom, it was the same. A first conversation, a first time flirting, then a first date. Okay, so my first date with Tom was with me and five other girls, but still.

Tom seemed amazing and brilliant at first, too.

Except he turned out to be a complete wanker.

I wrap my arms around myself and frown.

But Maxime isn't Tom, I think. *He's more of a man than Tom could ever dream of being.*

Despite what my gut is saying, I barely know Maxime. I made myself a promise, and I need to be careful. My gut couldn't have been more wrong about Tom, and even though my insides are screaming that Maxime is different, I need to use caution.

"Oh my God, I need to shut up!" I cry aloud.

Great. Now I'm yelling at myself.

I'm losing it.

I'll blame the fact that I'm starving. I get cranky and absolutely nutters when I'm hungry.

That has to be it.

I bundle back up and head outside. The snow is continuing to fall, and I wonder how many inches will be on the ground by tonight.

I find Maxime waiting in his Jaguar SUV for me. I open the passenger door and slip inside, the warmth of the heated air once again wrapping around me.

We don't talk much on the ride back, but it's not a weird silence. I find myself gazing out the window at the Rockies, wondering what is happening between us. We're becoming friends. Will we become more? We've both been hurt badly by people we loved. While I don't know his story with Juliette, I can tell she is the one who hurt him, like Tom was the one who hurt me.

Can we take a chance on each other?

I feel the chemistry between us. I want to explore it, and I have a feeling Maxime does, too.

The drive back seems faster than the drive to Pearl Street, and before I know it, Maxime is pulling up in his circular drive. He puts his vehicle in park and clears his throat.

"Here we are," he says.

"Thanks for today. I had fun," I say, smiling at him.

"Me, too. It was a nice way to spend the day," Maxime says.

I wait for him to add more, and when he doesn't, I add, "Well, I should get going."

I open the car door, and Maxime follows suit.

"Do you want to let it warm up first?" he asks. "You can wait inside."

I walk over to my car and flash him a smile, despite my disappointment that our time has come to an end. "I'll wait in it while it warms up. Your warming service is going to spoil me. Thank you again for everything. I'll, uh, see you soon."

Maxime stands still, staring at me as I put the key in the lock. I study the fresh layer of snow on my car. I know I need to scrape off the windshield, but all I want to do is drive off, with my disappointment as a parting gift, and go home.

I slip inside the frigid car, turn the key in the ignition, and let it start running. My teeth are chattering as I reach for the ice scraper, which is on the passenger side floorboard. I retrieve it and get back out, and I find Maxime is still standing in the driveway. The snow is drifting down over him, but instead of moving toward the house, he comes toward me.

My heart begins to pound as Maxime stops a few inches from me. The snow is swirling between us, dusting his gorgeous cheekbones and long, dark eyelashes, and I forget how to breathe.

"While I was waiting for you to come down from your apartment, I found on my mobile there's a New Mexican restaurant about twenty minutes from here," he says. "Nothing fancy. Small. Seems like the kind of place you'd like."

Now I'm shaking, and it has nothing to do with being cold. I stare up at him, happiness bubbling through every inch of me as I wait for him to speak again.

"Skye, I never thought I'd be asking you this, but I am. I want to spend more time with you. I feel as if I have been granted a second chance today. That rarely happens, and I want to make the most of it.

"Tomorrow night is Valentine's Day," he continues. "I was wondering if you would have dinner with me."

CHAPTER EIGHT

I'm going out with Maxime on Valentine's Day.

I AM GOING OUT WITH MAXIME ON VALENTINE'S DAY!

Yes, I'm shouting at myself in my head, but this is a shout-worthy sentence, even if I have to do it mentally.

I run up the stairs to my apartment, my body humming with excitement about Maxime's invitation. He's going to pick me up tomorrow night around seven. I make a plan as I thrust the key into the lock and enter my apartment. I need to find a date-appropriate outfit. Do I have anything suitable? I haven't been on a date since *Is It Love?* last spring.

A date.

I'm going on a date.

On Valentine's Day.

With Maxime Laurent.

I close the door behind me and exhale.

I can't decide if this is a sign. I first laid eyes on a

man on the other side of the Atlantic, and he has now re-entered my life. Does that mean this is meant to be? Or have I learned nothing from *Is It Love?* Am I setting myself up for another romance that might end with my heart being ripped apart and scattered into the winds?

I doff my winter gear, setting my boots beside the door and hanging up my coat in the closet. I move over to the sofa, drop down to the floor, and find my sweet kittens huddled together, staring back at me with wide eyes.

"Hi, sweethearts," I say gently, smiling at them. "Mommy is home for the night. Remember Maxime? He asked me to be his date on Valentine's Day. I'm so happy I could yell, but that would scare you, wouldn't it?"

I spy the bag of treats Maxime was using and dump some out on the floor. Natasha immediately moves closer, ready to partake in my equalizer, but Boris is not having it.

"You're a smart one, Boris," I say, pushing a treat toward him. "You don't trust easily, do you?"

Maybe Boris is here as my reminder to be careful with Maxime, I think. *Have dinner. Have fun. But don't go full-on thinking romance and potential for love after one date.*

Or five dates.

Or even the twentieth date.

I need to be guarded until my judgment is clear. Like Boris, I'll approach Maxime with caution. Once I feel safe, I'll make decisions about where things should go, if we go anywhere after this first date.

I will, however, allow myself to be excited. Nobody was ever hurt by looking forward to an evening out.

Especially if that evening includes eating New Mexican food with a sexy, sophisticated, European hockey player.

I have to share this news with someone other than the kittens. I get back up and grab my phone. I know JoJo is at work—and most likely in a development lab working on a new recipe—but even if she can't respond right away, I have to tell her.

I'll message her and Sierra in our Connectivity group chat.

I open up the chat box where the three of us talk almost daily. I sink down on the sofa and begin typing:

Me: Okay, stand back. Brace yourselves. I'm going out with Maxime tomorrow. He saw my pics online yesterday, we began chatting, and we met up for a cup of coffee. Then he asked me to go to dinner. I said yes, but don't worry, I'm going to be very cautious. It's dinner. JUST DINNER.

Then I hit send.
Within seconds, my phone goes off.

JoJo: WHAT?!?!?

Sierra: OMG BEST NEWS EVER!

Me: Aren't you two supposed to be working?

JoJo: AHHH! I am so excited! Maxime is a GREAT GUY!

I burst out laughing, as JoJo has inserted a GIF from *The Golden Girls* into our conversation that shows Bea Arthur saying, "I can dig it."

Sierra: I can multitask while writing a report. So can JoJo. BUT I AM DYING!

Sierra: We need ALL the details.

JoJo: ALL OF THEM. Come to Denver on Friday night for drinks and dinner. Mandatory girls' night out!!!

I'm grinning as I read the comments. I message back:

Me: Girls' night out, yes. But don't expect me to have much to report. We are having DINNER. That's it.

I chew the inside of my lower lip.
I wonder if Maxime will try to kiss me.
No. He won't.
We're both cautious people, and I have a feeling he's

been as burned by his past as I have. It would make more sense if he didn't kiss me.

But what if he does kiss me?

I might self-combust.

JoJo: Maxime never asks ANYONE out. I've been with Cade since September. Not one girl has been on the scene. In fact, no girl has been on the scene since he's been with the team, and that is going on three years now.

I'm fixated on JoJo's comment. Not one girl? Nobody?

Maxime has held back, just like I have. I needed someone exceptional to even think about dating; apparently, it's been the same for him, too.

Sierra: Except for you, Skye. That night you were at our apartment, the second he walked in and recognized you, nobody else existed. Now you're in the same town, and he's going for it AAAHHHH! It's like one of those second chance romances I love! Except it's REALITY!

JoJo: I know you're being cautious, and if anyone gets that, it's me. However, Skye, I promise you, without a doubt, Maxime is a GOOD man. There's a reason he was named one of the alternate captains this

year. He's respected by his teammates.
He's steady. He leads on and off the ice.
He is worth taking a chance on.

I read JoJo's words over and over, taking them to heart. JoJo has had her heart broken in the past, just like I did, and she was hesitant to follow her heart with Cade.

But JoJo did follow her heart and found love as a result.

I finish up our conversation, teasing them to get back to work and to come up with something fabulous for me to taste test.

I draw a deep breath of air.

Maybe something wonderful will happen between chips and salsa and dessert.

I exhale. I need to do something other than sit around and feel like an eager teen waiting for her crush to show up for their date tomorrow night. I check my emails, noting one from Charlotte, who chided me for looking like a desperate mess who was seeking solace in donuts and cats instead of America's Sweetheart yesterday in public. For good measure, she attached several tabloid pictures of my embarrassing moment.

Anger flickers over me as I read her words. I begin to type back that I'm far from desperate. I'm a real-life woman who doesn't always want to wear makeup. I can eat the occasional donut and wear sweatpants if I want. If she doesn't want to represent a real woman, she doesn't have to.

I abruptly stop typing. My mom would tell me to sit

on it for twenty-four hours. I click out of the email, sighing deeply, and sink back against my white sofa cushions as I click through the rest of my messages. I stop when I see another one from Charlotte, this time regarding the book opportunity:

To: SkyeReeve@flashmail.net

From: CStone@stoneclarkandwhite.org

Date: February 13th

Subject: Book proposal

Skye, you need to make a decision on this. I've held the publisher off as long as I can. I think we can come up with a way to make everyone happy. I know you refuse to write a tell-all book, and I respect your sweet, not-wanting-to-upset-anyone nature, but surely you can find a way to talk about your time on the show in a way that is comfortable to you yet entertaining for the public. You're already helping so many women like yourself, those who have been dealt the cruel blow of a broken heart. Think of how many more we can reach with a book. I propose a life guide, with just a few, tiny personal stories thrown in.

Skye, you also need to think like a businesswoman. This will bring you not only an advance, but I'll negotiate a top-rate for royalties. Plus, we can discuss an audiobook, international rights, a book tour, and speaking engagements. This can catapult you out of Colorado and into a reporting career in a big market. Don't let sweetness stand in your way. You can find a way to be both.

Best,

Charlotte

I put my phone down and think for a moment. I know she's right about this being a tremendous opportunity, but I'm wrestling with it. I know the publishing house is going to want the stories from *Is It Love?*—the juicier the better—and I refuse to do that. I'm not going to talk bad about the other girls in the house or Tom, even though he is a wanker. I'm not going to dive into the details of our relationship for the masses to read, even if our romance played out on TV and my silence now screams of hypocrisy.

I'm not a hypocrite if I refuse to gossip and provide details that nobody else needs to know, I think stubbornly.

The idea of writing a book does appeal to me, though. I could share some things I've learned and maybe help people. A book would give me far greater reach than my blog. I could talk about transitioning from a university student to a reality TV star to a working woman. I can share what it's like to show your real self to the world after being on an unreal TV experience.

It might be worth it.

But I'm starting this new TV job on Monday, so when will I have time to write a book? When will I learn *how* to write a book? On top of that, I still have my Instagram and blog and responsibilities as a social influencer.

My mom's twenty-four-hour rule comes to mind. I'll answer Charlotte tomorrow after I've had a chance to think about it. I know my dad, the TV executive, would tell me to seize every opportunity that comes my way. He would insist that you never say no in this business and the fact that there is still an interest in me after my repeated no's is nothing short of a miracle.

However, there is one thing that has come my way and caught my interest, and that is one thing I do want to think about right now.

Maxime Laurent.

Our date tomorrow night cannot come fast enough.

CHAPTER NINE

Celebrate Life with Sprinkles—The Blog
Happy Valentine's Day

I PULL OUT A TUBE OF MASCARA AND CAREFULLY BEGIN applying it to my lashes. I remember how the *Is It Love?* team always put fake ones on because the producer said my natural blonde ones were non-existent. I pause as I study my reflection, thinking of how I look now, as opposed to when I had a team of makeup artists working on me.

Watching endless hours of makeup tutorials on YouTube has paid off, as I know how to use brushes and sponges now to create a dewy, luminous finish on my gold-tinted skin. I create a sun-kissed glow, much lighter than the heavy makeup I wear on TV. I dusted my cheekbones with some bronzer and followed with a highlighter cream on the top for some shimmer. My eye makeup is a neutral palette, with champagne as the color near the brow bone and a cappuccino color for the lid that I've blended with my brush. I selected a dark chocolate brown to smudge into the corners and a similar color to line close to my lashes, which I winged out just a touch for emphasis.

I finish applying mascara and stare back at my reflection.

I'm ready to go out with Maxime.

I put down the mascara and realize the last time I got ready for a date was on my final day with Tom. I remember the excitement I felt while getting ready. I was eager for the rest of my life to begin with the man I loved. When Tom broke my heart, I was convinced I would never want another man to touch me ever again. There would be Tom, or there would be no one. I would never want to take a chance on love, as obviously I had no clue what it was. I didn't know how to tell real intentions from a bunch of promises whispered in my ear before kisses landed on my lips.

Yet here I am.

I've taken extra time to do my makeup. My hair is in beachy waves that cascade down my back. I've dug through my wardrobe moving boxes to find a cream, velvet camisole top; a long, thick charcoal duster cardigan; my distressed Paige jeans; and my suede, over-the-knee black boots.

As opposed to the pink tones the show put on my face, to give me that sweet, innocent look, my appearance now reflects the golden, California girl I am inside. I'm not dressed in the trendy short skirts and crop tops the show had me wear to emphasize my body. Instead, I wear the clothing I like, such as this cozy sweater and cami that feel good next to my skin. I love texture, I love feeling warm, and I love clothing that makes me feel wrapped and secure.

This is me.

This is the woman I want Maxime to get to know tonight.

I flip off the light and walk back into the living room, where I get down on my knees so I can peek at my fur babies underneath the sofa. I heard them come out last night; the sound of chewing kibble gave them away and made my heart melt. They came out to eat canned cat food this morning, but then they retreated under the sofa. I keep giving them treats and talking to them so they get used to my voice.

"I'm going out as soon as Maxime gets here, so please feel free to explore," I say.

Natasha stretches, and I think she is going to be the brave one. My little *Dora the Explorer,* I think, remembering the cartoon my cousin's daughter, Violet, loves so much.

But Boris—he's going to be much more cautious.

"You're my reminder," I say softly, turning my attention to Boris. "I'll take my time getting to know Maxime, just like you will with me."

Ding!

Oh! He's here! I stand up, and nerves and excitement fight for control as I head for the door.

I put my hand on the doorknob and press my eye to the peephole.

Oh, I'm in serious trouble.

Because through the peephole, I see Maxime is holding a beautiful bouquet of bright red poppies.

He brought me flowers.

On Valentine's Day.

I turn the lock and open the door, drinking him in as I do. I take in the stunning brown hair with blond streaks, the piercing blue-green eyes, the sculpted cheekbones and full lips.

Maxime does the same, taking me in from my face down to my boots before quickly bringing his eyes back up to meet my gaze.

"*Tu es superbe,*" Maxime says.

I can't breathe from hearing those beautiful words escape his lips.

He just told me I'm gorgeous in his native language.

"*Merci, tu es aussi très beau,*" I say, thanking Maxime and telling him that he looks handsome, too.

A huge smile lights up his face. "I like that you can speak my native language."

I put out my hand to stop him. "Don't get too excited. I'm not an expert in French by any means."

"I think you're underestimating your French," he says. Maxime then extends the bouquet to me. "These are for you."

I take the poppies from him, and the second our fingertips brush, I feel a delicious warmth fill me inside like I've never experienced before. It's a feeling of excitement and anticipation mixed with comfort from the brief contact with his skin.

Comfort.

Like the clothes I'm wearing, I feel as if those hands

would protect me. Comfort me. Make me feel adored and safe.

With a jolt, I look back into his eyes and see something so genuine it nearly takes my breath away.

"These are beautiful," I say, wondering how I can feel all these things for one man, a man I barely know. "Please, come in."

Maxime walks past me, and for a brief second, I can smell that wonderful, warm cologne that is lingering on his skin. I wish I could get more of that lush bourbon-vanilla scent, but the second he steps away from me, the scent is gone. It's obvious you have to get up close to him to breathe it in.

Heat fills me from that thought.

"They reminded me of you," Maxime says, turning around and flashing me a smile.

"Huh?"

"Um, the flowers. They reminded me of you."

GET IT TOGETHER SKYE, I think, mentally slapping myself upside the head.

Before you ask Maxime if you can lick his neck to see if he tastes as divine as he smells.

I clear my throat as a reset. "How so?" I ask, moving into the kitchen to find something to put them in.

"Bright. Cheerful," Maxime says. "Beautiful."

Oh, this Belgian's sweet words make it difficult to be pragmatic.

But I have to try.

"Thank you," I say, rummaging through my half-filled cabinets and retrieving a glass. I'll need to cut the stems to make them fit, but it's the best I can do for now.

"They are lovely. I'm curious, though. What made you select poppies?"

"It's the national flower of Belgium, where we should have met, but didn't."

My heart flutters rapidly.

The flowers are more than a gesture.

They have meaning.

"I love that," I say, carefully untying the string around the cellophane wrapping and mentally deciding that if we start dating, and months and months later we fall in love, poppies will forever be our flower.

Of course, that's a totally unrealistic thought, and since I'm being pragmatic and taking my time, there's no need to think of poppies in my future.

At least that is what the rational, mature, learn-from-the-past side of my brain informs me.

However, the other half of my brain, the one connected to my heart that tends to override my rational side, is feeling all the THINGS. I feel butterflies and goosebumps and eagerness inside, and a gut feeling that I crossed Maxime's path in Belgium, and again in Denver, for a reason.

A reason of the heart.

I carefully lift the flowers out and reach for my scissors, which are still laying on the countertop from earlier. I glance up, and Maxime has moved back to the sofa and is down on the floor talking to Boris and Natasha.

"They're sleeping," Maxime reports back. "I bet they will come out and explore while you are out."

I cut the stems of the bouquet, and Maxime continues to talk to the kittens.

"I'm eager to hold them and play with them," I say. "I can't wait for them to feel at home, but I understand they need to take their time. They are afraid of trusting me right now."

Maxime rolls over on his side, and his sweater creeps up. I get a flash of the most chiseled six-pack I have ever seen, with a trail of dark hair leading down to the waistband of his jeans. I feel my jaw drop as I stare at his definition.

I quickly shift my focus back to arranging the flowers in the glass.

"You'll earn their trust quickly. They will know they are safe here, and then you won't be able to keep them off you."

"There is nothing better than puppy kisses or kitten snuggles," I say. I pick up the glass filled with the vibrant poppies and smile. "I'm going to put these on my nightstand and shut the bedroom door, just in case Boris and Natasha get really brave and decide to enjoy eating some flowers."

Maxime nods, and I steal another look at his glorious abs, which are still exposed. "I'll Google if poppies are toxic to cats. I should have thought of that before bringing them to you."

"Maxime, don't even say that. They are gorgeous, and I love them."

He pushes himself upright, and my view of his amazing stomach is gone.

Dammit.

"I still want to know if they are toxic." He stands up and retrieves his phone from his coat pocket.

"Okay," I say. "I'll be right back."

I head into my bedroom and place the flowers beside my bed, smiling as I know I'll love seeing them when I come home tonight.

I exit my room and shut the door behind me, making sure it's securely closed before leaving.

"Skye, come here," Maxime says.

I move back down the hall and find Maxime staring at his iPhone in the living room. I move next to him, feeling small against his towering frame, and glance down at his phone.

"I brought poison into your home," Maxime says seriously.

I read what he has pulled up, and sure enough, poppies can cause an excited or euphoric state in cats.

"You're trying to get my babies high," I tease.

"No, no, I'm not," Maxime says, laughing as he shakes his head. "I would have brought roses if I knew poppies were toxic to them."

"You brought *drugs* into my home," I continue. "What kind of man are you?"

Maxime slips his phone into his pocket and stares down at me. "Apparently, I'm a dangerous man, introducing you and your fur babies to fringe elements and leading them down a dark path of no return."

My heart flutters as I see the teasing glint in his beautiful blue-green eyes.

"I need to watch out for you, Maxime Laurent."

Oh, do I ever need to watch out for him, my head

reminds me. I could fall fast for him, which is the one thing I cannot do.

No matter how sweet and mature and sexy he is.

"Are you ready?" Maxime asks. "We don't want to be late."

"I'm starving, so no, we can't be," I say, retrieving my coat and slipping into it. "I hope they have great chips and salsa. Really spicy salsa. With warm, freshly fried chips that are liberally salted."

Maxime stares at me. "Have you ever thought about doing one of those food shows where you travel around and eat at different places?"

"No, I haven't."

I pick up my purse and keys, and we move out into the hallway. I put the key into the lock, and as soon as it clicks, we begin our walk to the stairs.

"You should," Maxime continues. "You have a way of describing food that makes me want to eat it. I could see you doing that."

An idea flashes through my head. "I can suggest that for *Boulder Live*," I say as my thoughts come together. "Maybe I could do a roving reporter thing around Boulder where I try different restaurants and discuss the food with the chef, try it on-air, etc."

"Yeah, I can see you doing that," he says as we walk down the stairs.

"I love to eat, so this speaks to me. When I start work on Monday and get my assignments, I'll bring this up. In the shows I've watched, they'll have chefs come in and do a cooking segment, but I haven't seen a reporter out on the town going to restaurants on a regular basis."

"You'd be good at it. You make me want to eat spicy food, and I'm usually not a huge fan," Maxime admits.

I stop walking. "Maxime, you realize you are taking me out for New Mexican food, stuff like enchiladas and green chile stew. It's *hot*. Why are we going here if you don't like spicy food?"

Maxime stops next to me, and I gaze up at him.

"Because it's something you love," he says simply. "You brought up stacked enchiladas and a hole-in-the-wall restaurant and a margarita. I can make that happen. Why wouldn't I give you this meal if that's what you want?"

I find joy surging through me.

You're exceptional, Maxime, I think, *and I don't think you have any idea of how amazing you are.*

"Come on," Maxime says, and we continue to walk down the steps and out into the winter wonderland around us. It has stopped snowing. The sky is a beautiful inky black, and the air is crisp and frozen.

"Hmm, if I were to return the favor, where would I take you to dinner? What would be your ideal date meal?" I ask as we walk toward his car.

Maxime laughs. "You couldn't find it here."

"Here as in Colorado?"

Maxime opens the passenger door toward for me. "No, as in not in America. I mean, maybe you could, but it's best at home."

I climb into the car, my teeth chattering.

I think I'm going to be a block of ice for the rest of my life.

Like Elsa from *Frozen.*

Until love saved her.

Jeez, I'm the queen of overanalyzing. I think that shall be my new title instead of America's Reality Show Sweetheart.

Maxime gets in beside me and interrupts my thoughts. "I'm sorry I didn't start the car. I figured we weren't upstairs that long."

"No, it's okay," I say. "So, what would your ideal meal be?"

"I miss *vol-au-vent*," Maxime says as he puts his seat belt on, and I follow suit. "It's this round puff pastry, and the center is cut out and filled with meat and a cream sauce. My mom makes the best *vol-au-vent*. My favorite is one filled with chicken, leeks, and mushrooms. It's the first meal I want when I go home after the season. She serves it with fries on the side."

I picture this dish in my head. "Anything with puff pastry has to be good. What else do you miss from Belgium?"

Maxime eases into the stream of traffic. "Beef stew with fries."

I furrow my brow as I begin to defrost, thanks to Maxime's heated car seats. "Beef stew with fries?"

"And mayonnaise."

"Wait, you eat beef stew with mayonnaise?" I ask, cringing.

Maxime laughs. "No, no, with the fries."

"What? Mayo with fries?"

"It's the only way to eat fries. You dip them in mayonnaise."

"Ew, no, no, no, you have to have ketchup," I declare. "Mayo sounds wrong."

"Ketchup is wrong."

"You might need to take me home, Maxime," I tease. "Because I hate mayo."

"Hate is a strong word."

"I have strong negative feelings toward mayo, so it's appropriate."

"How can you hate mayo?"

"It grosses me out. It's gloppy and smells weird. Blech."

Maxime stops at a red light and turns to me. "I've never been with a woman who hates mayonnaise."

I see his mouth curve up in a sexy smile, and my heart flutters in response.

I raise my eyebrow. "I've never been with a man who can't handle the heat."

A devilish grin passes over his face, and I realize what I said sounds totally different from what I meant to imply, which was spicy *food*.

"I can handle the heat. In fact, sometimes heat is good, don't you think?"

Hello, we are *not* talking about enchiladas here.

"Yes, heat can be good, like seat warmers," I say, winking at him.

We haven't even arrived at the restaurant, and we're already off to a great start. We are laughing and flirting, and the conversation is natural.

This first date is going to be different from any other because of this man. Maxime is different. Our chemistry is different. It's exciting, and we're connecting, and there's something unique about our interactions. I didn't have this with Tom; that is becoming more apparent with every second I spend with Maxime.

This is wonderful.

It's real.

I have a reason to be excited.

And I can't wait to see how the rest of the evening unfolds.

CHAPTER TEN

I TAKE A MOMENT TO SLIP OUT OF MY PUFFY PARKA AND drape it across the back of my red plastic chair. Before sitting down at the small table for two, I pause to take a good look at the restaurant I've found myself in tonight.

It's textbook hole-in-the-wall, tucked inside an old brick building that looks like it used to be a gas station, judging by the ancient gas pump that greets you outside the door. The restaurant is narrow, with tables squeezed close together to get maximum seating. The décor on the walls is an eclectic mix of old road maps and vintage travel prints from both New Mexico and Colorado. Holiday lights are strung every which way across the ceiling. The kitchen is open to the restaurant, and the staff is hustling to bring dishes to customers. There are metal napkin dispensers on each table, along with a tiny vase with a single fake plastic rosebud in it. Plastic-coated menus are parked between these items.

Delight fills me.

It's fantastic.

"You said you wanted a dive," Maxime says, interrupting my thoughts.

I sit down in my chair, grinning happily at Maxime. "It's *exactly* what I wanted it. You couldn't have picked a better restaurant. This is me."

Maxime removes his knit cap, which reveals that gloriously thick hair of his. He takes a moment to rake his hand through it.

Oh, he's beautiful. He looks more like a model than a hockey player.

Hockey player.

I keep forgetting that fact about him.

Because to me, he's Maxime—the sensitive soul from the coffee house in Brussels.

He shoves his hat into his coat pocket and removes it before taking a seat. Once he's settled, he studies me for a moment before speaking.

"You are an incredibly genuine woman," he says.

"That's a wonderful compliment," I say.

"You're very grounded. Not what I expected when I found out you were on *Is It Love?* I'll be honest, I thought you would be different."

I retrieve the menus and slide one across the table to Maxime. "Did you think I'd be Hollywood fake?"

Maxime exhales. "Yes. But as I talked to you that night at JoJo and Sierra's apartment, you didn't seem that way at all. You were so kind. But I've read women wrong in the past, and I wondered if I was repeating the same mistake in trying to figure you out without knowing you."

He misjudged Juliette, my instincts tell me as I think of

his previous girlfriend. *Somehow, like I did with Tom, he fell for a woman who wasn't what she seemed.*

"What made you change your mind?" I ask.

"I started reading your blog. Your emotions were in all those posts, and you can't fake that. You put your heart in those words. You're real."

"I'm glad you believe that this is me."

"I don't just believe it." Maxime hesitates a moment, and to my surprise, he lifts his hand and reaches across the table, placing his large hand over mine and squeezing it gently. "I know it."

Every nerve I have leaps alive the second I feel his skin. His hand covers mine, and it's both warm and rough at the same time. I don't want him to remove it. Maxime slowly turns my hand over and entwines his fingers with mine, sending ripples of delight down my spine as our hands link together.

"Hello," a young woman greets us, causing us both to look at her. "How are you this evening? My name is Tara, and I'll be your server tonight."

Maxime doesn't let go of my hand while Tara places a plastic basket filled with warm chips in front of us, followed by two bowls of salsa.

Ooh! There are blue corn tortilla chips mixed in with the yellow corn ones.

The chips look crisp and fresh, and oh, I can see the flecks of salt on them. I've found my happy place in Boulder.

Absolute food porn.

"Hello," Maxime says, and I follow suit, tearing my

attention away from the chips long enough to focus on the woman who will be serving us tonight.

"Are you two celebrating Valentine's Day this evening?" Tara asks, grinning at us.

"Yes," Maxime says, not hesitating to answer. "The lady wanted authentic New Mexican food this evening, so that is what she will get."

Tara looks positively swoony from Maxime's super sexy accent. I bite my lip to keep from laughing, as I'm pretty sure I look the same way.

"Where are you from?" Tara asks.

"Belgium," Maxime says, smiling at her. Then he cocks an eyebrow at her. "And where are you from?"

Tara begins to blush, and oh, Maxime's unexpected devilish side has to be one of the most intriguing things about him.

"Um, Boulder," she mumbles as her face continues to turn red. Then she goes all business. "May I get you something to drink this evening?"

I flip the menu over and find the beverages.

"What would you like, Skye?" Maxime asks.

"I'll have a margarita on the rocks," I say.

"Very good," Tara says, nodding. "And for you, sir?"

Maxime studies the list for a moment. "Which craft brown ale do you like?" he asks.

Tara bites her lip and gazes down at the selection of beers. They discuss a couple of options, and Maxime decides on a local craft beer brewed here in Boulder. While she goes off to get our drinks, I turn my attention back to Maxime.

"Are you a craft beer fan?" I ask.

"I like good beers. I prefer the ones back in Belgium, but Cade has found me some good beers here in the States. That is a guy who is serious about his beer."

"Yes, he is. I'm more a wine or margarita girl. And if I'm eating a cupcake, I love a glass of bubbly with it."

I reach for a blue corn chip, as I can no longer resist, and Maxime does the same, all while keeping his other hand entwined with mine.

I stare down at the salsa bowls, one filled with a bright red salsa and the other with a green tomatillo salsa verde, rich with New Mexico Hatch chilies.

I can never resist a red salsa, so I dip my chip into that bowl first.

"Mmm," I murmur, as I taste the wonderful spicy blend. "So good!"

"I'll try this one," Maxime says, loading his chip up with the green salsa.

Before I can warn him that the green salsa verde is hot, according to the number of chili peppers next to it on the menu, Maxime pops the chip into his mouth.

As soon as he does, his eyes flip wide open.

Maxime starts coughing.

"That's really hot," he sputters.

He releases my hand as he continues to cough.

I see his eyes are watering. He's turning red.

I go to shove a glass of water toward him, and as I do, my elbow hits the red salsa bowl, flipping it up and splattering salsa across my chest and boobs. I feel a glob resting on my cheek.

Now Maxime is staring at me while choking, and I hear the couple at the table next to us laughing. I thrust the water at him and quickly grab a napkin as the salsa slides down into my bra.

I'm frantically stuffing paper napkins into my camisole as salsa drips off my face and onto my hand, and the situation is so absurd I do the only thing I can do.

I burst out laughing.

Maxime takes a swig of his water, and as soon as I start laughing, he starts laughing, and unfortunately, the water he drank shoots out of his nose and lands on the table.

"Oh shit!" he cries, grabbing his napkin and throwing it on the table.

Now I'm dying. Tears are streaming down my face, and Maxime is turning blood red in embarrassment.

He quickly reaches for more paper napkins from the dispenser to blow his nose, and I continue to blot salsa off my chest.

At this point, Tara reappears with our drinks. As soon as she sees the mess we've made, her brow crinkles.

"Is everything okay here?" she asks as she places the margarita and beer on the table.

I take one look at Maxime, and we both burst out laughing.

"It's perfect," I answer truthfully.

"Except for one thing," Maxime says, clearing his throat.

"What is that?" Tara asks.

"We need more red salsa."

Which makes both of us crack up again.

Tara scoops up the mess on our table, dumping it all into the chip basket.

"How about we start over here? I'll bring you a new basket of chips and salsa and then your order."

"That sounds like a good idea," Maxime says.

As soon as she leaves, Maxime grabs another napkin, but this time, he reaches across the table and gently blots the side of my face.

"How about we start over here?" he asks.

I shake my head, and a piece of onion flies out of my hair and lands on Maxime's hand.

He grins as he flicks it off.

"We will absolutely not start over," I say firmly. "This was fantastic. Perfect. Hilarious."

"Real."

I see the intensity shift in his beautiful eyes.

"Yes," I say, nodding. "It was real."

I take the napkins off my chest and drop them to the side of the table. Maxime relinks his fingers with mine, and the butterflies take off in full force.

And I can't think of a better start to our dinner than this one.

———

"THIS WAS THE BEST MEAL EVER," I DECLARE HAPPILY.

I put my fork down, having polished off an entire plate of stacked enchiladas, topped "Christmas" style with both red and green sauce and a fried egg.

"I can't tell by your plate," Maxime teases.

I grin. "I told you this was my idea of a great date: casual dress, hole-in-the-wall spot, and amazing home-style New Mexican food."

Though the food wasn't the best part.

Maxime was.

We laughed at ourselves and shared details of our lives. I learned that Maxime grew up in Belgium, but his passion for hockey took him around the world. He has two siblings, like I do, and is close to his family like I am.

I was amazed at how much he opened up, telling me how he loves reading fantasy books and can quote passages from anything written by Tolkien. The two places Maxime can leave everything behind is in a book or on the ice.

Maxime shared how much the game means to him. No matter what is going on in his life, hockey is his one constant. When he steps onto the ice, everything that is bothering him disappears and the game is all that matters. He loves the speed of the game and how his brain is challenged by how fast things happen. He enjoys the rush of beating a good defenseman to score a goal. Maxime stressed the need to stay calm in pressure situations, to think of solutions, and to point out mistakes made by younger players to help them improve. I can easily see how his quiet, calm demeanor made him an easy choice for alternate captain this season.

There were many things I didn't know about being a professional hockey player. Maxime normally follows a nutrition plan, laid out by the team nutritionist, and tonight's burger was an exception to that plan. On off days, he has practice and goes early and stays late to work on his weak points with the coaches.

I have a feeling hockey is the thing that distracted him from his broken heart after his relationship with Juliette ended. I can see how that could happen. When Tom dumped me, I didn't have a job. All I had was the media and fans reacting to every moment of my relationship as it aired on TV, and all I could do was re-live it.

Now I'm in a different spot, as is Maxime. He's the alternate captain of the Denver Mountain Lions and one of the best players in the league. I'm starting my new reporter job next Monday, I'm blogging, and I may even get a book deal.

We've both moved forward.

And we're moving forward with each other.

"Do they have any desserts that won't make my throat burn?" Maxime teases, interrupting my thoughts.

"We could get *sopaipillas*," I suggest. "It's deep-fried dough that puffs up, and it's served with honey."

Maxime reaches for the menu again. "Is there anything with chocolate?"

"You're a chocoholic, aren't you?"

Maxime smiles at me. "Yes. You know how you love sprinkles? That is how I feel about chocolate."

He glances down at the dessert section of the menu, and a cute, crestfallen expression passes over his gorgeous face. "They have a chocolate cake, but they put red chile in it." Maxime puts the menu back. "You win."

Tara reappears to sweep up our plates, and Maxime

orders sopaipillas, tripping over the pronunciation of the word and melting my heart in the process. As soon as Tara leaves, he sighs heavily.

"Why ruin a chocolate cake like that? I don't understand," he asks aloud.

I can't help but giggle at the adorable expression on his face. "Maybe I'll have to make you some chocolate cupcakes. I can't bear the disappointed look on your face."

"You can make them for me when I get back," Maxime says. "I leave for a road trip through Canada this week."

"How long are you gone?"

"Eleven days."

My heart sinks into my stomach. Eleven days? I'm having the best first date ever with him, and now I won't get to see him again for ELEVEN DAYS?

"Oh," I say, knowing my face is giving away the emotions I'm feeling inside.

Maxime reaches for my hand, once again linking his fingers through mine. "I'm sorry. It's one of our longest trips of the year, and I hate that we're having this great date and I have to leave so soon." He pauses for a moment and clears his throat. "What are you doing tomorrow night?"

My heart soars from his words.

"My calendar is fairly open, I think," I say, already knowing I'm free tomorrow.

"Would you want to go to the game? Maybe we can get a late dinner afterward?"

I squeeze his hand. "I would love that."

Maxime flips my hand over and begins drawing his fingers across my palm, causing heat to burn though me from the sensual feeling of his fingertips dancing across my skin.

"Good. I've got to get my time in before I leave. You might meet some guy and forget me while I'm on the road."

"True," I say, smiling at him. "But this new guy I might meet—he probably wouldn't have Dutch chocolate sprinkles in his pantry. That's an unforgettable quality in a man."

"I see," Maxime says, a smile tugging at the corner of his mouth. "What else is unforgettable about me?"

"Your accent," I say, feeling myself go weak as he continues to stroke my palm. "Your aversion to spice."

Now he's grinning.

"It's pretty hard to forget a man who shoots water out of his nose on your first date."

"Or a girl who has salsa all over her sweater and camisole."

"So, we're meant to have a second date tomorrow."

"Absolutely."

A basket of piping hot sopaipillas is brought to the table, along with a bottle of squeeze honey and some wet wipes, as they can be sticky to eat.

I breathe in the scent and stare at the golden puffs of dough in front of me, beckoning for a drizzle of honey.

My food porn continues.

I let go of Maxime's hand and eagerly pick up the bottle of honey, squirting it all over the top of a sopaipilla before handing the bottle to Maxime.

"I should have warned you these are messy, but I find some of the best things in life are," I say, taking a bite as the honey drips down my fingers.

I glance across the table, and Maxime is watching me eat with abandon.

"Messy is good," he says slowly, his gaze dropping to my mouth.

Suddenly, I don't want dessert anymore.

I want him to kiss me.

The urge is strong, and it's all I can think about. What would it be like to have those full lips on mine, exploring me for the first time with a kiss? I want to feel his hands on my face. I want to slide my hand up his neck. I want to feel his hair underneath my fingertips. I want to breathe in that bourbon-vanilla cologne I know is lingering on his skin. I want to feel his breath on my face. I want it all.

Now.

From the look in his eyes, he's feeling it, too.

We each manage to finish a sopaipilla, and Maxime pays the bill.

"I'll go start the car," Maxime says as he rises from his seat.

"No, I want to go with you."

"You'll be cold," Maxime protests.

No, I won't, I think, staring back at him.

"I'll be fine," I say, rising and slipping into my coat.

I come around the side of the table, and as I do, Maxime puts his hand in mine. My heart is racing with anticipation as we leave the restaurant and go out into the snowy landscape, my mind whirling as we walk to his car.

Will he kiss me? It's a first date. Maxime might not make that move.

Or he could leave me with a simple goodnight kiss.

I begin anxiously running my fingers through my hair as he opens the car door for me. I slip inside, wondering what will happen next.

Maxime comes around to the driver's side, climbs in, and starts the car. My heart is pounding so hard I can see my velvet camisole move. I begin to shake, but it's not from the cold. It's from a sudden fear that grips onto me.

I shouldn't want this so badly. I promised myself I'd be cautious. Is it normal to want a kiss so much that I feel like I can't breathe? That I need to taste his lips and feel his skin and be held by him so soon, and that I'll feel incomplete if it doesn't happen?

I turn to look at him, and Maxime is staring at me.

My heart is now roaring in my ears. I shake when I see the look in his eyes, a look that tells me he wants this moment as much as I do.

He places an un-gloved hand on my face, cupping it gently.

"You're cold," he murmurs.

"I'm not," I whisper back.

Maxime moves closer, and I can smell the sensual cologne lingering on his skin. I draw a shaky breath, and he carefully tangles his fingers through my hair.

"I believe in the moment more than the place," he says softly, lowering his forehead to mine. "I told myself if I felt it was right, I'd give you a kiss goodnight at the door. I wasn't going to let attraction drive things with you, and if it wasn't the time, I wouldn't do it. I had to listen to my gut, to my head."

I swallow nervously as I dare to reach up and touch his face. My pulse soars as I feel his warm skin against my fingers when I brush them against his strong cheekbone, all the while keeping my forehead to his.

"What does your head say?" I whisper.

"My head says what matters is that I like you, Skye. *I like you.* I like that you make me laugh and that you are genuine in who you are. I couldn't forget you from that moment I saw you in the café. When I saw you again, I couldn't believe it. I didn't know what to make of seeing you again, or your TV fame, but it didn't matter because I was sure I'd never see you again. When I saw your picture this week, I had to do it. I had to reach out to you. It turned out to be the best decision I've ever made."

I lift my head so I can look at him. "I'm glad you did. I told myself I wouldn't take a chance on anyone unless I thought they were worth it."

Maxime continues to stroke my hair. He lowers his lips dangerously close to mine.

"Am I worth it?" he whispers as I feel his warm breath against my flushed skin.

I lick my lips. "Yes. You are."

I dare to move my hand to his chest, feeling the fine fabric of his cashmere sweater and more than that, how his heart is racing like mine.

"*Tu es splendide,*" Maxime repeats, telling me I'm

beautiful. "My head says this is the place. This is the time. I need to kiss you right now."

Then his lips find mine.

CHAPTER ELEVEN

MAXIME PARTS MY LIPS, HIS MOUTH DESPERATE TO explore me. Heat surges through me as I feel his tongue slide against mine in a slow, sensual rhythm, kissing me deeply. His hands move through my hair, and he takes hold of it and sexily winds his fingers through the strands as he continues to kiss me.

I lift my hands and cradle his face as I lose myself in this kiss, this kiss that is turning my world upside down. It's sexy, it's exploratory, and it's drugging all my senses. Our mouths move together, increasing the intensity, wanting to take more and more with each kiss. I love the way Maxime is kissing me. It's not a shy, tentative kiss, but the kiss of a passionate man who *knows* what he wants—and that is to bring me to my knees with his sensual mouth.

My heart pounds as his lips take more command. Our mouths are caught up in a frantic need to stay connected and never break apart. I'm burning up. I've never been kissed like this. I move my hands to his wavy locks, and Maxime moans as I glide my fingers through his silky waves. His hair has a glorious scent, one that I want imprinted in my memory.

I realize he likes having his hair touched, so I move my hand through his thick locks, down to the nape of his neck, and lightly graze my fingertips across the back of it. Maxime responds by drawing me closer to him, his hands skimming down to my waist and pushing my coat aside. I gasp as he finds my camisole, his fingers touching the curve in my waist, and I shiver against him, which causes Maxime to kiss me harder.

Maxime eventually breaks the kiss, and we take a moment to catch our breath. I move my hands to his face, framing it in my hands, feeling absolutely treasured by the way he's looking at me.

"That kiss," Maxime murmurs, brushing his fingertips over my swollen lower lip. "That kiss ... I don't even know what to say."

"It was incredible."

He dips his head and presses a sweet kiss against my lips that is gentle and soft and sends happiness through my veins.

"A perfect Valentine's Day kiss?" he murmurs against my mouth.

"Yes," I say back, smiling.

We kiss again, holding each other's faces in our hands as we engage in a slow, caressing kiss.

I break it first this time and look up at him. "You would tell me if I tasted like onions, right?"

Maxime's face lights up in the biggest grin.

"That wouldn't be very gentlemanly of me," he says, dropping another kiss on my mouth.

I furrow my brow. "Do I taste like onions? Is that why you can't say that?"

Ew, I hope not.

"You happen to taste like honey, but I would still kiss you that way if you tasted like onions. One, because your kiss is that good, and two, because I get to kiss *you*. That's all that matters."

Maxime gives me another kiss. I lose myself in him again, and I know one thing for sure.

This is, without a doubt, the best date I've ever been on.

There's no yacht.

No exotic beach.

No candlelight, champagne, or decadent foods.

Just Maxime. And like he said, that's all that matters.

And I can't wait to see where we go next.

———

Celebrate Life with Sprinkles—The Blog
The Game is On

GETTING NO SLEEP WAS SO WORTH IT LAST NIGHT.

That's what I keep telling myself as I look at the horrible dark circles under my eyes. I pick up my Juice Beauty concealer and dab some on my makeup brush, warming it up on the back of my hand before applying it to the large shadows under my eyes.

These are different dark circles. They aren't from

insomnia, or staying up crying over Tom. They weren't caused by anxiety over awful things being said about me on social media.

These are happy circles.

I grin as I apply concealer to the other eye. Maxime and I kissed in his car, and then again when he walked me up to the door. I invited him inside, but, being a gentleman, he declined and said he would take me up on that next time. Maxime said he wanted to end the evening the right way for a first date—with a sweet, gentle kiss at my front door.

As soon as he left, I told Boris and Natasha all about our date and then got ready for bed. I kept reliving every moment of THAT KISS over and over in my head, from the feeling of his hands on my waist to the sexy scent lingering on his thick hair.

Apparently, Maxime had the same problem, as he texted me to see if I was still up, and we chatted well past midnight before he signed off.

This man makes me happy, and I think he could make me happy for a long time if I decide to let him.

I made plans to meet up with JoJo and Sierra in Denver. We're going to grab dinner and then go to the game together. Maxime said I'd have a credential and ticket waiting for me at will call, and I'm so excited I could burst.

Knowing tomorrow he's leaving for a massive road trip through Canada is the hard part. Maxime's going to be gone for eleven days, but it's probably for the best. Maybe his being on the road will allow me to slow down my heart and think rationally about him instead of being overwhelmed by the surging feelings I have now.

Of course, texting Maxime today has done nothing but continue to create feelings of excitement and anticipation in me. I told him how I went out to some resale places looking for funky accent pieces for my new place. I also made the dreaded trip to the grocery store to fully stock my kitchen. Of course, more pictures of me showed up online, but at least this time I didn't have cat food cans shoved in my coat pockets or kibble in my hair.

I'm winning at life today.

"Meow."

I gasp and turn to find Natasha watching me from the edge of the bathroom door.

My heart is a puddle as I see her sweet, tiny face studying me.

"Hello, sweetheart," I say softly, putting down my makeup brush.

"Meow."

Then, to my absolute shock, she arches her back, stretches, and comes to me.

Tears fill my eyes as I slowly lower myself to the floor. Natasha rubs around my leg and begins to purr.

She let me in.

I gently place my hand on her and begin to stroke her super-soft fur. Natasha flops down next to me, purring happily as she allows me to pet her.

"You trust me," I say aloud, moved by her affection. "I promise I won't break it, sweet girl."

I glance up at the doorway.

There's no sign of Boris.

I draw a breath as I continue to pet Natasha, thinking of how these two kittens represent my heart so well. Natasha is going with her gut, trusting me quickly, wanting to give her affection and receive it in return.

While Boris remains very uncertain. It's too soon for him to reward me with trust. I have to earn it from him. He's not going to be hurt by me. He's cautious. Boris is protecting himself.

"I need to be more like your brother," I say to Natasha. "Maxime has been wonderful so far, and I can see myself falling for him, but I've been wrong before. What if I'm letting my heart repeat the same pattern?"

I can't take a chance of falling for Maxime and being that wrong again.

Because I have a feeling if Maxime broke my heart, I'd never get it back again.

I draw a breath and exhale slowly as Natasha crawls into my lap. There are still so many things I need to learn about him. About myself. About how we would be together.

"We're at the beginning," I remind myself, scratching her tiny little head, "and Mommy is going to see where this can go. I like him, Natasha. I think he could be special, but I won't know yet for a long time, will I?"

Natasha purrs in approval.

"I'm glad you approve. I do, too. Tonight is a big deal, though. I'm going to see Maxime play hockey. It's huge that he asked me, don't you think?"

Natasha rolls over and exposes her belly to me, so I smile and rub it.

It is a big deal, I think happily.

And I can't wait to see him play in a few hours.

CHAPTER TWELVE

"LADIES," SIERRA SAYS AS SHE PICKS UP HER WINE GLASS, "a toast is in order. To Skye being in Denver and to being able to see her all the time."

I smile as I pick up my glass. We're sitting in a cozy wine bar near the Mountain Lions Arena, on a huge sofa under dim lights, enjoying some small plates and a bottle of wine before heading over to the game.

"I'll drink to that," I say, putting my glass against theirs.

"Cheers," JoJo says. "I think we should add 'cheers' to seeing our men play hockey tonight, too."

I shoot JoJo a look before taking a sip of my wine. "Maxime is not my man."

"Not *yet,*" Sierra says knowingly.

I use my menu as a distraction, shifting my gaze down. "Life is not a Hallmark movie," I declare. "It's not about meet cutes and happily ever afters."

"True. Sometimes it's about going halfway around the world and meeting someone who noticed you months earlier in a romantic moment of fate," JoJo declares.

"A *second chance* love story," Sierra reiterates.

"As much as I hate to ruin the romance movie plots you two are so brilliantly scripting, we had one date. ONE. That's not a love story."

But it very well could be the start of one.

I reach for my wine, taking another sip and trying to focus on my choices for a light dinner.

But Maxime is all I can think about.

"We should get a charcuterie board," JoJo says, changing the subject. "I want to try the boar sausage."

"Yes," Sierra says. "I want to do a guide to summer grilling with game meats, and that might be the perfect thing to add."

I smile as I continue to read. Part of being around JoJo and Sierra is that their science minds are always sampling new foods and trying to break them down in their heads. Apparently, recipe tester brains never shut off.

"Ooh, and that smoked goose breast sounds amazing," JoJo adds.

As they go on about the cheeses and how each one complements the flavors of a different meat, something catches my eye.

"I think I want the steamed mussels," I say. "I love mussels."

"Did you know that is a popular dish in *Belgium?*" Sierra asks.

I look up, and both of them are grinning at me.

"I had no idea. He didn't talk about mussels," I say.

"Probably because mussels are a second date topic," JoJo teases.

I can't help but grin. "I'll be sure to bring it up later tonight."

The server comes by to take our order. We go with the charcuterie board, mussels, and lobster pot stickers. After he leaves, I take another sip of wine before bringing up the question I've been dying to ask my friends.

"I need to ask about something you all said the other day, in our group chat," I say. "Is it true Maxime hasn't dated anyone in a long time?"

"Not even casual dates," JoJo confirms. "Cade said Maxime seemed shut off from the idea of dating after his last relationship."

I nod. "I understand that all too well. It's terrifying to take that chance again."

It still is, I think.

"I think Maxime likes simplicity," JoJo continues. "A drama-filled relationship isn't for him. Since I've known him, he has had very defined relationships: one with his teammates; another, deeper one, with close friends on the team, like Cade and Jude; and one with the game itself. It's been his world for the past three years."

"There's a reason why there's an A on his sweater," Sierra says, pausing to take a sip of her wine. "He's devoted everything to the game since he arrived in Denver. Jude says Maxime is the guy who leads by example, on and off the ice. He doesn't have much of a reputation online. You won't see pictures of him partying or in bars. In fact, he avoids those pics if he can when the guys are out."

I know that's true. He only has a private account that he never posts on. There aren't even product placement promos, even though he has a platform that would earn him significant money if he were to develop it.

I think about how opposite we are in this regard. I've dated on TV. I'm visible across multiple platforms, with my blog and Instagram and website. My visibility will increase with my TV role on *Boulder Live*.

Then there's the book, where I'll have to dive into my past.

A pit begins to form in the bottom of my stomach. Maxime knows my story. He knows the journey I'm about to take with my career. Will this someday be too much for him? Me being everywhere while he hates being visible anyplace except on the ice?

Whoa. That's leaping way ahead of myself.

We've had one date.

We're having another one tonight, but it might not go beyond this, so it's crazy to even entertain such thoughts.

This is how you got into trouble with Tom, my head whispers. *You started thinking ahead before you even knew him.*

"I'm glad they gave Maxime the alternate captain title; he's a great balance to Gavin," Sierra says, interrupting my thoughts.

I heed the warning my brain has thrown up and decide to focus on the present, and this conversation with my friends, instead of worrying about what will happen if we continue to date.

If.

I know my brain is right, so why does my chest grow tight at the word "if"?

"Gavin is the fiery, passionate leader," JoJo says, oblivious to my internal torment. "Maxime is the yin to his yang."

Gavin Tremblay is the team captain and someone who is very vocal in the locker room. He uses his passion to fire up his teammates. During my internet search, I read that Maxime is the perfect, calming counter to Gavin's emotional leadership.

I can see that, I think. I read that Maxime comes to practice early and stays late. His summers are spent working on improving his body and mind for the next season. Diligent was a word that came up a lot in the articles I read about him, too. His hard work inspires— and challenges—his teammates to follow his lead.

"Jude says Maxime helped him transition to the league by guiding him on how to work out his problems," Sierra says.

"Cade has said the same," JoJo adds. "Maxime is only a year older than Cade at twenty-four, but has the leadership skills of someone who has been around much longer."

"I read that about him," I admit. "In all the articles written about Maxime, it's mentioned how calm he is under pressure. He has discipline and diligence on the ice that inspires that same work ethic in his teammates."

"All true," JoJo says. "You know how you'll see Cade

and Jude post funny pictures on Instagram? Or how they'll tweet comments during a TV show they are watching? You won't see that from Maxime."

Once again, that pit forms in my stomach. Maxime lives his life much differently than I do.

"JoJo! Remember how Veronica asked if he's asexual?" Sierra says. "She's such an idiot."

"*What?*" I cry.

"Okay, first of all, Veronica is Gavin's horrible, nasty, viper-like girlfriend," JoJo explains. "You will get to meet her tonight, and she'll try to get at you because her only joy in life is being nasty and thinking she is the center of the WAGS universe. The rest of the WAGS are lovely so don't let her put you off."

"She's the one bad apple in the bunch," Sierra adds. "All the other women are wonderful. Except for Veronica the Viper."

I know the WAGS are the wives and girlfriends of the players.

"I can't wait," I say dryly.

JoJo snickers, and Sierra continues the story.

"Anyway, she loves to spread dirt, and she decided during one game to dissect Maxime's lack of dating life with all of us. At least until JoJo went Sophia Petrillo on her."

"Sophia like *The Golden Girls?*" I ask, confused.

JoJo grins. "I told her to shut it. Bluntly, Sophia-style."

I laugh. "And did she?"

"Oh, she did," Sierra says. "JoJo doesn't put up with crap, and Veronica knows it."

"It made me so mad," JoJo says. "First of all, like it's anyone's business, and second, just because he isn't dating doesn't mean he's asexual. It appalled me she thought that was a conversation to be debated in the group during a game."

I feel anger rise within me. I know how it feels to have people openly debating your kissing style, your sex life, and other personal details in a public forum. At least I put myself in the position to have people talk crap about me by being on a dating show, but Maxime hadn't.

"Just make sure you set your boundary with her right away," Sierra says. "Veronica backs off women she can't push around."

"I learned that the hard way," JoJo says. "I was the recipient of some of her hurtful comments, and it shook my confidence in Cade. But you know who came to my rescue that night? Maxime."

My emotions shift in an instant. "Maxime?"

"He saw I was upset, and he talked to me. Maxime was level and rational and made everything clear," JoJo says. "You have a good guy in Maxime, Skye. I know what you've been through, and I wouldn't tell you to date him if I thought he'd hurt you. I honestly think in my heart he could be the best thing to ever happen to you if you let him in."

Let him in, my brain repeats.

I've already taken a few steps in that direction, by being vulnerable and open in sharing my *Is It Love?* experience with him. I accepted that first date on Valentine's Day and kissed him freely at the end of the evening. Now I've accepted his offer to come to his game tonight and go to dinner with our friends afterward.

We are at the beginning, I think, absently running my finger around the rim of my wine glass. *But it's a good beginning.*

And I can't wait to see him play tonight as the next part of our journey.

CHAPTER THIRTEEN

MY HEART IS GOING TO BE SLOW AND CAREFUL WITH Maxime, but it's not with the sport of hockey.

Because I've fallen head over heels in love with this game.

We're only halfway through the first period, but the thrill of seeing a game live is like no other sport I've ever experienced. I love how quickly the game moves, how the difference between a goal going in or missing the net can be mere inches, and how the players jump over the wall and get right into the flow of the fast-moving game. I love the sound of the skates cutting the ice and the puck ringing off a goal post. The cold air on my skin is even tolerable in this environment.

I snuggle up in my black, bell-sleeved sweater, layered under a black leather jacket, as a TV timeout is called on the ice. I'm sitting next to JoJo and Sierra in the seats reserved for WAGS, and while I don't understand much about the game itself, I know I'm amazed at what I see. It's so much faster in person; I can't believe the speed of these players. The hits seem harder, more physical, as I hear players bang against the Plexiglass and see the way it absorbs the impact of their bodies.

Of course, the most exciting thing is watching Maxime play. I'm locked in on him at all times, even when he's on the bench. I'm in awe of how quickly he can turn direction on the ice. Maxime always seems to instinctively know where he needs to be. Right now, he's on the bench with Gavin, and Maxime is pointing something out on the ice with his gloved hand. I watch as Gavin nods in agreement as Maxime talks to him, no doubt plotting some strategy against the Orlando Bobcats.

A woman moving down our row catches my attention. To my left is a girl named Ana, who is from the Czech Republic and dating a player who has been her boyfriend since they were teens. She made a point to welcome me and chose to sit by me for the game. We exchanged some small talk before she began talking to another WAG.

I study the tall, beautiful woman moving toward me, and since I've met everyone except for Veronica, I have a feeling I'm about to meet the captain's girlfriend.

"Ana, would you mind switching seats for a second? I need to introduce myself to this new face here," Veronica says, flashing me a smile.

"Sure," Ana says, nodding. "It was nice chatting with you, Skye," she says, rising and moving to exit the row.

"Likewise, it was a pleasure," I say, smiling at her.

141

As soon as she leaves, Veronica takes her seat. A cloying, heavy perfume invades my space, telling me this woman doesn't know the meaning of the word subtle.

"You're new," Veronica says, studying me with interest. "I'm Veronica, and I'm Gavin Tremblay's girlfriend."

She drops her Balenciaga bag next to her exquisite black stiletto heels—making sure to turn her foot so I can see the famous red sole of her Louboutin shoes— and extends her hand to me.

"And you are?" she asks pointedly.

"Hello, I'm Skye Reeve," I say, shaking her hand firmly. "Nice to meet you, Veronica."

Her glossy lips part and a gasp of surprise escapes her mouth. "You! I knew you looked familiar! I guess I didn't recognize you since you aren't crying like you were on the last episode of *Is It Love?*"

I feel JoJo stiffen in her seat. I keep the smile frozen on my face and lean forward to block her so she can't go Sophia Petrillo again on Veronica.

I can handle Veronica myself. If it's one thing I can thank the tabloids for, it's learning how to deal with people who think you are worth nothing because you were on a dating show.

"Yes," I say, smiling brightly at her. "Thank goodness for waterproof mascara, right?"

Veronica's mouth goes back to a tight smile.

JoJo and Sierra were right. Veronica was hoping I'd get upset with her dragging up my worst moment on the show.

Ha. What a rookie. She'll have to do much better than that if she is going to get under my skin.

"I was just joking," Veronica says, putting her hand on my jacket. "So, who are you here for? These seats are reserved for wives and girlfriends, not reality show *runner-ups*."

"She is with us," JoJo snaps, not trying to hide the anger in her voice.

"I wasn't aware we had seat designations broken down by if we starred on a reality show or not," Sierra adds.

"I merely wondered if she was getting celebrity treatment, Sierra; no need to get snippy. I thought maybe you were placed here by some team lackey in PR," Veronica insists.

"I'm friends with Maxime Laurent," I say, shifting my attention back to the ice now that play has started again.

I feel Veronica looking at me as I continue to stare straight ahead.

"*Maxime?*"

"Yes."

I see Maxime jump over the boards with Gavin as they take to the ice again, and I wish Veronica would quit talking to me so I can focus on the game. They skate back on defense, as the Bobcats have control of the puck and are passing it down toward the other end of the ice. I shift my eyes to the large video screen so I don't miss anything while they are down on that end.

"Interesting," she says. "You don't seem like Maxime's type."

I don't reward her by looking at her. I'm about to say something when JoJo jumps in.

"Funny, you told me the same thing about Cade," JoJo says, her voice extra sweet as she addresses Veronica. "Yet, here we are, engaged and getting married this summer. Maybe you don't read men as well as you think you do, Veronica. Oh, just kidding!"

Oh, she's so not kidding, and it's all I can do not to laugh.

One of the Bobcats takes a shot on goal, but Gavin deflects the puck, and it sails into the boards behind the net. Maxime is instantly back there, chipping at it. He frees it around to the other end, where it's picked up by another Mountain Lions player. He passes it back up the ice, and I see Gavin move the puck across center ice.

"Maxime doesn't seem like he'd be into a reality, um, you know, I don't even know what to call you, but I guess a reality *personality*, you know?"

"Skye is a TV reporter," Sierra says bluntly. "She's going to work on *Boulder Live.*"

Veronica gives us a fake laugh. "Oh, a small market, how fun!"

"I'm happy, and that's what matters," I say, keeping my voice sweet and light.

Gavin works the puck around the net, passing it to Cade Callahan. I watch as Maxime positions himself off to the left.

Give it to Maxime, I will Cade.

Cade shoots the puck to Maxime. My heartbeat picks up as I watch Maxime move it around. I want him to shoot it so badly, but Maxime remains diligent, working for the best shot available and willing to pass the puck to a teammate who has it.

He passes it back across the ice to Gavin. Gavin fires, but the puck bounces off the top of the net, and everyone in the arena groans.

Of course, Veronica is oblivious to the game and continues to zero in on me.

"Isn't that the reason anyone would do a reality TV show like *Is It Love?* To use the exposure to get a real career?"

Her words slap hard across my face because they're true.

I know some people think less of me for doing the show. I'm going to have to fight this the rest of my life because I entered the show with those aspirations. My credentials from UCLA don't matter to most people, nor does the fact that I know how to write my own scripts, record voiceovers, and edit my own video.

What I can do, however, is an excellent job on *Boulder Live.* I'll prove to everyone I work with at the station that I belong there just as much as they do, and that's what matters.

The puck is turned over, and Maxime's line heads off the ice as they go back toward the other end.

I turn back to Veronica. "Sorry, I was concentrating on the game. Back to your comment. I did get exposure on the show, which is huge. I'm grateful for that. However, that will only give you a chance. You need to work hard to keep opportunities that are given to you, and that's exactly what I will do while on *Boulder Live.*"

My phone buzzes in my lap, and I flip it over. It's our group conversation thread.

JoJo: You're slaying her. Keep going!

I smile and put my phone face down in my lap.

There's another shift change, and the score remains tied at zero.

"True," Veronica says, swinging her foot back and forth as she adjusts the cuff bracelet on her left wrist. "I still can't imagine Maxime with someone who was in such a public role. He's so reserved. He doesn't even post pics on his Instagram account, which is *weird*. Yet you are splashed all over the place, Skye. I can't imagine Maxime seeing someone who, you know, has been on the cover of icky tabloids and will continue to be until the public gets tired of your run as a reality show sweetheart."

I reach up for my hair, beginning to braid it as a distraction from the horrible feeling sweeping through me. She's right about this, too. Maxime didn't seem to care when I told him my story, but will he like seeing awful stories about me if we're dating?

Stories that could potentially involve him?

I can't think about it. I can't.

Because if I had any sense of decency, I'd walk away from him now, rather than risk putting an amazing man like Maxime, who values his privacy and protecting his image, through this. Even though the tabloid attention will wane eventually, when you are living in it in real time, it's awful.

And while I can promise it will wane, I can't promise it will die.

"Obviously, it doesn't matter to Maxime," Sierra says, keeping her eyes on Jude, who has taken to the ice now. "He knows what he gets with Skye, which is a brilliant, wonderful, kind person."

"Oh, I didn't mean anything by that," Veronica says, touching my arm again. "Just thinking aloud about how different you two are. But you know, opposites attract, right?"

I see JoJo typing frantically on her phone, no doubt sending another message about Veronica, but I'm rattled.

Veronica is right. She's one hundred percent right, and if Maxime dates me, I will drag him into a world he will want no part of.

"Go, Jude!" Sierra yells excitedly, interrupting my painful thoughts.

I watch as Jude breaks down the ice, toward our end, with the puck on his stick on a breakaway. We all rise to our feet as Jude approaches the net. He makes a fancy move with the puck, faking out the goalie before releasing a wicked shot toward the net.

Bam! The puck hits the back of the net, and the goal horn sounds as the crowd leaps to their feet.

The entire arena begins cheering and yelling "JUUUUUUUUUUUUUDE." JoJo snaps a pic of Sierra celebrating her fiancé's goal, which she uploads to Snapchat.

The goal song plays as Jude is hugged by the Mountain Lions on the ice. They skate back toward the

AVEN ELLIS

bench, exchanging high-fives, and I watch as Maxime affectionately taps the top of Jude's helmet.

As soon as the puck is dropped at face-off at center ice, we all sit back down. Veronica has moved on to texting on her phone, but her words are still rolling around in my head. I know JoJo has texted me, but I haven't read it. She and Sierra are trying to engage me in conversation, but I'm lost.

In so many ways.

I know Veronica is right about Maxime, about what will happen if we start seeing each other and this private man is dragged into the one place he never wants to be.

Into the spotlight.

Maxime jumps back on the ice again, and my throat grows tight as I watch him play the game he loves so much. He's willing to put up with the media for this game, but the spotlight attached to me will be much harsher.

It might have been fate that we reconnected, but believing in fate doesn't mean blindly ignoring reality. And it doesn't mean Maxime should be dragged through the mud in gossip blogs or tabloids.

No, that doesn't have to be his future, I think. *I must do the right thing.*

And that is to end things tonight.

CHAPTER FOURTEEN

I NERVOUSLY BRAID MY HAIR IN THE WAGS LOUNGE AS we wait for the guys to come out. All the other women are celebrating the Mountain Lions victory tonight. The Mountain Lions won 2-0, with Jude and Gavin scoring the only goals in the game and Maxime making a brilliant pass to assist Gavin.

I'm sitting with Sierra and JoJo in a corner of the plush lounge, and they keep trying to engage me in conversation, but I can't. I should be eagerly checking the time, impatient for Maxime to appear in the doorway.

But I don't feel excited or happy at the thought of seeing Maxime. In fact, I feel dread. I feel anguish thinking of what is to come in a matter of minutes.

While my head knows I'm doing the right thing, my heart tells me I'm letting go of someone truly incredible. He is a man that could have been everything but, instead, will be someone I'll never get to know beyond our date last night.

I know I'm doing the right thing. I had the rest of the night to think about it and picture how disastrous things would be if we continued to date. My next romance will get coverage, even more so because I will have "replaced" Tom with a professional athlete. That has star power to it. Maxime would hate being tabloid fodder; that's not him. He has to deal with the public because he plays professional hockey, but nothing like this. He would hate the sleazy invasion into his dating life, however temporary it might be. I can't imagine him on a tabloid cover, or as the subject of some breezy gossip report on an entertainment channel.

He would eventually hate me for it.

I braid my hair faster, my fingers moving at a rapid rate. I couldn't bear it if he ended up resenting me down the line for putting his life out there by default. I would die if all of this ended up embarrassing him and causing him to regret ever seeing me.

No. I won't do that.

I'm going to tell Maxime I need to speak to him alone and that I can't go to dinner with our friends.

I will tell him I can't see him again.

"I hope Veronica isn't in your head," Sierra says, interrupting my thoughts.

I don't break from looping my hair over and under, working through the locks to keep from getting teary.

"No," I say, which is the truth. "These are all my thoughts. My decisions. Veronica simply made some valid points."

In a flash, JoJo's hand is on my arm. "Wait. What does that mean?"

I don't look at her. "Maxime and I. We ... we aren't a match."

"Skye, you can't be serious," JoJo urgently whispers. "Listen to me; she's an idiot. She is a horrible human who gets her kicks out of two things in life: spending Gavin's money and getting inside people's heads. Don't give her this power."

"She's not wrong. Maxime is *private*. You both know that. My life is not. Can you imagine Maxime in a gossip magazine? On the cover? With some stupid made-up story about us? Because that's reality. It *will* happen. What happens when his peace and privacy are ripped away from him?"

I see JoJo and Sierra digesting my words. The sick feeling in my stomach worsens.

"I'm right," I say with defeat. "You know I am."

"Doesn't Maxime have the right to decide for himself if he wants to make this kind of trade-off?" Sierra insists.

"How can he decide that when he has no idea what it will be like?" I counter. "I thought I knew what the ramifications of being on a reality TV show would be on my life, but I had *no clue* the depths of it until I went through it. The biggest difference is that I wanted it. I wanted to be on TV; I still want a career on camera. Maxime doesn't."

JoJo opens her mouth to protest, but before she can, players start trickling into the room.

"I know this is for the best," I say firmly.

I look toward the entrance. Anxiety fills me as I watch for Maxime to appear.

As a stream of unfamiliar faces passes by, nausea rises within me. Soon I will see a face I do know.

One I will say goodbye to.

Jude walks into the room, and a sharp pain runs through me. Maxime won't be far behind him. He smiles and comes straight toward us, and we all rise to greet him.

"Hey, baby," Sierra says, reaching for him and holding his face in her hands. "You were on fire tonight."

Envy grips me knowing I'll never be able to congratulate Maxime like this.

He drops a sweet kiss on her lips. "Thank you, love. We'll need to ask your Magic 8 Ball if I'll score more goals on this coming road trip."

Sierra grins at him. "I'd say, 'It is decidedly so.'"

They both laugh, and my gaze shifts toward the door.

Gavin is next to walk in, and Veronica is busy talking to some of the other WAGS as he approaches her. Sierra and JoJo have told me he's super nice, and they don't understand their relationship at all.

I decide I don't want to start this conversation here, with all these people around. I want to catch Maxime in the hallway so we can go somewhere private. I owe him that much.

"Excuse me," I say. "I'm going to look for Maxime."

"Please don't," JoJo says, pleading with me to change my mind. "Don't do it. I think it's a mistake."

"Do what?" Jude asks, a crease forming across his brow.

"Nothing," I say. "And it's not."

I walk through the lounge, the sick feeling coursing through me as I move. I exit into the hallway, and as soon as I turn to my left, I see Cade and Maxime heading toward me.

The second I see Maxime, I realize how hard this is going to be. I take him in, but it's not the exquisite charcoal-gray suit, that is tailored to fit his athletic frame, or the way his thick gold-brown locks are fantastically tousled on his head that causes me to stare.

It's his expression.

I swallow hard as I see the light shining in his gorgeous blue-green eyes. They lit up the second he spotted me, and a brilliant smile flashed across his handsome face. No man has ever looked at me that way before.

When I watched *Is It Love?*, I realized Tom looked at every woman the same. There was nothing unique or genuine. His expression was always fixed, and he wore the same smile throughout filming.

But the second Maxime's eyes landed on me, his expression changed. He went from smiling and talking to Cade to looking deeply happy simply from seeing me.

Maxime's eyes are his soul.

How can I stop seeing him? How? My heart is wrenching. I know he's special. I know this man is a *good* man, who is funny and sweet and intelligent, and who has kissed me like nobody ever has, with desire and emotion. He made me feel like he's never kissed another woman in the same way. He remembered me from that café in Brussels and regretted not asking if I was okay, because he can already read what is in my eyes.

You have your answer, my head whispers. *You have to let him go for all these reasons. Maxime is a good man who doesn't want his life splashed across tabloids in a grocery store. He deserves better than this.*

Stopping this now, before he ends up resenting me, is what I have to do.

"Hey, Skye, how are you?" Cade calls out as they approach me. "Welcome to Colorado."

He reaches in to give me a friendly hug, and I manage to avoid looking at Maxime for a moment. Looking at his handsome, expressive face is unbearable, knowing I'm about to change everything between us. While he thinks we are going out for sushi with friends to celebrate the victory tonight, I know the truth.

I'm going to hurt him, and that thought kills me.

I force a smile on my face as I step back from Cade. "Thank you. I'm happy to be here."

"We're all glad you're here, too," Cade says, flashing me a grin. "I know JoJo is thrilled. I think Maxime is, too. Aren't you, Maxie?"

He winks at Maxime, and I detect a bit of a flush sweeping across Maxime's etched cheekbones.

"Why don't you go find JoJo and let her put up with your annoying self?" Maxime jokes.

Cade laughs. "I'm just glad I can finally tease you about someone."

With his words, the lump in my stomach becomes a heavy boulder.

"So where is my girl?" Cade asks, oblivious to my torment. "I thought you'd all be together."

"She's in the lounge with Jude and Sierra," I explain. "I came out to get some air."

"Are you feeling okay, Skye?" Maxime quickly asks, assessing me for any sign of illness.

No, I think, staring at him. *I'm not okay.*

"Skye?" Maxime asks again.

"Um," I say, the words sticking in my throat because my heart doesn't want to let them out, "can you walk with me, Maxime?"

I feel Cade's eyes on me and then Maxime.

"We'll wait for you guys in the lounge," Cade says, taking his cue.

"What is it?" Maxime asks, closing the gap between us and putting his hands protectively on my face. "Are you sick? Do I need to take you home?"

The second he touches me, I know this is the last time I'll ever have the warmth of his hands on my face or feel the roughness of his skin against mine. It's the last time I'll see him gaze down at me with nothing but concern for my well-being.

To my surprise, tears flood my eyes. I shouldn't be this upset. I've had one date with him, *one.* How can I have a feeling of loss like this?

"Skye?" Maxime asks, his voice growing with alarm. "What's happening? Tell me."

People pass us in the corridor, and I don't want any of his teammates to see this.

"Is there somewhere private we can go?" I get out, my voice shaking.

155

Maxime furrows his brow and looks around. Next to the family lounge is a media room, which is vacant since the players have already done post-game interviews.

He puts his arm around my shoulders and escorts me to the vacant room. There are white tables and folding chairs and bright fluorescent lighting. It's cold and unwelcoming, and I'd rather be anywhere but here, having to say what I need to say to Maxime.

"You should sit," Maxime says, moving in front of me and unfolding a chair.

"Maxime, no," I say.

He stops and stares at me.

"Maxime, I'm not sick," I begin. A huge lump swells in my throat, and I can't speak. I swallow hard several times before I can. "I don't think we should go out again," I say softly.

He stares at me in disbelief. One hand grips a folding chair as Maxime freezes in place.

"What?" he asks.

"I've thought about this a lot tonight," I say. "Maxime, please understand that I like you. I like you a lot, which is the problem."

My heart catches as Maxime doesn't move. I see his chest rise and fall, his beautiful eyes a sea of confusion.

"I don't see a problem," he says simply.

"That part is not, but I am," I say, my voice cracking. "We're very different people. I'm afraid we won't work in the long run."

Maxime's hand has tightened on the chair. I think I'm going to throw up.

"Usually women wait to get to know me before

making that assessment," he says as his knuckles turn white.

"Maxime, no," I plead. "You're an incredible man, the most incredible man I've ever had the honor of going out with."

Maxime drops the chair, and I jump back from the sound of it clattering on the concrete floor.

"I don't understand," Maxime says, his eyes searching mine for an answer. "Everything was fine last night on our date, and in our conversations today. You kissed me like you *meant* it. So, yeah, I'm confused right now. What happened to make you change your mind?"

"You have done nothing wrong; this is all about me. I just don't think our lifestyles will match up in the long run."

Maxime exhales loudly. "You're making it very clear it's me. The way I live would eventually bore you. *I'll* bore you. I should thank you for picking up on it now rather than later. I've been there. I won't go through that again."

Juliette, my brain calculates. Something went wrong after Maxime fell in love with her.

"No, no, that's not it," I say urgently, not wanting him to think this.

"Don't humiliate me by lying. If you don't want to see me, you don't have to. We can be friends. That's what you are going to suggest next, right?"

"I'm not lying," I cry, shaking my head. "Do you really think I *want* this?"

"You're the one asking for it," Maxime snaps, raking

157

his hands through his hair in frustration. "Of course, you want this."

My carefully controlled emotions suddenly erupt from me.

"You will hate me if we start dating!" I blurt out.

"*What?* What are you talking about?"

"Do you want to be on the cover of tabloids? Do you want awful things written about you just because you are dating me? Because you will. I like you so much that I have to think about the ramifications on your life if we continued to date. If you are with me, people will talk. They will take pictures and gossip, and you guard your privacy so fiercely. It will all go to hell if you date me. Even when the tabloids get tired of the story and move on, it will never end on social media. I can't do this to you because I *do* like you. After that one date, I like you a lot, more than I should, and I know if I keep seeing you, that will grow. As much as I want to date you, and, believe me, I want that more than you could ever know, I won't destroy your life like that. As much as this kills me now, I would rather stop seeing you than see resentment in your eyes when you look at me. This is the truth. I can't ruin your life like this. I won't."

I'm shaking as I turn and walk toward the door. I've said more than I wanted, but my heart did all the talking. I'm leaving Maxime behind, when all I want to do is run to him. I blink back tears, the what-ifs of what we could have had haunting me before I leave the room.

I could have fallen for you, Maxime Laurent, I think as I reach the doorframe. *Now I'll never know what that could have been like.*

I'm just about to step through the door when Maxime slams the door shut angrily with one hand. I gasp in shock, and Maxime turns me around and presses my back against the door, framing my face in his hands.

"I'm not walking away from you," Maxime says urgently.

I fight back tears. "Maxime, please. You should."

"No," he says, his voice strong. "I'm not. Not now. Not after that date. Not after what you just said. I'm a man. I can handle what I choose to handle. And I choose this. Us. I choose *you*."

Then his mouth urgently closes over mine.

CHAPTER FIFTEEN

Maxime's kiss is deep, his tongue desperately seeking mine, with a passion telling me there is no way this man is walking away from me now.

Hunger for him takes over, and I thread my fingers through his thick hair, kissing him back with the same urgent need. I feel tears slip from my eyes, mingling with his skin as his lips burn against mine. Heat burns within me, a fierce need to be with him taking over. Maxime's body is pressed against me as his mouth continues to take all that he can, all that I can give. His hands move my leather jacket aside so he can touch my blouse. I instinctively take his hand and move it under the silky fabric so I can feel his hand on my bare skin, with nothing between us.

A groan of desire escapes his throat. He seizes my lower lip with his teeth, lightly biting it, and the move is so hot, a violent tremor runs through me.

"Oh," I gasp, closing my eyes as his lips go to my collarbones. Maxime responds by running his mouth across my neck with hot, powerful kisses that cause me to break out in a sweat. I lift my leg, wrapping it around him, and then Maxime lifts me up and pins me to the door as he finds my mouth again.

I've never wanted anyone as much as Maxime. This man wants me. All of me. He's possessing me with his tongue and his mouth, and I want more. I could do it right here, against this media room door, and have no regrets.

Maxime's hands span across my lower back, caressing my skin. I feel him go hard against me. I kiss him fiercely. I breathe in his vanilla and bourbon scent and allow myself to dip my head to his neck. Then I allow myself to taste him, the rich cologne, my lips greedily opening and allowing my tongue to flick across his skin.

"God," Maxime groans. "I can't take this."

I continue to kiss him, harder and harder, sucking on his neck as Maxime shivers violently against me.

"I love the way you taste," I murmur into his golden skin.

"Je voudrais t'embrasser. Maintenant," Maxime says urgently, his mouth reclaiming mine as he tells me in French he wants to kiss me. Now.

I'm lost in this moment, in this kiss—the sexiest, steamiest kiss I've ever had. We both have all our clothing on, but it doesn't matter. We're connecting through these intimate kisses, and I find it both sensual and romantic.

"Anybody in here?" a voice calls out, followed by banging on the door. I nearly let out a startled cry, but

Maxime silences me by kissing me again on the mouth. Then he throws one hand up against the door while holding me in place.

"Yes, just finishing up," Maxime yells back, and I stifle a laugh. "Be right out."

"Okay, thanks," the voice on the other side says.

I cradle his face in my hands. Maxime is gazing at me with nothing but affection, and my heart soars as a result.

"You should probably put me down now," I say, smiling at him.

Maxime brushes his lips against mine again, but this kiss is slow and gentle, telling me he cares about me and enjoys kissing me just as much this way, too.

He breaks the kiss, and I feel him smiling against my mouth.

"Okay," he says, gently lowering me to the floor.

Maxime takes a step back from me but reaches for my hands and draws me to him. "I think that kiss tells you I will handle any attention we will get, Skye."

For a moment, reality fights through my happiness.

"Maxime, this will be intense," I say, lacing my fingers through his. "Please believe me when I say you don't know what it's like until it's too late. You will not have the same life you have now if we're together. I don't want you to ever resent me for taking away your peace. It would break my heart if that happened, if I hurt you in any way."

Maxime is silent for a moment, and his expression turns to one of both softness and seriousness.

"We've both been hurt," Maxime says slowly. "We've

both made miscalculations with the opposite sex. If you had told me I would want to go out with a TV personality a year ago, I would have run. But that was before I met *you*."

He pauses and affectionately grazes my cheek with his fingertips. "I have my own baggage, Skye. You might decide the guy who is a homebody and hates parties is too boring for you. The logical side of me should be terrified I'm taking this chance, knowing that could be the outcome. I've been wrong before. Wrong in a way that devastated me. You could leave just like Juliette when you've had enough."

I search his face, knowing that none of that matters. I'm about to say so when Maxime continues.

"Your actions tonight, the fact that you wanted to spare me pain, that you were willing to do something that hurt you to protect me, tell me I have to take this chance. You're sexy and beautiful and smart, but more than all of that, you have a beautiful heart. I'm going to take this chance. I need to see where this goes. If you still want that, Skye."

I blink away fresh tears. "I don't have the best judgment," I say, my voice thick. "But I'm trusting it now. I want to see where this goes, too."

He draws my hands to his lips and presses a warm kiss across my knuckles. "Do you still want to have dinner with our friends?"

I nod. "I do."

"Afterward, we can lay out our plans for dating during the next eleven days."

I laugh. "I love that we're already long-distance dating."

"See? You have tabloids, and I play a game that takes me away for eleven days at a time. Mutual baggage."

I squeeze his hands. "It's not, but I adore you for framing it that way."

"Come on, let's go," Maxime says, holding my hand as he opens the door.

Elation doesn't describe what I feel as I walk down the hallway with Maxime. All seemed so lost a few minutes ago, and I was so close to losing the chance to date Maxime. While there is no guarantee where this will go, we have a chance.

I've decided my judgment of Maxime's character is right. My judgment that this could be something different and wonderful is right.

Now we'll just take our time and see where it goes.

———

Celebrate Life with Sprinkles—The Blog
Starting the Day off Right

Everyone knows a good breakfast is a great way to start the day, right? I love all kinds of breakfast. Overnight oats. Steel-cut oats. Eggs and bacon. A new favorite, and follow me on this readers, is butter-slathered brioche bread with Dutch-chocolate sprinkles covering it from top to bottom. You all know I love sprinkles, but these imported ones raise the game to a whole new level. I know, you're skeptical. You don't trust it. But sometimes

life is about putting your judgment aside until you try it. You might be surprised and find something magical as a result.
XO Skye

"YOU KNOW, I SHOULD BE ANGRY WITH YOU," I SAY TO Maxime. "It's freezing outside, it's eight o'clock in the morning, and after spending half the night making out with you and then texting you when I got home until I fell asleep, you take me out for breakfast. We should be in bed snuggled under the covers."

Maxime shoots me a wicked grin. "*We* should be in bed?"

Oops.

I blush furiously. I'm sitting across the table from Maxime at an old-school breakfast café in Boulder, and I'm lucky enough to have a breakfast date with this sexy Belgian man.

"Snuggling with you in a warm bed with an electric blanket would be nice," I admit.

Okay, that's the blurred-reality version.

The real version is much more X-rated and would include me snuggled up against his bare chest, running my fingertips down the trail of hair that leads to the waistband of his boxer-briefs. That's what I'd really like to do, but I'll keep those details to myself.

"Electric blanket? I'd sweat to death. Though I am used to having dogs all over the bed."

"Would there even be room for me?" I flirt back.

Maxime's eyes dance at me. "We can find out when I get back from my road trip."

Ooh!

Our server appears and places two menus in front of us. I order a cup of coffee, Maxime requests a cup of tea, and she leaves to let us study the menus.

Despite plowing through all that sushi last night, I'm ravenous.

"So, no coffee for you?" I ask, knowing the exact reason why.

"If I wanted water, I'd ask for a cup of coffee."

He flashes me that cute smile, and my heart melts in response.

I begin studying my options. "Pancakes sound good. I think I'll have those."

"American pancakes are crazy," Maxime says, shaking his head. "They are the size of my SUV tires."

I shoot him a quizzical look. "You act like this is a problem."

Maxime grins. "You're cute."

I feel warmth in my cheeks. "Thank you. I think you're kind of cute, too. So much so, I'll share my huge pancakes with you."

"Ugh, no, you can keep your huge pancakes. They sit in my stomach like rocks."

The server returns and places a steaming cup of coffee in front of me, which I use to warm my hands, and we place our orders. After ordering pancakes, I listen as Maxime goes through his order.

"I'd like three eggs, scrambled. Wheat toast, no butter. One bowl of oatmeal. A side of fruit," he says, pausing as he continues to read the menu. "Turkey bacon. Oh, and a side of potatoes."

"I think the only thing you didn't order is pancakes," I tease.

The server laughs and leaves to place our orders. As I watch her walk away, I notice some people a few tables over recording us with their cell phones.

My stomach drops out. I reach up for the end of my braid, a sick feeling washing over me.

I turn toward Maxime, who is studying me with a concerned look on his face.

"What's wrong?"

"How do you know I'm upset?"

"You play with your hair when you are upset."

"Maxime, you know me better than people who have known me for years. How is that possible?"

"I can't explain it, but I do."

He reaches for my hand across the table, but knowing we're being filmed, I move it away.

"Skye, you haven't changed your mind, have you?" he asks, anxiety rising in his voice.

"Oh, no, no," I say, shaking my head firmly. I lean closer. "There are people filming us a few tables over. I'm sorry, Maxime. If I could change this, I would."

"How do you know they aren't filming me?"

I laugh. "Fair point. You're a hockey star and incredibly sexy. I'd film you, too."

A pink tint sweeps across his chiseled cheekbones, and my heart dances the second I see it.

"You blush," I say in delight.

"I do not," Maxime insists, ripping open his tea bag and dunking it into his mug.

"Oh, yes, you do! And if we weren't being filmed, I'd caress those blushing cheekbones."

Maxime's expression turns to one of seriousness. "Touch me."

"What?"

"I don't care if we're being filmed."

"But, Maxime, when people take pictures of you in public, it's different. They end up on Twitter or Tumblr, Instagram or Connectivity, and that's it," I say softly. "With me, you could end up on a tabloid in a supermarket or on TV in a reality show update. On *Is it Love?* blogs. Why do we want to give that to them? We've only had three dates. You don't want that onslaught now, Maxime."

To my surprise, Maxime reaches across the table and places his hand on the side of my face, caressing it gently.

"I don't care. I want to see you. I want to touch you. I will handle whatever onslaught comes my way. Oh, and as far as grocery store tabloids go, I get home delivery. Problem solved."

I reach for his hand and wrap mine over it, placing it on the table between us and squeezing it firmly.

"I don't know how I ended up in that coffee house in Brussels this past summer," I say, "but I'm grateful I did. That doing a food magazine shoot led to me JoJo, and JoJo led me back to you. So many coincidences."

"We were meant to meet, Skye. I believe that."

"I believe that, too."

Maxime draws my hand to his lips and kisses it. "Let

the tabloids run with this, instead of saying you are pining for Wanker Tom with a bag of donuts."

I giggle, and he smiles warmly at me.

"I know this sounds crazy, since we're still getting to know each other, but I'm going to miss you when you are on the road, Maxime."

Maxime sighs heavily. "Normally, our trips aren't eleven days long. This one is bad timing. I'm going to miss you like crazy, too."

"We'll have Connectivity video dates," I assure him. "No matter what the time is."

Maxime's phone buzzes on the table.

"Damn, I forgot to turn it off," he says, reaching for it. He picks it up and furrows his brow. "Gavin's calling me. He always texts me."

"Take it," I encourage. "It might be important."

"I won't be long," Maxime says before answering. "Hello?"

I start going through my phone as Maxime talks to Gavin, but I notice Maxime isn't saying much.

"*What?*" Maxime gasps.

I glance up. Maxime has a look of disbelief on his face. His brow is furrowed, and he's listening intently.

I know something is very wrong.

"Shit, Gavin. Are you going to the police?" he asks.

I freeze. I wonder if a player is in trouble.

Maxime is silent for another long period.

"I'm so sorry," he says. "We'll talk about it on the way to Montreal. Want me to pick you up? ... Okay ... Right ..."

Shortly afterward, Maxime disconnects and exhales loudly. "Christ."

"Something is wrong," I say. "Can you tell me?"

Maxime rakes his hands through his hair. "You can't tell anyone."

"No, I won't," I reassure him. "I want you to know whatever you tell me, no matter the topic, will stay between us."

He leans across the table and lowers his voice.

"Gavin's accountant called him with suspicions about Veronica," Maxime says very quietly. "At first, Gavin blew it off and made it clear to the accountant that she had complete access to his credit cards, etc. Gavin told me he was pissed because the accountant had asked him about it several times during the past year. Finally, the accountant asked if he had approved various accounts in his name. He insisted Gavin listen and began reading them off. Gavin didn't know *any* of them existed."

My hand flies to my mouth in horror. "She ... she was opening accounts in his name behind his back?" I ask, shocked.

"Veronica opened multiple accounts in the past year, and they are all maxed out. Everything from gas to expensive department store credit cards. All maxed. Gavin hired a private investigator and insisted it was urgent. Apparently, in addition to the credit cards, she's been moving Gavin's money into a private bank account. She's stolen thousands and racked up almost a hundred thousand dollars in debt in his name."

"Oh my God," I whisper, feeling beyond awful for Gavin.

"Everything was a lie," Maxime continues. "I don't know if he'll ever recover from it. He's broken, Skye. You should have heard him on the phone. He threw her out last night."

My heart breaks for Gavin. If I was scarred by my judgment of Tom, I can't imagine how Gavin will ever trust another woman again after being deceived by Veronica.

"I feel awful for him," I say, shaking my head.

"I do, too. I'll try to get him to talk on the plane this afternoon. I think he will need me to listen more than anything. Nobody else knows."

"He trusts you," I say.

As do I.

A feeling of gratitude surges through me. *I'm so grateful you wouldn't let me end us,* I think. *I'm grateful you are willing to take on the spotlight that comes with me.*

With Maxime, I've found the man I want to take chances with. To trust that my gut is right. I believe him when he says he can handle my life and the crap that comes with it, like I will with his.

My heart has been given new life. I'm ready to trust him.

Just like my experience with chocolate sprinkles and butter and bread, I was skeptical, but I trusted it would be good and went all in.

It was amazing.

And I hope this beginning with Maxime will turn out the same way.

CHAPTER SIXTEEN

Celebrate Life with Sprinkles—The Blog
Time to Get Cozy

I GET HOME FROM A GIRLS' NIGHT OUT WITH SIERRA AND
JoJo in Denver and slip into my apartment. As soon as I
flip on the light, Natasha comes out from underneath
the sofa and takes a moment to stretch. A tiny meow
comes out, and my heart melts with joy.

"Hello, sweet girl," I say as she comes toward me,
rubbing around my boots. "Mommy is back in for the
night. Just enough time to take off my makeup and put
on my thermal PJs before having a date with Maxime."

I grin as I think of it. He's getting reality Skye, not
blurred, for this evening. Best of all? I'm confident
enough in my sexiness, in myself, to show him my fresh,
bare face and thermals on one of our first dates.

I shimmy out of my winter gear. The drive back
from Denver was slow, and the snow made me tense, but
it was worth it. Sierra and JoJo took me to an old-school

Italian place, and I'll be dreaming of my next trip for the incredible wood-fired pizza.

It was obvious that neither one of them knew anything about the Veronica scandal. Gavin must have only confided in Maxime. I'm sure I'll learn more tonight, but my heart absolutely aches for him. I was broken over Tom, and it was *nothing* like the deception that Gavin has to face.

"Meow."

I can't get over how one sound can make my heart so happy. I'm about to scoop her up when Boris tentatively comes out from under the sofa.

Oh! This is huge. Boris has *never* come out in my presence. I've been sliding him treats under the sofa every day, and Maxime suggested I put them in my hand to feed him, to show him nothing will happen if he gets close to me.

I pick up Natasha, who purrs the second I cradle her to my chest, and I place a gentle kiss on the top of her head.

"Let's get treats," I say.

I retrieve some new freeze-dried tuna treats and take a seat on the floor, making sure to keep a safe distance from Boris. I place Natasha in my lap and rip open the treats. She goes crazy the second she smells the tuna, and I put some pieces in my palm and lower it to the floor for her to eat.

Boris watches with interest, his nose twitching as he picks up the scent of the tuna.

"Come on, Boris," I encourage him.

I hold my breath as I wait for him to approach. *Come*

173

on, sweet boy, I will him. *You don't have to be afraid. You can trust me.*

To my surprise, he makes his way over to me. I pull a Hansel and Gretel and make a trail of treats leading up to one I've parked on my jeans. Boris eats them one by one and ever-so-bravely takes the treat off my thigh.

"Good boy," I say gently, daring to touch the top of his head.

Boris winces but doesn't move because he's eating.

As soon as he's done, he backs away from me, but I feel as if I just made tremendous progress with him.

I head down the hall and flip on the light to my restroom. I turn on the hot water and let it warm up while I retrieve my braided headband to slip over my blonde locks to keep my hair out of my face. I go about my cleansing routine, which I'm constantly changing because I'm obsessed with finding the perfect skin care line. That, and I get bored using the same things and the lure of new products is my Achilles heel. If I'm flipping channels and find a shopping channel with a skin care program on? Game over. I'm sucked in for the next hour, itchy fingers on my phone, wondering if I should order it now before they are out of stock and feeling fidgety as I watch the stock number go down. Will I regret it if I don't get in on this deal for the hottest new Korean skin care routine?

I pause for a moment. I probably don't want to know how much I've spent on skin care products since college.

It might be enough to buy a new car.

Which I need way more than glowing, radiant skin.

I adjust the temperature on the water and splash it on my face. Okay, so that's an embellishment, but I've probably spent enough to buy a moped, at the least.

I also don't want to know how many hours of my life have been spent reading skin care product reviews online, or pinning products to my skin care board on Pinterest.

Hmm. My dirty secret of overspending on products might come in useful, now that I think about it. I know from Instagram that skin products are a hot topic, and I can start a regular review of them on my blog under a beauty topic header. I wouldn't do paid advertising, but I'd write about brands I choose to try myself. Of course, I can't count anything I used over the summer. Extreme stress due to a reality show, constantly changing climates, ridiculous hours spent filming, and last but not least, falling for a total wanker caused my skin to go all kinds of crazy.

I put a gentle cleanser on my fingertips and apply it to my face in a circular motion. My current trial is an organic line infused with the magic of coconut milk and coconut water and whatever else they can get out of a coconut.

I grab a thick washcloth and dampen it before applying it to my face to remove the grime of the day.

I'm in a harsh winter climate now, so my skin should be dry, skewing my current results, too. I should need something ultra-hydrating, yet my skin somehow looks superb. I turn off the water, thinking that while the organic coconut line might be excellent, I also know my frame of mind is contributing to my good complexion.

Joy.

I turn off the water and reach for my white towel, carefully blotting my skin. As soon as the word dances through my head, I notice my cheeks pick up a natural pink blush, one that makes me look healthy and happy. I'm embarking on a new adventure. I'm starting a new job on Monday. I'm in a new city. I have friends here, and life seems rich with opportunity.

With one opportunity being a chance to date Maxime Laurent.

I turn and look down at Natasha, who is studying me with her bright, inquisitive kitten eyes.

"Come on, let's get cozy in bed so we can talk to Maxime," I say.

"Meow."

I grin. "I knew you'd agree. He's irresistible with that accent, isn't he?"

I head into my bedroom and open my top drawer, retrieving a pair of fresh pajamas. I have another confession: In addition to luxurious skin care, I'm also obsessed with pajamas. I have two drawers packed so full of them, it's hard to slide them open. Tonight, I select my ski lodge-themed sleepwear set, red with tiny prints of skiers, skis, evergreen trees, and deer in white.

I work my hair into a long side braid and put on my glasses. I pick up my tablet and sit on the edge of the bed, grateful for my duvet cover and the extra throw blankets I've piled on top, then slip inside, sitting against the fluffy pillows I've stacked across my headboard. Maxime said he'd send me a Connectivity Video Connect tonight once he was back from dinner with Cade and Jude in Vancouver, which is one hour behind.

I figure he should be calling me soon. In the meantime, I'll just do my social media catch-up.

As I power up my tablet, a slight feeling of nervousness washes over me.

Will there be more pictures of us online yet?

I found a few yesterday, but so far, no tabloids have run with anything. I know I'll be the focus of a "New Couple Alert!" sooner rather than later, but the anticipation is brutal.

Natasha jumps on the bed and curls up next to me. I stroke her fur instead of playing with my hair as anxiousness fills me.

I know it's only a matter of time now. If not today, it will come tomorrow or the next day. Maxime says he can handle it, but I can't help but have this nagging fear that he doesn't understand how invasive this is going to be.

I hear a chirp, and Boris lands on the bed.

My mouth drops open. I watch in awe as he carefully approaches Natasha and drops beside her. His bravery surprises me.

Maybe Boris is trying to tell me something, I think. That I should trust Maxime will be equally surprising when it comes to handling the baggage that will drop into his life because he's seeing me.

Steeling myself, I go on Twitter and plug in my name, which is always a crapshoot. There is always gossip and the fan-favorite meme of me saying, "I'll always love Tom. ALWAYS," after we broke up. I'm tearful and lip-quivering in the clip and oh, God, I want to puke now whenever it pops up in my feed.

What people don't know is that the confessional was filmed after a lot of prodding by one of the producers. I was barely holding back sobs in front of the camera when I realized they were going to hammer until they got something from me, something emotional and sad. I gave them the least I could.

And my heartbreak is now a meme used around the world.

Yay, me.

Ugh.

Shit. I hope Maxime has never seen it.

Ding!

I reach for my phone and pick it up from the nightstand. It's a text from Charlotte, and I cringe. I know she needs an answer about the book. I tap it open to read it:

Skye, I need an answer no later than tomorrow about the book. Again, this is a huge opportunity, and you shouldn't keep them waiting.

I exhale. I have mixed feelings. I know I should do it. I'd be an idiot to turn it down, but I want to do it on my terms. I want to write a lifestyle book with advice about everything from learning to cook to trusting your heart.

Wait a minute. That's exactly what the answer is. I want to tell my story *after* the show, my journey from that impossibly low place to now. I can describe how I'm learning to redefine myself with the help of all my experiences and the people who have been by my side.

Which might very well include Maxime.

They'll want some Tom, but I'll give them post-Tom. If Maxime is a huge part of my life, I'll want to talk about all the gifts he's given me, too.

Inspiration fills me. This is exactly what I want, to write about my ups and downs and self-discovery. I want it to be inspirational and positive and help others on a path toward finding self-love.

I know Maxime might not want to be mentioned, but that's a bridge we can work though if we get there. I can always leave his name out, and I wouldn't share super intimate stuff. This is not going to be a kiss and tell, after all, and respecting his privacy is a priority.

Oh my gosh. I want to write this story. I'm still worried about having enough time to juggle everything, but I will find a way.

I need to do this.

I quickly type Charlotte a text back, telling her I want to do the book, outlining my content ideas, and insisting on no Tom-bashing. As I hit send, excitement runs through me. I want the publisher to go for this idea. I want to show people you can be kicked down and get up and be the best you ever because of it.

Beep!

I glance down at my tablet and see that Maxime is requesting a video chat with me.

I accept his request, and his gorgeous face lights up the second we connect. But when I see him, my throat goes dry.

Maxime's lying back in bed, holding the phone up to talk to me, and all I can see is his gorgeous, golden brown hair against the stark-white hotel pillow. He's wearing a red and black plaid flannel shirt, unbuttoned a notch or two with a hint of chest hair peeking out the top, teasing me to imagine what he would look like if I were to unbutton the rest of his shirt.

I swallow. There's something incredibly hot about the fact that I know Maxime has chest hair. It's *so* masculine, and I can visualize running my hands over that broad chest and feeling the hair that covers his contoured pecs as I move my hand down the trail leading to his—

"*Bonsoir*," he says, interrupting my thoughts.

I blink. I wish I weren't wearing thermals because I'm uncomfortably hot. The sight of his handsome face, the visual of his chiseled chest, and the sound of him greeting me in French are all super sexy.

"Hi," I say, feeling the heat creep into my face. "How are you?"

"Better now that I can see you."

Swoon.

"Me, too. How was dinner?" I ask.

"Good. We went to a steak house," Maxime says. "How was girls' night out?"

"Also good. Pizza was involved."

"I know. I saw your Instagram."

I cock an eyebrow at him. "Creeping on me again, Maxime Laurent?"

This time, I notice a flush sweep across his sculpted cheekbones. "I think I would call it having a vested interest."

I laugh. "If you had an active Instagram, I'd creep on you."

Maxime grins. "You make creeping sound adorable."

"It all depends on who is doing the creeping. Confession: I like the fact that you follow me."

"You give me a reason to look at my social media accounts. How many pictures of Pot Noodle cups can I see on Jude's anyway? You are much more interesting."

"Yeah, Jude does love his British Pot Noodle cups," I say.

"Want me to share a confession with you?" Maxime asks.

"Are we playing a game of confession tonight?"

Maxime shoots me a sexy smile. "We can."

I'll play any game he wants as long as he continues to smile at me like that.

"Go ahead. Confess," I say.

"After we met, for real, in Denver months ago, and you and I followed each other on social media, I always checked your accounts when I woke up in the morning, hoping to get another glimpse into your world. Not the world the tabloids gave me, but your reality. I'd try to think of something to say, but I felt like an idiot who let you slip through his fingers twice and had no way to go back."

I stare at his open face, the one sharing a confession with me from his heart. Maxime regretted letting me go and not making a move. He is confident, an in-control leader who always seems to make the best decisions on the ice, but he is admitting his vulnerability when it comes to me. He's not trying to be brave in this moment, or projecting the image of a badass professional athlete, but he's showing me his real self, the one he keeps locked away to everyone else.

The fact that he's letting me into his world, *his reality,* unfiltered and raw, means more to me than he can ever know.

Despite my determination to go slowly, I know I'm willingly handing him over a piece of my heart.

"My turn," I say, running my fingers through Natasha's silky fur and taking a breath, "Every time I received a notification that you had liked a post of mine, I always hoped you would leave a comment so I could comment back."

Recognition flickers in his blue-green eyes. "We both wanted the same thing."

"We did," I admit softly.

"Then I'm glad we have it now."

My heart is racing from his admission. "Me, too."

His eyes linger on me, and I know if we were side by side, he'd be kissing me with those slow, sweet, searching kisses.

He clears his throat. "New confession: You're beautiful in your glasses and pajamas."

"I like being cozy," I say.

And I'd do anything to be cozy with you right now.

"Blankets, coffee, fireplace? Is that kind of your thing?" Maxime asks.

Oh God, I'm picturing this with Maxime, and I am losing all my focus.

"I'll go retro on you with my answer. It's totally my jam."

He groans. "My jam. I never liked that expression."

"Sounds like another confession."

"At least I know that one. Between Gavin and Cade, I'm always using Urban Dictionary to decipher their speak," he says, grinning.

"Hey, speaking of Gavin," I say, "how is he doing? He's been on my mind all day."

"Nobody knows but his family, me, and you. I hope you don't mind, but I told Gavin I told you and that you might be someone he can talk to when he's ready. I know you would understand better than anyone what he is going through. You know what it's like to be led to believe one thing and find out another by a person you care about. I know I should have asked you first, but he's gutted by this. I don't know how he's going to get his head right to play on this trip."

I nod in understanding. "Veronica makes what Wanker Tom did look like nothing, which in comparison to what she did to Gavin is just that—nothing."

"I gave Gavin your number and encouraged him to talk to you. I hope he takes you up on it."

"You're a good friend, Maxime," I say. "I'd be happy to talk to him."

"Gavin and I didn't get close until training camp. I don't know what was different, but we spent time talking about the direction of the team, like how he wanted me to be an alternate captain this year because he thought I was already serving in that role in the room. We're different. Sometimes what draws you to someone is their differences. Like us."

"Like us," I repeat happily.

We talk and flirt for hours longer, and I don't care what time it is because I'm savoring every second I have with Maxime. Finally, the late hour catches up with me. I yawn, which Maxime picks up on.

"You need to get to bed," Maxime encourages.

I nod with regret. "I know, but I don't want our night to end."

"I don't either. It's crazy, but I miss you, Skye."

"I miss you, too."

"I'll talk to you tomorrow," Maxime says. "We'll set up another video date."

"Okay. Have a great game tomorrow. I'll be watching."

Maxime's face lights up at the news. "I'll try to score a goal. I need to impress the girl I'm dating."

Oh, Maxime, if you never scored a goal again, I wouldn't care, I think happily. *You already impress me by being the man you are. The man who worried about me the second he saw me in Belgium and who could instinctively read my thoughts.*

We say goodnight, and as soon as he signs off, I hold my tablet over my heart for a moment.

I know I need to go slow with Maxime. I know this.

I also know I'm starting to fall for him.

My Maxime, I think, setting my tablet aside, *is worth the risk of falling.*

With that wonderful rush filling me, of a new relationship that could become something magical, I turn off my tablet and set it on my nightstand. I fall back into my pillows and close my eyes.

Ready to dream of all the wonderful things that are happening in my life.

Starting with Maxime Laurent.

CHAPTER SEVENTEEN

Celebrate Life with Sprinkles—The Blog
Career Day!

I remember my first career day at elementary school vividly. We had Jasmine Jones, a TV hostess from Love Home Life Network, talk to us. I was in the fourth grade, and I remember sitting crisscrossed on the floor in the front row. When Jasmine walked in, I remember a sense of awe filling me. She was beautiful, with long raven-black hair and brown eyes. She was impressive in her suit and her high-heeled pumps. When she spoke, I was as enraptured with her as some kids are with reading Harry Potter books. She was full of energy and life and positivity. She talked about how much she loved hosting her home and family show and making people happy through her work, and I knew in that moment that's what I was going to do. I was going to bring some light and joy into the lives of the audience through TV. I would show them how to make wreaths or bake something yummy, just like Jasmine did with her guests. I never lost sight of that goal. I worked on the student TV network in high school. Then I went to UCLA to study broadcasting. I did everything and anything to learn the business. I interned every year I was in college.

Today, my hard work has paid off. I'm starting my very first day on the job at Boulder Live, *as a lifestyle correspondent. I'm excited to take this new road in my life! I can't wait to explore Boulder and bring interesting stories and features on-air. If you don't live in Boulder, you can still catch me, as all of our shows are available on the web (see link below). I'm thrilled to be a part of the Boulder Live family and can't wait to be live today at one o'clock! XO Skye*

I ADJUST THE WIRELESS MIC PACK ON MY BACK AS I WALK across the set. This is really happening. My dream is starting right here, right now. I move across the studio floor, mindful of the cables dotting my path. Adrenaline is surging through me, and I can't wait to sit on that red sofa and talk to the hosts and TV audience.

I've had my hair made "TV News Show" ready, which is translation for puffier than I like. I've attended the morning staff meeting to discuss how the show is going to roll today and what segments and features will be in the blocks that make up the show. I'm in the second block, and the hosts of the show will interview me and roll some footage from my time on *Is It Love?* We'll banter, and then I'll join them in the last segment, where we will all learn how to force blooms indoors from a garden expert to bring some spring into dreary February snow days.

Of course, the day started off brilliantly, when I received a delivery at the studio of another bouquet of poppies from Maxime, wishing me luck today from the road. Last night, Maxime scored a goal in Vancouver, but Gavin was the one on fire—getting a hat trick on the road. Apparently, he's fueling all his emotions about Veronica into his game, which I give him credit for. They're playing in Edmonton tonight, and I have plans to get some Chinese food and watch Maxime play. Hopefully, by the time we talk again, we'll be celebrating another Mountain Lions win along with my first day on-air on *Boulder Live*.

Life is good, I think as I take my seat. *And it's about to get even better.*

I turn my attention to my co-hosts Aly Meyers and Rick Peterson, who are sitting in two plush, oversized chairs, reading their tablets, while I take my seat on the guest sofa. Rick is in his mid-forties, with hair starting to gray at the temples, but Aly is my age, and this is her first year on the show, according to her bio on the station website. I met them both for the first time this morning. I felt that Rick was genuine, but Aly was reserved, telling me she might need to see what kind of person I am before embracing me and my role here.

"Are you nervous?" Rick asks, smiling at me.

I shake my head. "No. I'm excited," I say. "I can't wait to go live."

"You dated on live TV; I'm sure a little show like *Boulder Live* is nothing, right, Skye?" Aly asks, her eyes locking on mine as she takes a sip of coffee from her bright yellow *Boulder Live* mug.

Is that a dig? Throughout this morning's staff meeting, I've caught her staring at me with a displeased look on her face. I thought maybe I was being paranoid, but now I'm wondering if I was right.

I keep a smile fixed on my face. "Actually, I've been used to cameras since my broadcasting days in high school," I say easily. "I find that same energy every time I'm on TV doing what I love."

"Of course," she says, smiling back and putting her tablet aside and scooping some papers off the coffee table in front of us.

One assistant hands me a mug filled with water, and I take a sip and park it on the table. The stage manager begins her countdown, and we all look at the camera she's directing us to. She flashes up numbers with her hands, and at zero, Rick begins reading off the teleprompter.

"We're back, and we're here to welcome the newest member of the *Boulder Live* family to our show," Rick says.

Aly picks up the next part. "We're thrilled to announce America's Reality Show Sweetheart, Skye Reeve, is joining us as our new lifestyle correspondent. Welcome to *Boulder Live*, Skye!"

"Thank you so much," I say, placing my hands over my crossed knees. "I'm happy to be here."

Rick goes into a bit about my back story, and I answer questions about wanting to be a lifestyle correspondent and what drives me. Then we get to the part I've braced for.

My *Is It Love?* past.

"You are famous for being the, well, the one Tom

rejected last season on *Is It Love?*" Aly says, nodding empathetically at me.

I manage a small laugh. "I lost Tom, yes, but looking back, I don't think we were right for each other. Time gives you an amazing ability to see things clearly and an opportunity to learn from your previous decisions."

"Mmm-hmm," Rick says, doing the sage newscaster thing. "Getting perspective is an amazing gift, isn't it?"

I love Rick.

"It really is," I say, nodding. "So no matter how hard some moments were, I can't say I regret it."

"Especially considering being a reality TV personality opens doors," Aly says.

I notice she's trying to furrow her brow, but she has so much Botox in her forehead she can't make a crease.

"It has certainly given me exposure," I answer honestly. "But I also know I've studied and worked very hard for a career in TV."

"Speaking of *Is It Love?*, what made you decide to go on the show?" Rick asks. "Were you looking for love?"

My stomach grows into a knot. I want to tell the truth, but I know I can't say "to get exposure to land a job like this one." I mean, I could, but that's a truth better left unsaid if I want to build credibility with this new TV audience.

"I had just graduated from UCLA, and it seemed like a fun opportunity to do something different. I knew I'd meet people and get to travel. I wasn't expecting to find love. That was a surprise," I say.

"Mmm-hmm," Aly says, nodding. "You know what

else fascinated me on the show? Besides your love story, which I was so *sad* to find out was only one-sided."

"I think Tom loved everyone," Rick interjects in that jovial morning show host way.

"Oh, no, Tom *loved* Miley, and we'll get to that in a moment," Aly says, wrestling her question back from him. "But there's one thing I always found *interesting*, especially considering your background and desire to be in broadcasting. When the show was filmed in the spring, you said you wanted to open a cupcake bakery. That's a rather, um, *unusual* career switch, isn't it?"

"Well, yes, I—"

"I'd almost say *implausible,*" Aly interrupts. "I can't imagine the great newswomen we know saying right after graduation, after doing all these internships for a *broadcasting career*, that they suddenly not only want to be on a reality dating show but now want to bake *cupcakes* for a career. I'm curious about your thought process here."

The single knot in my stomach now feels like a scout has tied it into twenty secure, hard knots. She has every right to ask this question, but I need to be very careful how I answer. I would love to scream the truth, to own it, to admit it was a huge mistake, but I can't. Not if I want any credibility as a reporter.

I've never hated myself more for not fighting against Charlotte and the cupcake lie than I do now.

"Like I said, I was trying to discover who I was, and I did love cupcakes," I say, sounding like a complete flake. "The show focused on that in the edit, but in the end, I knew my heart was in broadcasting."

"Aly, move off this," Stephen Wembrick, the producer, quickly interjects into our earpieces.

"Well, we're glad you chose TV over frosting, aren't we, Aly?" Rick says gamely, laughing.

"Oh, you bet, Rick," Aly says, her voice dripping with fake happiness. She gives a pinched smile and pauses to sip her coffee.

Aly has just put on boxing gloves in my head. She hates me and wants to score the knockout punch.

Ha! If this past year has taught me anything at all, I've learned that I can take the punches.

Not only take them, but remain standing at the end.

"Let's talk more about the romance on the show," Rick says.

I remind myself we can't talk about *Is It Love?* for the whole segment, and eventually, this torture has to end.

"Okay," I say, smiling brightly.

"I have to be honest," Aly says, leaning forward and turning her mouth into a serious, hard line. "Was there really *love* on *Is It Love?* It all seems, um, how should I say it? Rather *unrealistic* to find real love on TV."

I'm beginning to hate how she does dramatic enunciation every five words whenever she's addressing me.

"Oh, it can absolutely happen," I say. "What I felt for Tom was real."

"Love. Complicated enough on its own, probably more complicated on TV," Rick says.

"So, you were *really* in love with Tom?" Aly asks, wearing her concentrated hostess face.

Bleurgh. She is going to ask me the same question on repeat.

"Or did you second guess that like you did your broadcasting career?" she asks as a pointed follow-up question.

I blink in surprise. Boom! She just landed one on my jaw. I keep my face arranged in a smile, but now my guard is up. She will not hit me again in surprise with a question like that.

"No. I didn't second guess my feelings. It absolutely was love for me. The cameras disappeared, and it became my love story with Tom. Even though it didn't end in the way I had hoped, my feelings were all real at that time."

A TV screen comes up from behind us, positioned between Aly and me.

"Why don't we let the footage tell the story," Rick asks. "Skye, let's take a look back at your season, if you're ready."

"Oh, yes, let's relive your *love story* with all those *magical* moments," Aly says eagerly.

Right. I have a feeling her favorite magical moment will be the one where Tom sends me packing.

"Here we go. Our own Skye Reeve on *Is It Love?*" Rick says, turning toward the TV screen.

The footage rolls, showing me meeting Tom and going on dates with him. It's as if I'm watching someone else's life now, as what I'm starting with Maxime is so beyond this whirlwind I got swept up in on TV.

And it's so much better.

When it ends, Rick smiles at me.

"Is it hard to watch?" he asks.

"No, not anymore, I've moved on," I say, thinking of Maxime. "That seems like a different life."

Which it was.

"I can imagine! Then, you were all about *cupcakes* and *Tom,* and now, you're here in Boulder with us," Aly says excitedly.

I want to shove a cupcake in her face right now.

"Yes, and I'm excited to be here as part of the *Boulder Live* family," I say, using this opportunity to shut the door on my *Is It Love?* past and move onto my life now.

"Well, I'd be excited, too, if my life in Colorado involved a super sexy *hockey player!*" Aly says brightly.

My heart leaps out of my chest. I feel the color drain from my face. She must have seen the pictures on Snapchat and Instagram.

"A hockey player?" Rick asks, rolling with the change in topic, one we didn't go over in the production meeting this morning.

"Yes, you've moved on with a certain *European* hockey player, isn't that right?" Aly asks, her eyes sparkling with delight. "I guess celebrities *attract* celebrities, right? I figured you wouldn't mind us asking about *Maxime Laurent,* the alternate captain for the *Mountain Lions,* you know, since you had *intimate* overnight dates on *camera,* right?"

"Aly, quit the crap; this isn't a gossip show!" Stephen roars into our earpieces.

"Okay, my producer is telling us to move on to your role here on *Boulder Live,* but before we do, you two have looked awfully *lovey-dovey* on social media. Can we say, this time, it's love? For *both* parties instead of just *one?*"

I need to recover. Quickly. Without further embarrassing Maxime.

"Maxime and I are spending time together," I say, flashing a smile despite nausea rising within me. "I enjoy his company."

"Spoken like a woman who is going to keep this one out of the public eye," Rick says, smiling.

"That seems like an impossible task being that you are *everywhere,* Skye," Aly says sweetly. "Everyone wants to know how *America's Sweetheart* is healing her heart. Apparently, a sexy *hockey player* is just the thing to do the trick, according to Twitter."

She's enjoying this way too much. She wants to diminish me in front of the audience, to make me look like a celebrity wannabe who is hooking up with local athletes to stay in the spotlight.

"Speaking of moving," Rick says, hitting the transition button, "you moved out to Boulder to join *Boulder Live.* What have you discovered since being here, Skye?"

My brain immediately shifts with Rick, and I bring up Pearl Street and the funky eateries and unique stores. I mention the Flatirons and snow and how I love being in Colorado. Then I talk about my role on *Boulder Live* and what I plan to bring to viewers of the show. I somehow do all of this on autopilot while my stomach is in knots, furious at Aly for pulling this crap on me and scared to death about what Maxime will say when he sees this.

After we're counted out to break, and as soon as we are at commercial, I turn to Aly.

"I wasn't expecting to talk about Maxime today, Aly," I say, not letting her pull this shit on me.

"Oh? Why weren't you?" Aly says, picking an imaginary piece of fluff off her short wool skirt. "*You're the one who has aired your love life on TV. I didn't know Maxime would be off-limits.*"

"A heads-up would have been nice," I say. "Please give me that courtesy in the future, Aly."

"Oops. Sorry." She rises and stares down at me. "If you'll excuse me, I need to move over to the kitchen for the next segment. Maybe you can join me the next time we do *cupcakes*, okay? That would be so *fun!* You know, because you are a *baking expert* in addition to a *broadcasting major.*"

I watch her walk away, anger consuming me. Aly is not a woman who will lift other women up, but try to tear them down to make her feel better about her position. About herself. All she sees is Reality Show Skye, and she's going to make me pay for it.

Fine. She can think I'm an idiot. That I don't belong here, that I can't report. And, yes, I did lie about the cupcake bake shop, but I know what I'm capable of. I do belong here. She can take her crappy attitude and shove off because I'm here to do my job, and I can do it with or without her support.

"Skye, I'm sorry about that," Stephen says in my ear. "That won't happen again."

I hit my talkback button. "It's okay; it's all good," I lie, not wanting anyone to know how rattled I am.

I leave the set, smiling as I do and trying to appear as if this ambush hasn't rattled me. I practice some breathing, listen to the producer and director in my earpiece as they discuss what's going to happen for the cooking segment, and I head back toward my cubicle. I reach for my phone with one thought now dominating my brain.

Maxime.

He's been outed on TV.

The national media will be running this within a matter of hours. My stomach rolls over as I imagine the online articles that are most likely being written as I stand here. It's going to hit him hard, and some of these articles will embarrass him. I'm going to text him a heads-up, but I feel sick with worry.

He doesn't understand, I think, feeling as if I'm going to throw up.

He's about to be discussed in ways that will be humiliating to a man who has kept his personal life very private. His life as he knows it is about to disappear, and he's oblivious to what is about to happen to him.

And there's nothing I can do to stop it.

CHAPTER EIGHTEEN

I ABSENTLY SHOVE SOME SALTINES INTO MY MOUTH AS I
wait for the third period to start. The Mountain Lions
are up over Edmonton 3-1. Gavin has been on fire again
tonight, scoring two out of the three goals, with the
other one scored by Cade and assisted by Maxime.

Normally, I'd consider today a day to celebrate. I
started my TV job and got the contract started for my
book deal. Seeing Maxime get an assist on a goal would
be the icing on the cake and reason enough for cupcakes
covered in an abundance of sprinkles and a glass of
bubbly champagne.

Instead, I can't eat. I'm nauseated. The only thing
I'm indulging in is a sleeve of crackers, which I'm
using to try to calm the anxious sea roiling in my
stomach.

The articles have started appearing online about me
seeing Maxime.

Bile rises in my throat. I texted Maxime from the
station to let him know, and he responded that he knew

it was coming, he wasn't planning to read the articles, and the media attention is irrelevant to us.

I haven't read them, but I have skimmed the headlines: *Skye Moves on with Hockey Player! Is It Love? Between Skye Reeve and Pro Athlete?* Blah blah. I have received phone calls all afternoon from media outlets, but I haven't returned them. Charlotte is giddy about Maxime. I told her it was still new and to have no comment if anyone asks her.

I keep checking my social media feeds for new posts, but so far, the tabloid that has been the worst in its coverage of me—*Dishing Weekly*—has only run a brief spot on their rumor page. That is the one I fear the most, and I know it's coming, but today is apparently not going to be the day.

I groan and put the half-eaten sleeve of crackers on the coffee table. Boris and Natasha are chasing each other through the apartment without a care in the world. I need to be more like them. I need to shelve the worry and focus on the game. Live in the moment, focus on what I can control, and quit worrying about when the bomb will drop in *Dishing Weekly*.

I also shouldn't think about the other thing I can't control: Aly Meyers.

I screw up my face. She was okay during the flower potting segment, but she did "innocently" ask if I had enough of dirt, ha-ha, as in tabloid coverage.

I gamely played if off, chuckling that it was part of being on reality TV, blah blah, and went about potting my bulb in between her and the guest gardener.

After the show, the producer, Stephen, apologized

and said Aly would be spoken to about what happened on set. Rick came and talked to me privately, too. He said Aly was territorial with other women who have worked on the show in the past and that it had nothing to do with me being on a reality show but me being a strong talent. He said I was a real natural on-air, he was happy I was on the show, and I shouldn't let Aly get under my skin.

Oh, and Aly? Not a word to me as soon as the cameras were off.

Rick's comment confirmed what I had already suspected, though. Instead of seeing me as someone who could bring value to the program, I was a threat. One Aly wanted to rattle and diminish as best she could to cement her position as host.

I snort. Whatever. I can handle her. If I am grateful to *Dishing Weekly* for one thing, it's for making stuff like this seem so irrelevant when horrible untrue things are published and splashed on covers and put up in supermarket checkout lines for my family and friends to see.

Aly is an amateur. Her behavior won't change how I feel about doing my job.

I only hope Maxime can deal with the tabloids in the same way.

Stop it, I think. You need to trust Maxime and what he says. He's going to deal with it. I have to trust my judgment and believe him when he tells me he can handle the crap that is going to head his way.

I reach for a thick-cabled throw blanket on the end

of the couch and tuck it around me. It's not snowing today, but it's still below freezing outside.

I watch another commercial roll by and wish Maxime was here to get cozy with. I'd love to kiss and snuggle with him under a blanket. I want all the sappy romantic things with him at home. I want a fireplace, blankets, warm clothing. Wine. Candles. Kissing. Caressing. Me snaking my hand underneath his sexy, lumberjack, plaid shirt and feeling his chest, raking my fingertips through that dark hair and finding the contours of his pecs as my mouth leisurely explores his—

I blink. Okay. That was a good diversion—imagining a sexy, intimate date with Maxime.

He can't come home soon enough.

The game comes back on, and I listen as the announcers reset the scene. They talk about the great plays of the top line—Gavin, Maxime, and Cade—and the solid goaltending of Westley Pratt, whom the Mountain Lions got in a trade a few weeks ago.

Maxime heads to center ice for the face-off, and I eagerly watch as he places his stick down, the camera zeroed in on his intense face as he waits for the puck to be dropped. I find myself holding my breath as the Edmonton player and Maxime both go for the puck. Maxime wins the draw, and it sails out of the circle, where a Mountain Lions' defenseman brings it back up the ice. I watch again in amazement as Maxime positions himself in front of the net, ready to take a pass, but it's intercepted by an Edmonton player who makes a break toward the other net.

Gavin and Maxime take off in the other direction, to get back on defense. Gavin gets to the other end first and becomes entangled with an Edmonton player for the puck. The Edmonton player hits him from behind, and Gavin slams into the boards with his right leg first. I gasp as I see it bend backward.

"Gavin was hit hard," John Lewis, the Mountain Lions play-by-play announcer, says gravely. "His leg just buckled there."

Play stops as the team trainers rush toward Gavin. I watch in horror as Gavin's leg remains bent back. He puts his hands on his head, then his leg, then back to his head, and tears sting my eyes as I know he's in agony.

"Oh, Gavin, no," I whisper, my hands flying to my mouth.

I see Maxime is standing behind him. Everything is still. The doctors are hovering over him now. I want to throw up. I feel awful for Gavin. He doesn't deserve this. Not after what he went through with Veronica.

"Gavin is just so fast, so strong on his skates," Martin Czeck, the color analyst, says, as they replay the gruesome injury again. I close my eyes. I can't bear to see it again. "But as you see right here they get tangled up, and he goes awkwardly into the boards."

I open my eyes and see more doctors around Gavin, along with Maxime, who hasn't left his side.

"This arena is *silent* right now," John continues. "They know."

Their words blur in my head as I see Gavin writhing in pain on the ice. It seems like he is there forever before a stretcher comes out.

"Oh my God," I whisper aloud.

They go on to talk about Gavin as the captain, what he has brought to the team and what it means to lose him as they fight to stay in position for a playoff spot.

I watch as they take off his helmet, his golden blond hair standing out against the sheet of ice. Another trainer slides a towel under his head.

This game is dangerous. I knew it was, but now I'm seeing it firsthand.

Next time, it could be Maxime lying on that ice.

Tears fill my eyes. I know I shouldn't be thinking of Maxime when Gavin is the one who is hurt, but I realize how much Maxime means to me already. I would be devastated if he was in another country, hurt, where I couldn't get to him—

I choke back a sob. I couldn't bear it. I couldn't.

A team of people carefully get Gavin onto a stretcher. The players tap their sticks on the ice, and the crowd stands and applauds as Gavin is taken out of the arena, where no doubt an ambulance is waiting for him.

"Now the Mountain Lions will have to find a way to regroup with their captain gone," Martin says.

"We'll see how they can do that when we come back," John says before they go to break.

I say a prayer for Gavin. I pray for God to keep Maxime safe on the ice, too.

A heaviness fills my heart as I think of Gavin and Maxime.

The team has lost their beloved captain.

And now the leadership of the team, and everything

riding on their playoff dreams, has just fallen onto Maxime's shoulders.

———

I CLIMB INTO BED, BUT I KNOW I WON'T BE ABLE TO sleep until I hear Maxime's voice. The Mountain Lions went on to win the game, 3-1, but I watched it play out in a numbed state. Seeing Maxime play without Gavin hurt my heart. They kept showing Maxime on the bench, talking to his teammates, and there's no doubt in my mind he was keeping them together tonight with his calm, steady, focused leadership.

Natasha and Boris jump up on the bed with me, and while Boris stays a safe distance away, Natasha curls up next to me, purring happily. I nuzzle her sweet head, thinking how glad I am to have these babies with me tonight. I need them more than they could ever need me, and their presence is helping me stay sane.

My mind flashes back to the third period when, with absolute shock, I watched Maxime get in a fight with another Edmonton player. He dropped his gloves and began throwing punches at a defenseman. I screamed at the TV as his opponent, who was twice his size, practically took Maxime's head off with one punch. When I saw his cut-up face in the penalty box up close, all I wanted to do was hold his face in my hands and make it better. Maxime is not a fighter, but I know why he picked that fight.

He had to show his team he could be the fiery leader that Gavin is in his absence. On top of all of this, the second he looks online, he'll see his name linked with mine in cheesy screaming headlines.

Maxime doesn't need my crap in his life right now, I think sadly. *If he told me he didn't want to see me anymore, I'd totally get it. He has enough going on without my baggage.*

As if on cue, my phone rings. I swipe it off my nightstand, and it's Maxime. I answer, desperate to hear his voice.

"Maxime," I say before he can say a word. "I'm sorry about Gavin. And I'm sorry you felt like you had to fight in his absence." I have to stop because of the lump forming in my throat. I shove it down so I can continue. "I'm sorry about those awful headlines. I know you don't need this shit that I bring with me wherever I go," I say, and my voice begins to wobble. "I'm sorry, I'm sor—"

"*Arrête, chérie,*" Maxime interrupts.

His words reach up and wrap around me, and I listen to his command.

Maxime clears his throat. "Sweetheart, stop," he repeats in English. "If you think I'm concerned about being called a 'Super-Hot Euro Babe,' you underestimate me. In fact, I rather like being called a super-hot Euro babe. I watched that segment online on the bus to the arena. Aly was a bitch to you. But you— you held your own. I'm proud of you. You were amazing."

"Thank you," I say. "I'm shooting my first report on Thursday with some new theme decorating service that is opening in Boulder. Wait until you see me report. With no Aly, I'll be so much better."

"Dealing with Aly proves how skilled you already are."

"Maxime? I want to go back to something."

"What?"

"I kind of like that you called me your sweetheart," I admit.

"It's not too soon?"

"No," I say without hesitation.

I swear I hear him exhale. "Good."

"It's very good. Are you blushing?"

"What?"

I grin. "You blush when you get flustered. It's rather cute."

"I'd rather you think of me as a super-hot Euro babe."

We both laugh, and then I clear my throat.

"How is Gavin?" I ask.

"He's in surgery. It's a broken femur."

I gasp aloud. "Oh my God."

"It's bad," Maxime says quietly. "We're going on to Winnipeg right now. I'm about to get on the bus. Gavin will stay here and then fly home to Denver when he's able."

"Let me know when he is," I say. "I'll get together with the girls. We'll make some dinners for him and bring them over. I'll go first. It might be a good time to talk to him, too."

Maxime is silent for a moment.

"What? Is that okay?" I ask.

"You have a beautiful heart," Maxime says.

A happy flush radiates through me, warming my skin from head to toe. "Thank you."

"You do. I'll never understand why Tom let you go, Skye."

"I can say the same thing about Juliette."

"She had her reasons," Maxime says softly.

"Maxime? What happened between you two? Because I honestly can't see why she would ever let you go."

"Laurent!" I can hear Cade's voice in the background. "Time to get on the bus."

"I've got to go," Maxime says. "I promise we'll have this conversation tomorrow night. I'll tell you everything. And Skye?"

"Yes?"

"I hope you aren't the one wanting to end things after you hear it."

CHAPTER NINETEEN

Celebrate Life with Sprinkles—The Blog
Fear of the Unknown

Sometimes, I find myself worrying about things that could go wrong. Perhaps if I had done that before going on Is It Love? I would have never signed up for the show. Back then, I ran on positive energy. Put good things out in the world, and you'll get them back.

As I learned, life doesn't always work that way.

I admit I had a hard time dealing with everything that happened after the show ended. I didn't feel positive. I felt as though I had been reckless. With both my judgment and my heart. I vowed to never risk both so brazenly again.

Funny, though, how time heals things.

While I'll never be the same girl I was before I went on Is It Love?, I'd like to think it has helped me grow up and shape me into the woman I am today. I've also found myself being too careful, too safe, in making some life decisions, out of fear of the unknown. Afraid that I'm not using the best judgment. It's amazing how that negativity can get in your head, and soon you are scripting a reality that might never happen.

I found myself doing that this morning: projecting the worst-case scenarios for a particular situation. Then I realized I had to stop it. Can something bad still happen? Yes. But am I spending a lot of energy worrying about something that could be nothing? Also yes.

I stopped myself. I'm going into the situation with an open —yet cautious—mind. I won't spend hours scripting endings that might never happen.

Sometimes, you have to let life unfold and see where you end up, and that's what I'm doing today. I can't control the future. I can't continue to worry about it. All I can do is let life take the turn it's going to take and see where the road takes me afterward. XO Skye

It has taken all my energy to follow the advice I doled out in my blog post today. Sure, I was able to shelve my brain during the *Reality TV Show Roundup* segment with Aly and Rick, recapping the previous week of shows and giving my *Skye's Eye On* tidbits for the upcoming week. It's a new feature, created with my addition to *Boulder Live.* Aly looked absolutely thrilled to be doing it during the pre-show meeting, as in she would have been happier having an ingrown toenail pulled than discuss reality television with yours truly.

But once I was done with work, my brain shifted right back to worry, about the one topic that has had me scripting horrible scenarios in my head.

What did Maxime do to Juliette?

Have I read him as badly as I read Tom? I tossed

and turned all night, coming up with all kinds of things that would make me want to stop seeing him. The list included:

- He cheated.
- He dumped her in a state of duress, like a pregnancy, accident, or medical issue.
- He's married, which is idiotic, but once I start scripting, I can't stop.
- He didn't spend enough time with her and neglected her for hockey. Again, from what I know of him this doesn't make sense, but could this be what happens down the line?
- He doesn't want children. We haven't gotten that far in our conversations, but I do want to be a mother someday. In the far-off future, that is.
- He is bad in bed. My guess would be this isn't the case based on his kisses. And just because Juliette thinks he's bad in bed doesn't mean I would. I'd have to find this out for myself.

I stopped myself at six. I could torture myself all day with wondering if knowing this piece of his past will change my mind about him, but what if it doesn't? What if it has nothing to do with the relationship I'm forming with him? I trust him to tell me the truth, and I trust myself to think carefully and make the right decision for myself after hearing his story.

I trust that I do know this man. What we have is

real, and no matter what he tells me, we'll be okay in the end.

I pull into my apartment building and park my car. It's warmer today, a practical heat wave at forty-eight degrees. I think back on my day as I head upstairs. I haven't heard anything from Maxime, which is weird. Normally, we text during the day.

Does his silence mean something?

It could be bad.

Or it could be nothing.

Ugh.

I step inside my apartment, heaviness settling over me. Natasha is curled up in a sunny spot on the hardwood floor, her gray fur glittering in the ray of light warming her tiny body. I think I'll follow her lead before dinner and curl up in my bed and take a nice nap, letting the sun peek in through my window. Sunshine always improves my mood, and I think I could use it right now.

I head back into my bedroom, and even though it's only four o'clock, I change into my pajamas, crawl under the covers, and let the sunlight fall across my skin. I close my eyes and drift off, hoping I'll wake up in a much better mental place before I talk to Maxime tonight.

———

My phone is buzzing. Somewhere. It feels like it's in my ear.

I lift one eye. My room is pitch black. I find my

phone underneath my pillow. Wait. What? I took a nap. Why is it so black in here?

I glance at the clock.

It's eight.

Eight?

Shit!

I was supposed to talk to Maxime at *seven.*

I just missed a phone call from Maxime; there is also a stream of missed texts.

I don't read them. I'm sure Maxime thinks he scared me off with his cryptic comment and now I'm avoiding him. I quickly redial his number. One ring … two rings … three rings …

"Dammit, pick up!" I yell.

"Hello?" Maxime asks at the exact same time.

Great timing on my behalf for the second time this evening.

"Maxime, I'm so sorry. I crashed out in bed and missed your call," I say quickly. "Can we still have our date?"

"So you aren't avoiding me."

It's a statement, not a question.

"No, absolutely not. In fact, there's nothing more I want than to see your gorgeous face on Connectivity right now."

"Let me disconnect and do a Video Connect."

Maxime doesn't sound right, I think, looping my fingers around the ends of my hair. I don't hear the lightness in his voice that I've come to know whenever we talk.

Worry eats away at my stomach.

If he does have a wife, I'll kill him.

Within seconds, I get a Connectivity Video Connect request from Maxime. I accept, and his face pops up on my phone. My worry immediately flips to full-blown alarm. Gone is the brilliant smile. The sparkling eyes. The face that normally shows excitement whenever my picture comes up on his screen looks worried.

"Hi," he says softly, anxiously raking a hand through his hair.

"You're scaring me," I whisper.

"I'm scared," Maxime admits. I watch him swallow. "I don't want to lose you, and I know I might after I tell you this stuff about me."

"Maxime," I say, pushing down my fears, "I don't think there is anything you can say that would change how I feel about you. Unless you have a wife. Or you murdered someone."

There. I see a smile tug at the corners of his mouth. "No. Nothing on the criminal scale."

I don't let him see it, but I feel some of my doubts slip away.

"Okay," I say, sitting upright and crisscrossing my legs. "Let's get this out of the way. Tell me the story, and then I can tell you that it doesn't matter, and we can have a good evening."

Maxime's smile falls. "It's not that simple."

"Then tell me."

Maxime exhales. "Okay. I met Juliette when I was playing hockey in Belgium. I had gone out after a game with my friends, to a pub. It was a big win. We were having beers. There were some girls at the bar, and when it was my turn to go up and get another round, I

213

ended up next to Juliette. She started talking to me. Juliette was like a bright light. Bubbly. She talked and talked and used her hands," Maxime smiles at the memory. "She was outgoing. She made me laugh. Juliette was everything I'm not."

I want to counter that, to ask what universe he's in where he doesn't see these qualities in himself, but I know I need to simply let him talk.

"I think I fell in love with her that night," he continues, his expression turning serious again. "I asked her out for the next night since I didn't have a game. I didn't know her, but I know I had to be with her. I could never get enough of her."

I nod, knowing I'd felt the same way about Tom.

"I soon realized how different we were," Maxime says. "Juliette shines in every room she enters. People gravitate toward her. She feeds off that energy. She loved pubs and parties and nightclubs. She loved being out late. The more people she could be around, the happier she was.

"The very things that sustained her, though, drained me," Maxime continues. He pauses again, clearing his throat before continuing. "I'm not like that, Skye. I'm an introvert. I don't like parties and nightclubs and people looking at me. I'm not a dancer. I don't like being in large groups of people at pubs until the wee hours of the morning."

I try to reconcile the man I know and care about—*my Maxime*—in this world. My man, the one who loves books and his private lake and his Belgian coffee at home—doesn't sound like he would fit in this environment at all.

"I'd come home exhausted and resentful," Maxime says, running his hand through his hair again, making it messily stand up on his head in the most endearing way. "When I'd suggest we stay home, she would call me old. She said I wasn't fun, that I was too young to live a life holed up in my flat like an elderly man. We'd argue. I couldn't help feeling she was right. What twenty-year-old guy wants to stay in? My teammates didn't act like that. Neither did my siblings. I know I'm not normal. I'm not. Eventually, the fights grew worse. She picked fights with me if I wanted to leave a place before she did, and she pouted if I wanted to make a meal at home and watch a movie."

My heart breaks for him. Maxime doesn't see that this wasn't his fault. He thinks he was boring and left Juliette no choice but to leave him.

"Juliette and I stayed together for a few years. The reasons that drew me to her, that I loved, were all the same things that drove her to leave."

Relief washes over me. I didn't realize I was holding my breath until I exhale loudly.

"What?" Maxime asks, confused.

"Maxime Laurent," I say firmly, "If I could reach through this screen right now, I'd do two things. First, I'd smack you for scaring me with your cryptic ending of our phone call last night. Then, I'd take your gorgeous, adorable face in my hands and kiss you like mad."

"Skye, don't you see what I'm saying? You like being out. You're on *TV*. You have that light, that brightness,

215

and whenever I'm with you, I feel it, too. I'm afraid that one day, I'll disappoint you and you'll resent me and find me as boring as Juliette did. We're young, but I don't always act my age. I have an old soul. I was crushed when Juliette and I didn't work. I can't imagine how I would feel if the same happened with you. Because I think it would be even worse."

I stare back at him, shocked by his admission.

Maxime is emotionally invested in me.

This isn't slow in his mind, not like how he said he wanted us to be. His heart is taking the lead.

I'm silent, drinking in this moment in complete and utter amazement.

I know, right now, without a doubt, I'm falling in love with him.

"Maxime," I say at last, "do you realize this whole conversation makes me even crazier about you?"

Maxime blinks in surprise. "What?"

"All the things you describe about yourself are things that I draw energy from. I love your quietness. We have incredible conversations because you are wise beyond your years. I love that you treasure books and quiet and love your dogs and your coffee. If I want to go out to a club, I can do that with Sierra and JoJo when you are out of town, like when we went to the wine bar for girls' night. I'm right where I want to be, and I know what I'm getting. I'm getting you, Maxime, exactly the way you are. Exactly the way I want you to be."

Skepticism remains in his beautiful eyes. "You say that now."

"I'll say it later."

He lets go the second I say those words to him. I see the tension ease from his body as he relaxes his shoulders and exhales, and I long to be cuddled against him.

"This road trip needs to come to an end," he says. "I miss you."

"I miss you, too," I say, an ache filling me. "We're going to have the ultimate cozy night date when you get home. Pajamas required."

A sexy smile tugs at the corner of his mouth. "What if I don't sleep in pajamas?"

An image of a naked Maxime flashes through my head. My face grows hot. I'm about to tell him I like that idea when he starts laughing.

"I'll bring pajama bottoms," he says, his eyes dancing at me.

Hmm. I can totally take those off.

"Okay," I agree, keeping my plan to strip him naked to myself.

"I was hoping you'd fight that a little more."

"Maybe I like unwrapping things."

Maxime's cheeks get a light sweep of pink across them, and I fall a bit more in love.

I'm about to say something when my stomach lets out a hideous growl that, once again, echoes off the walls in my bedroom.

Maxime bursts out laughing, and I know my face is the color of a beet.

"You have the loudest stomach of anyone I've ever known, and I'm in a dressing room of guys all the time."

"I know," I groan, embarrassed by my Abominable Snowman growl. "I didn't eat dinner."

"I'll make sure I have groceries delivered before our cozy date."

"Ha-ha, so funny. But do put colored sprinkles on that list, please."

"Colored sprinkles ... Anything else?"

Condoms?

Thankfully that thought didn't slip out of my head.

But I will be sure to bring some, just in case. I clear my throat and think of other necessities we'll need for our date.

"Wine," I say.

"Hmm. Sprinkles and wine. Sounds like an interesting dinner."

"It will be perfect."

"What else will we do?"

"Oh, I think we're serious enough for me to introduce you to the *Island of Misfit Toys*," I say. "We're going to watch *Rudolph the Red-Nosed Reindeer.*"

"But it's not Christmas."

"And that matters why?" I challenge.

Maxime grins. "I guess it doesn't."

"Pajamas, wine, sprinkles, and a holiday movie; it's going to be the best date *ever.*"

"Fire in the fireplace," Maxime adds. "I'll cut some wood."

"You chop your own firewood?" I ask.

"Yeah, I like doing that. It's a good workout."

I get a quick picture in my head of Maxime outside in his flannel shirt, swinging his ax and splitting logs with his powerful, muscular upper body as snow gently cascades down on his thick, wavy hair.

Good lord. That's all kinds of lumberjack, manly hot. I absently tug at my thermal pajama top.

"It sounds very romantic," I say, heat rising within me.

"It does," Maxime says, his eyes locking with mine.

We don't say anything for a moment, but our eyes say it all.

We're going to have one very romantic evening when Maxime gets back.

One that will include making love for the first time.

He needs to come home now. I think I might die before this swing through Canada is over.

"I have one more request," I say, twirling a lock of hair around my finger.

"Yes?"

"Can I watch you chop wood?"

Maxime gives me a quizzical look. "Um, okay, but it's not very exciting."

"Maybe you can teach me how."

"Is that the reason you're asking? You want to learn how to chop firewood?"

"Maybe. Will you wear that red and black flannel shirt? You're kind of a sexy lumberjack in it."

Now he begins to blush.

"So, your fantasy is a date with a rugged lumberjack?"

"No."

"No?"

"My fantasy date is with *you*," I say. "I can't wait for you to come home, Maxime."

"I can't either."

My stomach lets out another growl.

"Hungry for me?" Maxime teases.

Now I'm the one blushing. "Apparently so."

As I take him with me to the kitchen, so we can talk while I heat up something to eat, I know tonight has been a turning point for us. Maxime trusting me with this story—and revealing how much he already cares about me—shows he's trusting himself.

He's trusting us.

And I intend to do the same thing.

CHAPTER TWENTY

Celebrate Life with Sprinkles—The Blog
Good Things Come to Those Who Wait

*Today, I'm shooting my first feature for Boulder Live, and I feel
as though I'm living a dream. I've waited for this moment;
sometimes, it seemed like it would never come. Sometimes, I
made questionable decisions, but my determination and patience
have paid off. Life doesn't always happen on the timetable we
want. Things don't go according to plan, and sometimes, they
even backfire spectacularly. But when the moment we've worked
so hard for, waited so long for, finally arrives, it makes that
moment that much sweeter. Keep focused. Fight for it. And
when your moment comes, savor it. XO Skye*

I ARRIVE WITH MY VIDEOGRAPHER AT A BEAUTIFUL SPLIT-
level home with lots of large windows. In my first feature
for *Boulder Live*, I'm interviewing a woman named
Whitney Green, a seasonal decorator. The company—
called Décor Bliss—is based in Seattle but recently

opened their second branch in Boulder. In my research for the interview, I learned that seasonal decorators come into your home and take decorating off your hands, creating a magical Christmas setting or the perfect table for a dinner party.

Whitney is going to show us this home in Boulder, which she has been hired to decorate for spring. She also said she would bring some St. Patrick's Day decorations to show us what a holiday-type service would include.

"First shoot, are you ready?" Hayes Blevins, the shooter, asks, turning off the engine. This *Boulder Live* van rivals my car in the competition of which will hold out longer before completely imploding.

I glance at Hayes. He's in his twenties like me, and we are both cutting our teeth together on *Boulder Live*. Hayes was hired only a month ago, from a small station in Iowa, so this is a step up, closer to the bigger Denver market. On the drive over, we discussed how lucky we feel for whatever breaks we get and how we plan to make the most of them. Our time together so far has been brief, but I can already tell I like him. If he knows anything about my time on *Is It Love?*, he's too polite to ask.

"I'm ready. I know a lot of reporters don't like these kinds of stories—the fluff pieces—but I do," I say. "These stories add balance to the serious news of the day. They give people something fun to think about, teach them something new, or inspire them."

Hayes nods as we climb out of the van. He goes around to the back to gather up his camera and the audio equipment.

"I agree. Although I still don't understand what the hell a seasonal decorator does," he teases.

"That's where we come in," I say, grinning. "We get to tell viewers *what the hell* a seasonal decorator does."

My phone buzzes, and I retrieve it from the pocket of my cream, wool swing coat, one perfect for the mild, mid-fifties that will be the temperature today. I swipe my phone and smile when I see it's a text from Maxime:

Good luck today with your first feature. I know you'll do great.

I'm so besotted with this man, I think smiling down at my phone. I begin to type back, but another message comes through from him first.

I miss you so much. I can't wait to come home.

Forget besotted. I'm so in over my head for Maxime, there's no hope of ever going back.

I don't want to go back.

I text him back as Hayes slams the back door shut on the van.

I miss you, too. So much it hurts. About to shoot seasonal décor. I'll ask if she has any tips for creating a cozy theme for our date on Saturday night.

Hayes and I begin walking up the winding sidewalk

to the house, and Maxime gets in one more message before I turn my phone off:

All I need is you.

Same, I think as I stare at his words.

I shut off my phone and drop it into my pocket, tucking his words inside my heart while my brain gets ready to go to work.

———

"So, Whitney, why don't you show me what things you have done in this home to bring in a spring feeling?" I ask, smiling brightly at her.

The light of the camera is shining on me and Whitney, a young, beautiful red-haired woman who is one of the decorators for Décor Bliss Boulder. The homeowner, Suze Joyce, is standing by with a giddy look on her face, pleased that her home is going to be featured on TV. I will interview her as soon as I'm done shooting with Whitney.

After a brief chat about on-camera basics—look there, don't be nervous, act like you are talking to a friend—Whitney is practically a pro.

"Sure, I'd love to," Whitney says, leading me over to the expansive dining room table. "One place I love to bring in the elements of spring is at the table. We often think of tablescapes for big holiday gatherings or parties, but I say, use the place you share your meals and make it seasonally beautiful."

I gaze down at the table, which reflects the bounty of spring with rustic wooden boxes filled with tulips and peonies in gorgeous shades of peach and pink. A cake stand holds a stack of artfully arranged apricots. A white-and-red-ticking-striped runner lays across the length of the table, with orange and cherry jams in mason jars, each tied with elaborate bows to coordinate with the flowers, anchored at each end. The place mats are the same ticking stripe, and a full place setting sits in front of each of the eight chairs.

"This is gorgeous," I say, picking up one of the mason jars. "This is such a cute idea. This is jam, right?"

"Yes, I sourced those from a local farm stand and added the bows," Whitney explains, her green eyes lighting up.

"And if someone hires you, you come in and make all this happen?"

"Absolutely. Our job is to do décor tasks, big or small, and make your home seasonally beautiful. We can work with what you have, or we can bring in everything for you."

"Even the plates?" I ask, picking one up.

"Of course. We can source plates for your table or lanterns for your living room. We can do it all, no matter what the occasion or holiday. The items are rented to you for as long as you want the décor up."

"That's fantastic. You make it so easy to give your home a refresh." Then I give her a skeptical look. "Okay, Whitney. The next holiday is St. Patrick's Day. What do you have up your sleeve for that?"

Whitney laughs, and I can't help but notice how much she loves her job. She's completely at ease talking about it, and her thoughts and words never waiver.

It's a dream interview to get me out of the gate with *Boulder Live.*

"I do have some things up this bell sleeve of mine," Whitney says, gesturing so her sweater sleeve swishes. "If you will follow me over to the living room, you can see I have done up a St. Patrick's Day mantle."

Hayes and I follow Whitney to the mantle, where she has placed a beautiful collection of bright green bottles filled with fresh white flowers.

"You can go whimsical, with shamrock bunting or garlands, but in this case, I wanted to capture the color of the holiday," Whitney explains. She moves over to the coffee table and picks up a stack of books. "Another way you can infuse a season into a room is through curated collections, like these books on Irish legends and the scenic countryside of Ireland."

"That's smart," I say, nodding.

I go on to ask her a few more questions, making sure I have more than enough footage to edit together a great segment, and then I move on to Suze, who has a frozen smile in front of the camera. I have to stop a few times to make her laugh and loosen up before I'm able to talk to her about why she hired Whitney and how she feels about the result. Then we call it a wrap.

"I'm going to shoot some close ups," Hayes says, moving around to the mantle.

I thank Suze for opening her home to us and tell her

I will email her as soon as I know when the segment will air.

"Would you mind signing an autograph for my daughter? And taking a selfie with me? She's a senior in high school, and she loved you on *Is It Love?*"

I nod. "Of course."

"Thank you. Our whole family loves you, Skye. Tom was an idiot."

"Things worked out the way they should have," I say, thinking of Maxime's messages on my phone.

Whitney walks out with us, and once we've stepped out into the sunny February morning, she pauses and clears her throat.

"Is it hard talking about your ex all the time?" she asks.

I shrug. "When the show first aired, and my feelings were raw, it was. But now? Nah. I've moved on."

Whitney nods.

I get the feeling she is thinking of an ex.

"My heart hasn't gotten that far yet," she admits, stopping next to her car. "I hope to be where you are someday. I thought coming here to Boulder might help. I'm here to launch the branch, and hopefully, by the time I go back to Seattle next December, I'll be where you are."

I don't know her story, but I see a bit of myself in her. There's a vulnerability in her voice when she speaks of her ex. I don't hear sadness or longing, but she's not fully healed, either.

"I think this temporary move will be good for you," I

say, nodding in assurance. "I know it was for me. Time is a great healer."

"Thank you," Whitney says. "Knowing your story, and seeing how happy you are now, I believe it can happen for me, too."

"I have a pretty good feeling you're not only going to be fine but better off," I say, thinking of how things turned out with Maxime and me.

As I did with Suze, I promise I'll let her know when the segment airs. We say goodbye and part ways, and I get in the passenger seat while Hayes reloads the equipment into the back of the truck. I retrieve my phone and turn it back on.

I text Maxime back:

Interview is done! I think it's going to be great. The décor consultant was very good on camera. Have a good nap this afternoon and know that I can't wait to kiss the cut on your cheek better when you get home. Which can't be soon enough.

Maxime replies:

I can't wait to see it. I know you did a fantastic job. Not much longer, two more nights, but it seems like forever until I can see you. I've got some news. Gavin is being released from the hospital and flying home tomorrow morning. Would

you mind checking on him for me? I'm worried about him.

Maxime is such a good man, I think. *How did I get so lucky to have another chance with him?*

While I might never know the how, I do know I will never, ever, take it for granted.

I send my response:

I'll be first up in the dinner rotation. I'll see if I can get him to talk. I know from experience burying your heartache only makes it worse. I'll bring something with sprinkles for dessert. That will make everything infinitely better. Just kidding!

Maxime types back:

You make everything infinitely better.

My heart fills with happiness. While he's been physically gone these past eleven days, we've been more connected than ever. Our video dates have allowed us to get to know each other on a deeper level as we talk for hours every night.

I can't wait to take our relationship to the next level when he comes back in two days.

In the meantime, however, I need to take care of Maxime's friend, and that's exactly what I'll do tomorrow night.

CHAPTER TWENTY-ONE

Celebrate Life with Sprinkles—The Blog
Inspirational Quote of the Day:
"Experience is the teacher of all things." —*Julius Caesar, Roman politician*

I REMEMBER READING THAT FAMOUS QUOTE BY JULIUS Caesar and saving it into my OneNote file on my laptop as something that should be my mantra.

I stare at my face on *Dishing Weekly*, with an outlandish headline above it, my hands frozen on the grocery store cart handle, trying to remind myself I learned things from my experiences on *Is it Love?*

One of them is that the tabloid media will rear its head from time to time.

But seeing the words splashed across my face—and Maxime's—makes me sick with fear. Of course, I saw it online this morning, and even shared a picture with Maxime, but seeing it in person is much worse. It makes it more real.

Why today? I think, anxiously biting my lip. I've signed my book contract. Maxime is coming home tonight. I should be on top of the world, but all I can do is stand in front of the magazine rack, regretting that my past is now toying with my future in a sidebar picture on the tabloid.

IS SWEET SKYE HITTING THE PENALTY BOX WITH BELGIAN HOCKEY HUNK?

Is It Love for real this time? Page 12.

I pull a copy of the magazine from the rack with a shaking hand. The article is going to be painfully cheesy and humiliating. I quickly thumb through the pages, dread increasing with each flick of the page as I get closer to "my story." Finally, I find it: a two-page spread filled with photos of Maxime and me at breakfast last week. There is one snapped of me leaving the TV studio, and another of Maxime leaving the rink on the day he left for the road trip, with this hideous caption underneath it:

Looking sullen at the thought of leaving his luscious reality show love, Maxime Laurent prepares to jet out for a long road trip.

I swallow hard. The rest of the WAGS don't drag their boyfriends and husbands into this quagmire of crap. I feel horrible, inferior.

Because I know the article is always worse than the

headline. If this one isn't, one full of hurtful things and absolute lies will be coming.

I chuck the magazine facedown into my cart. I'll read it at home. The last thing I need is for people to take pictures of me reading about myself in the store. Then the headlines would be "Spotlight-loving Skye can't stop reading about herself! We caught her flicking through our article on Friday!"

Maxime can handle this, I reassure myself as I keep my head down and begin to push the cart through the store. He told me the tabloids didn't matter. I remind myself it's temporary interest, and as soon as the next season starts, they will shift their attention to the new contestants, but I know he won't like it. I also know it won't be enough to unravel what we have.

At least that is what I have to believe, or I'll go mad with worry.

I begin shopping for the dinner I'm making Gavin tonight. He is getting my one specialty; in other words, the one thing I can make without it ending in complete failure: my mom's chicken, broccoli, and rice casserole. You make it in one pot, and at the end, pop it into the oven for browning. My mom had it growing up, and she made our housekeeper add it to the menu when I was young.

It's the only thing I can make. Besides cupcakes from a mix.

I go through the list I neatly organized on my phone, acting like I don't notice people staring at me while I shop. It's an acquired skill. It's not easy to pretend you don't notice when someone is obviously gawking at you.

Bleurgh.

I work through the items on my list, throwing in a rustic loaf of whole-wheat sourdough bread, a bag of organic salad mix, and a bottle of natural low-fat dressing. I head to self-checkout so I can move quickly and get out without more people noticing me.

I head outside into the sunshine, purchases in hand. I open the passenger door and place my bags on the seat, then shut it and slip behind the wheel. I say a little prayer for my car to start, and it does. Curiosity gets the better of me, and I retrieve the tabloid out of the bag. I pass royal gossip and Hollywood scandal to get to my love story:

It looks like America's Reality Show Sweetheart, Skye Reeve, is no longer crying over Tom Broaden, who broke her heart with his declaration that he did not, indeed, find love with her on the season finale of Is It Love? last season.

Rather, our stunning blonde, sporting her hair in a stylish braid and looking casual chic in a cozy, pale gray V-neck sweater with a crisp white shirt sticking out underneath, seems to have found love with a dashingly sexy hockey hunk from Belgium.

Maxime Laurent, the model-like looker with cheekbones that could chisel stone, is the alternate captain for the Denver Mountain Lions. He only had eyes for his own reality star during their intimate breakfast for two on February 16th in Boulder, Colorado.

According to sources close to the couple, they connected when Reeve landed a job on the TV show Boulder Live this year.

"Skye has never been so happy," raves one source close to

the TV personality. "She's already planning for a lavish wedding in Belgium next summer."

I stop reading. What fresh hell is this? *Wedding?* Just a few weeks before, the tabloids had me drowning myself in donuts over Wanker Tom; now I'm running off to marry Maxime in Belgium?

I sigh and continue reading:

Laurent, for his part, has been quiet on the Denver dating scene and at Mountain Lions functions, never attending with a date.

Apparently, all he needed was for the skies to open up and drop Reeve into his life.

The two looked at each other with tenderness and adoration over breakfast, sharing not just pancakes and bacon, but also sweet whispers, hand-holds, and kisses—right in public!

While making out in front of the world isn't new for Reeve, it is for the quiet, off-the-radar Laurent.

"He couldn't keep his hands off her," says a patron who was at the restaurant that morning. "It was so sweet!"

The sexy hockey hunk, looking deliciously disheveled with rumpled hair and stubble across his jaw, also brushed tender kisses across Reeve's knuckles, gazing at her lovingly in the brief time they had together before he went on a brutal road trip through Canada.

While Laurent hated to leave his new love so early, insiders close to the hockey-playing star said he's confident in what they have.

"They are a true team," says a Laurent insider. "These two are meant to be together."

Friday is his last game on the road, and we look forward to seeing a happy reunion with our new favorite lovebirds!

Okay. Rather cringe-worthy, especially the wedding bit, but as far as tabloid fare goes, this isn't awful. It's actually favorable to us, and while I have a feeling his teammates will give Maxime shit about knuckle kisses and having chiseled cheekbones, I know Maxime will survive it.

And come home to me later tonight.

———

"I HOPE YOU ARE IN THE MOOD FOR RETRO HOME cooking," I say, carrying my casserole dish into Gavin's luxurious, modern kitchen. "Because I brought a broccoli, chicken, and cheese casserole. Canned soup is included in the recipe."

Gavin hobbles on crutches behind me. "It sounds perfect. I can't thank you enough for doing this. You spared my mom a trip from Toronto. I love her, but her fussing over me would have been way too much for me to handle in my current mood."

I place the casserole dish and the bag of groceries on his vast kitchen island. It's covered with stacks of folders and papers and a calculator. I bite my lip as I see there are piles and piles of credit card bills.

I know it's the Veronica mess staring me in the face.

I move to the state-of-the-art Viking wall oven and turn on the temperature I need. I face Gavin, who has dark shadows under his eyes and the start of a golden-haired beard on his face.

"Why don't we sit down? I'll let the oven pre-heat, and then I can bring everything to you."

He moves slowly on his crutches to a large, sectional, theater-style sofa and eases himself down, gently propping his broken leg onto a huge square ottoman.

I follow him and take a seat not too far down from him.

"It seems stupid to ask you how you are feeling," I admit, "but since I'm a TV reporter, I get to ask the dumb and obvious. How are you feeling?"

A small smile tugs at the corner of his mouth. "Let's see. My girlfriend never loved me and robbed me blind because I'm a clueless sucker. Now I've busted my femur, and it hurts like hell, and I'm out for the season. Other than that, I'm fantastic."

"We're going to argue on that first comment," I challenge. "You are *not* a clueless sucker. You fell in love. You took a risk. It ended badly, but you will come back from this and love again; I promise you that."

"Oh, hell no," Gavin says, setting his jaw determinedly. "I'll *never* be this stupid again. I'll hookup, and have fun, but I will be dammed if I'm ever this weak again. Do you have any idea how humiliating this is? She loved my money, Skye. Veronica had me wrapped around her finger like a——" he pauses, and I can tell he's searching for an appropriate word to use in front of me, "a fool. We'll go with that. A damn fool."

"According to this logic, I'm the bigger fool," I say.

"Why?"

"I fell in love with Tom on TV. He didn't want anything from me. I was a pawn he played for the cameras. My judgment is infinitely worse than yours, Gavin. I thought he loved me. I thought he was going to get down on one knee and propose to me. Worse, I was going to say '*Yes,*' to that wanker. So I win this round. He never thought of proposing to me, he lied with every word he whispered, and I had no clue it was all a script he was saying to every other girl on the show. I'm the sorrier one here."

Now a real smile appears on his face. "You've been hanging out with Jude," he says, referring to my wanker comment.

I smile back at him. "Jude is a good guy. So is Cade. I obviously think Maxime is, and so are you. You will be just as happy as they are once you heal from all of this."

The smile falls from his face. "No. I'll heal my femur. I'll work my ass off in rehab here and back in Toronto this summer, and I'll be ready for training camp next fall. But I will never get over what Veronica has done. I won't let myself. I will never be this vulnerable again."

"Gavin, I felt the same way. Sitting in that café in Brussels, I was at my lowest point. People were laughing at me, making GIFs out of things I said on the show, and having a field day with things that weren't true. I wanted to *die*, to hide, which is why I ran to Europe. And that's where I found Maxime."

Gavin reaches for his water bottle, undoes the cap, and takes a long swig. "That's still crazy how you guys were at that same café."

"I know. We were meant to meet. There will be,

when you are ready, some other woman for you to meet, too."

"I won't find anyone like you, or Sierra, or JoJo," Gavin says, his voice tinged with bitterness. "I can't read women. That's painfully obvious. So, I'm done. Sex and out." Then he glances at me. "Sorry for the bluntness."

I smile gently at him. "I'd like to think we're going to be friends, as I know you mean a lot to Maxime, so candor between friends is okay. So, my turn to be blunt. What are you going to do about Veronica's theft? Are you going to press charges?"

He lets out a long, painful-sounding sigh, and my heart aches for him. Gavin pushes down on his backward Mountain Lions baseball cap and keeps his light-blue eyes straight ahead, to the TV that is tuned to the channel where the Mountain Lions game will air in an hour.

"No," he says, his voice quiet. "I should, but then this will be all over the media. I can't take that humiliation. I'd rather eat the loss than put her in jail." He pauses for a moment, and I watch as he swallows hard. "I also can't put her in jail because I still love her."

A lump forms in my throat.

"I loved Tom for a while afterward," I admit. "I came around pretty fast, but when you give your heart, you give it. It would be nice if we could erase those feelings, but we can't. Now I see that it's part of life. It's part of the road you take to get to where you need to be."

"To Max?" Gavin asks, turning his attention toward me.

I can't stop the smile that spreads across my face. "Yes. To Maxime."

A true smile appears on Gavin's face. "He's *crazy* about you."

My heart flutters. "That's good to hear, because I'm crazy about him, too."

"We gave him so much shit for not hooking up," Gavin says. "We were like, 'Dude, you can hit anything. Why not at least ban—err, sleep with girls?'"

I repress the giggle that climbs up in my throat.

"That's not his style," I say.

"No, it's not. You're not who I pictured for him at first, to be honest. I watched *Is It Love?* with Cade and Jude. Maxime gave us shit for watching it, ironically. When I heard you two went out on a date, I was shocked. But sitting here with you now, I get it. You're *real.* You just happened to be on a TV show, that's all."

"Thank you. That means a lot to me."

"You're good for him."

"Maxime's good for me," I say. Then I clear my throat. "We've both had relationship disasters, Gavin. Once you heal, however long that takes, you'll be fine."

He snorts. I can tell the topic is going nowhere with him.

"Okay, okay, I'll let it go. For now. But I will bring it back up at some point because that is what *friends* do."

"Skye?"

"Yeah?"

"It's an honor to be your friend and get to know you."

"Same," I say as genuine affection for my new friend

fills my heart. "Now, why don't I get that casserole in the oven? We'll watch the game, and you can explain the intricacies to me so I can give Maxime some pointers when he gets home," I tease.

Gavin laughs. "Deal."

———

WE'VE SPENT THE REST OF THE NIGHT WATCHING THE Mountain Lions take on Toronto, the last game of this never-ending road trip. I've watch as Gavin cycles between elation at good plays and frustration when he sees things that are going wrong or mistakes being made on the ice.

There's a lot of swearing involved.

Now there are a few minutes left in the game, and the Mountain Lions are down 2-1. If Gavin could pace, I know he would. I'm chewing a hole through my lower lip. The Mountain Lions have headed back toward the offensive zone with two minutes and two seconds left in the game.

"Kelly hesitates for a moment, passes to Laurent," John Lewis, the play-by-play announcer, says.

I watch as Maxime rips a shot on goal that sails past the goalie and into the net.

I leap off the sofa and cheer.

"Hell yes!" Gavin yells.

"That's my Maxime!" I cry excitedly.

"Ka-bang!" Martin Czeck, the analyst, yells. "Maxime Laurent has tied it up!"

I watch as they replay the brilliant fake out by Brayden Kelly before slipping the puck over to Maxime, followed by another shot of the goal.

Maxime goes down on one knee after he scores and skates across the ice in a moment of rare exhibition. He gets up, and I see a smile of pure, unabashed joy on his face as his teammates hug him on the ice. Pride surges through me, watching him score the tying goal for his team.

"Wicked shot there, Max," Gavin says, grinning.

The camera follows Maxime as he skates to the bench, fist-bumping everyone as he goes down the line. My adrenaline is still high from the goal, and I have to remind myself to breathe as we watch the remaining time play out.

Gavin and I watch on edge, and when a Toronto shot rings off the goal post as time is about to expire, we both gasp with relief. Whew! We've made it to overtime.

Gavin explains how overtime works during a commercial break. It consists of three-on-three hockey, for five minutes, and if a goal isn't scored, they go to a shootout. Gavin has a natural ability to break things down to a level where I can understand, without making it sound like he's talking down to me.

He'd be a great coach for kids, I can't help thinking.

After the break, I see Maxime skate out as part of the first line to hit the ice in the overtime period. He skates next to Cade, covering his mouth with his glove as he speaks to him, and I see Cade nodding as he listens.

Maxime moves into the circle for the face-off. My

241

heart is pounding, and I'm braiding my hair as I watch the screen.

"This is intense," I murmur, anxiety filling me.

"It's *fun*," Gavin says. "God, I wish I was out there."

I'm about to acknowledge his comment when the puck is dropped and they take off. The pace is insane! I watch as Maxime passes to Cade, who fires a shot on goal that the goalie deflects. They race back to the other end, with Mountain Lions' defenseman Andrei Petrov blocking a shot by throwing his body in the way of the puck.

Gavin continues to swear. I'm now unbraiding my hair, and each shot on goal is a hold-your-breath moment, either praying for it to go in or praying for a save. It's both exhilarating and nerve-fraying at the same time.

The clock winds down as a Toronto player intercepts the puck and flies down to the other end of the ice.

"Shit!" Gavin and I both yell at the same time.

He fires a shot that looks like a sure goal when our goalie, Westley Pratt, comes out of the net and makes a huge save.

"Pratt with an incredible save!" John yells.

"What anticipation by Pratt," Martin adds. "He knew he had to come out to make that save!"

Overtime ends.

"Shootout time," Gavin says, taking off his hat and putting it back on.

"Who will take the shots?" I ask, my stomach in knots.

"Well, I'm usually one of them," Gavin says, sighing.

"My guess is they will move up Jude, as he has a sick set of hands and is awesome in the shootout. Then Maxime. If it goes further, then Phillips, Kelley, and Callahan. But let's hope Maxime can close this game out."

Gavin was right. After the shootout is announced, Jude takes to the ice.

"Here we go in the shootout! First up is Jude Parker," John says. "He grabs the puck at center …"

I hold my breath as Jude comes up the ice. He closes in on the Toronto goaltender, moving the puck one way, then the other, and then he shoots, and bam! He scores!

"Jude Parker scores!" John cries. "What a slick move to beat the Toronto netminder."

"Yes!" Gavin yells. "He schooled him!"

"Way to go Jude!" I cheer.

"What a beautiful move, a backhand, forehand, roof," Martin says.

Next up is a player for Toronto, who takes off from center toward Westley. He tries to fake him out, but Westley drops and deflects the puck with his stick.

"Yes!" I scream.

"Come on, Maxime. Get on the board," Gavin says, fixated on the TV.

I put my fingertips to my lips. I feel all the pressure Maxime must have on his shoulders right now, to put that puck into the net.

Maxime takes to center ice and puts his stick on the puck. I can't decide if I want to cover my eyes or not, but I keep my hands still, my eyes riveted to Maxime.

"Laurent brings the puck up the ice," the announcer says. "He slows up a bit …"

I'm going to have a stroke.

I watch as Maxime takes a shot on net, holding my breath.

"To the backhand and he scores!" John roars.

Gavin and I are yelling in unison now.

They replay Maxime's move, and then they show him skating over to the bench and high-fiving his teammates.

"If Pratt makes the save here we win," Gavin says.

Come on, Westley, I think. *Close this game out.*

The Toronto player skates toward Westley. I once again have my fingertips pressed against my lips, anxiety filling me.

The player goes back to make his shot. I watch he releases the puck, but it's snatched by the glove of Westley!

Gavin and I are both screaming in excitement now.

The Mountain Lions have come from behind and won the game.

They show the Mountain Lions players coming over the wall and forming a line to congratulate Westley on his incredible showing tonight.

"What a thrilling way to end what has been a great road trip for the Denver Mountain Lions," John says.

Pride fills me as I watch Maxime congratulate Westley by patting him affectionately on the top of his goalie helmet. They cut away from Maxime and show the announcers in the booth, but at this point, I don't hear what they are saying.

Maxime played *brilliantly*. There are no words to describe the happiness I have for him.

Best of all, he's coming home now.

And I can't wait to show him exactly how I feel about him tomorrow night.

CHAPTER TWENTY-TWO

Celebrate Life with Sprinkles—The Blog
Taking in the Moment

ANTICIPATION RUNS THROUGH ME AS I PARK MY CAR IN front of Maxime's house. I take a second to reflect on this moment, because once I walk through that door, everything between us will change. There will be no going back to the way things are now after tonight, when we make love for the first time. My mind is filled with thoughts of what his body will look like when I undress him, how he will feel against my skin, and how his body will join with mine.

Heat flickers within me from those images passing through my mind. I've never wanted to be intimate with someone as much as I do Maxime. With each date we had, whether in person or through video, I found myself wanting to know all of him more and more. I want the passion, the tear-your-clothes-off need to make love, as if no other man could fill my needs as he can. I want him to feel the same way about me, to want me in a way he's never wanted anyone else. I want to explore him and give him what he needs to drive him over the edge.

Sex, however, isn't the only threshold we'll cross tonight. This isn't just sex for me, and after my conversation with Gavin, I know it's not for Maxime, either. This is an emotional investment in each other. We are allowing ourselves to be vulnerable for the first time since our hearts were broken, and to see if the relationship we're building is moving closer to love for both of us.

There's something magical about firsts. The first touch of a hand. The first brush of the lips. Now we're entering the first time we'll bare everything to each other and make love.

The funny thing is, I'm not nervous. Not at all.

I feel as if Maxime is the one I've been waiting to find.

The one who could be my everything.

I climb out of my car, grabbing my tote, and dash up to his front door. This is our "cozy date," so Maxime told me he wanted me just the way I'd be at home for a snowy night in, as snow is forecasted this evening. I glance down at my outfit. I went all out, with my *Rudolph the Red-Nosed Reindeer* plush pajama bottoms, complete with Abominable Snowman, and a white lace camisole leaving nothing to the imagination, but one he can't see until he unties my white hooded cardigan, which I have belted so the camisole is just peeking out at the top.

It's soft and cuddly, and I can't wait for Maxime to take it off, I think with wickedly.

Oh, and to finish off the cozy vibe, I'm wearing brown suede moccasin slippers lined with fleece.

Don't say I don't know how to seduce a man with a sexy outfit, I think, grinning.

But the thing is, with Maxime, I know I don't need seduction. We have a connection that goes beyond the superficial, that is driven both by emotional and physical desires.

I ring the doorbell and hear his dogs barking. It feels like forever since I've seen Maxime.

I hear him talking to the dogs, and they both fall silent. The door opens, and it's all I can do not to gasp aloud.

Maxime has dressed to a T for tonight, with gray drawstring sweat pants, a white T-shirt, and the red and black flannel shirt I requested. He still has a cut across his left cheek from his fight. Maxime's hair is messily rumpled, the gold-streaked waves sweeping across his forehead.

I restrain myself from jumping him right there in the doorway.

I drop my tote on the floor. Maxime takes me into his arms, his hands sliding up to my cheeks, his eyes drinking in every detail of my face as he stares at me.

"You have no idea," he murmurs sexily, "how long I have waited to do this."

He lowers his mouth to mine. I eagerly open for him, my tongue parting his lips, tasting him, inhaling the glorious, unique scent of bourbon and vanilla mixing on his skin. I feel his hands climbing to my hair, tangling through my loose waves. I glide my hands over his powerful arms, stroking the muscles through the soft flannel, to his neck, then to his hair, looping the silken waves around my fingertips and moaning softly as Maxime's lips begin kissing the side of my face.

"I missed you," I whisper, closing my eyes again as his mouth moves down my jaw.

His hands span my back, drawing me into his hard body. I tilt my head back, and he trails his tongue down the side of my neck. Maxime gently moves my sweater aside so he can breathe a sexy kiss on the top of my shoulder, causing me to shiver in response.

"I've missed you, too," he murmurs against my skin. "God, how I've missed you."

He lifts his head and once again frames my face in his hands. I gaze up at him, touched by the look of adoration in his vivid blue-green eyes.

"All I could think about," he says softly, "was being able to touch you. To feel your silky skin with my hands, to kiss your luscious mouth, to bury myself against your neck and inhale your scent, which is imprinted on my mind. I see your eyes and the way you look at me, and I want nothing more than to be with you. I need to be with you tonight."

"I want you," I say, my voice low with desire, "to make love to me."

Maxime's eyes flicker with passion. We both know the moment is right now.

He picks me up, and I wrap my legs around his waist as his tongue parts my lips in a desperate way. I grab his hair and kiss him back, my mouth rapidly moving against his, heat filling every inch of me as we move

AVEN ELLIS

toward the living room. Oh, God, I've never wanted—
needed—a man like I do right now. I'm tugging on his
hair. I'm biting his lip. I'm greedy and taking everything
I can get from him as I return my tongue to his mouth,
deeply kissing him as a groan of desire escapes his
throat.

"I want you now," he pleads before kissing me again.
"All of you, I want to see all of you."

He puts me down in the living room, and I'm about
to undress him when I become aware of what he's done.
I gasp in surprise at what Maxime has created for us
tonight.

It's the cozy date I told him I had dreamed of for us.

The floor is filled with thick, plush blankets, all in
cream. There are luxurious pillows strewn about.
There's a fire roaring in the fireplace, which, along with
dozens of cream-colored votive candles, provide
intimate lighting in the room. I see two glasses of red
wine and a bottle on the coffee table.

My gaze stops there, because next to the wine
glasses are two pink cupcakes, covered in colored
sprinkles.

"You said sprinkles make everything better," he says
softly.

I turn back to him, overwhelmed with what I'm
feeling for this man. Maxime wanted to make tonight
everything I asked for.

It's not a date on an exotic beach. It's not on a yacht
off the coast of Monaco.

It's so much better.

Love surges through my heart as it beats frantically

250

inside my chest. One thing has become crystal clear, in both my head and my heart.

I love Maxime.

Love is what this is. Love drove this man to create this kind of moment, one that he knows will mean everything to me. Love is wanting to bring this joy to my face, just so he can see it. He wants it to be romantic and intimate for our first time.

I turn my attention back to him, this amazing man that I've fallen in love with. I'm going to give him all of me physically tonight, but now my heart as well.

"Maxime," I whisper, "it's *perfect.*"

His mouth reclaims mine, but this time the kiss is slow, sensual, as if he wants to savor every second of this intimate moment. It tells me the kissing is just as important as the act of making love.

Maxime skims his hands over my body, causing me to tremble. He undoes the knot on my cardigan, sliding his hands inside of it, where they find my waist. His fingertips slowly, achingly dance up and down, causing desire to swirl within me.

"I need to touch you," I murmur sexily against his mouth, causing him to groan.

I begin to unbutton his sexy lumberjack shirt, and once I reach the last button, I glide my hands up over his T-shirt, trembling as I feel the hard, muscular chest that is all mine to kiss and touch. I remove his shirt, allowing my fingertips to explore his sculpted shoulders.

Maxime continues his deep, slow kissing, his hands now sliding up to remove my cardigan. I let it fall to the floor, standing before him in a sheer, lace camisole.

251

With nothing underneath it.

"You're so beautiful," he says, his eyes moving over me. Maxime lowers his hand to the bottom of my cami and slowly, gently, raises it up, as if he's unwrapping a precious gift. He carefully lifts it over my head and bares my breasts to him.

He doesn't say a word, but his eyes say everything to me.

This man is going to love me with reverence tonight.

Maxime moves his hands over my breasts, touching them gently as he explores me for the first time.

As he does, his lips find mine, kissing me sweetly, carefully, with gentle intimacy.

I reach for his T-shirt and push it up, my hand skimming over his abs, and I sweep my fingertips across the contours of his defined muscles, shaking.

Maxime helps me push it up, and then he takes it off. I gasp upon the sight of him, the hard muscle, the developed pecs, and the sexy, glorious trail of dark hair that starts at his chest and leads down to his waist that dips into a V, where his sweatpants hang enticingly from his hips.

I stare at him, utterly amazed at how beautiful and powerful his body is. I run my hands over him, caressing him, and then I begin a trail of kisses from the top of his chest and move down slowly, kissing him, touching him, and stopping just as I get to his waistband.

Maxime is shaking. So am I.

He lowers me to the floor, cradling me on top of the blankets. The light from the fireplace flickers across his face, illuminating him in the darkness as his hands move down to my pajama bottoms. His hands carefully stroke the inside of my thighs as he lowers them down past my hips.

He kisses me again as he removes them, as if he needs to stay connected with these intimate kisses as our hands explore each other.

I feel loved.

"God, I want this," he whispers as he slowly traces his fingertips around the wisp of my lace thong.

I undo the drawstring on his pants. He removes them, and I swallow hard when I see how perfect he looks in boxer-briefs. I move my fingertips over the waistband, down to his backside, cupping his tight, firm butt in my hand as he lowers himself over me.

Maxime dips his head and kisses my neck, down to my breasts, slowly moving his tongue across my body, giving every inch of me attention. I'm shaking. My hips buck against him, and I bite my lip to keep from crying out for him.

He lifts a pillow and pulls out a condom before his tongue is caressing my mouth again. He gives me a long, deep kiss before breaking away.

"Now," I pant, desperation filling me. "I need you *now.*"

"No," Maxime whispers. "You need to be worshipped and touched everywhere. I am going to take my time tonight. You deserve to be made love to, to have all of you celebrated. For *hours.*"

A cry escapes my lips as he traces them with his tongue.

I close my eyes, happy tears filling them.

Maxime is going to make love to me in a way I've never dreamed existed. I will do the same, loving this man and his body as we become one tonight.

I love you, I think as I kiss him back. *I love you, I love you.*

And now is the time to show him how much.

CHAPTER TWENTY-THREE

"What are you thinking?" Maxime murmurs as he drops a kiss on my head.

We're snuggled up on the floor. Maxime is sitting up against the couch, and I'm in his arms, my cheek to his chest, cozy throws draped around us as we sip wine. He's added more wood to the fire, and I can hear the crackling of the flames along with the beating of his heart.

"I'm thinking," I say, turning so I can look up at him, "about how perfect this evening has been and how making love to you has been a life-changing experience."

Maxime's mouth curves up in a sexy smile that makes me hunger for him all over again.

"Life-changing?"

I nod. "You made me feel things I didn't know I could," I say softly.

Maxime lowers his mouth to mine, giving me a sweet, lingering kiss. I savor the taste of wine on his tongue, which I find very sensual, and slowly kiss him back, greedily taking as many kisses as I can get from the man I love.

Love.

I know without a doubt this is what real love is. It's not what I had with Tom.

Love, true love, soul mate love, *The One* love, is what I have with Maxime.

We made love for hours this evening, and now I love him more than I did before. He was passionate, giving, sensual.

I felt *cherished* by this man, as if I was the only woman he'd ever touched like this. The physical connection between us was powerful and emotional. Making love to Maxime was a reverent experience, one that has changed my life forever.

I want forever with you, I think as I kiss him with all the love in my heart. *Only you, my Maxime.*

Maxime breaks the kiss and gazes down at me with nothing but adoration in his eyes. He combs his fingers through my hair.

"I've never made love to anyone like I did to you," he says, as if reading my mind. "That was worth waiting for. I'd wait again if it meant making love to you."

A powerful wave of love washes over me, leaving a warm feeling radiating through my skin. I touch his face, and Maxime takes my hand and puts my fingertips to his full lips, brushing a kiss against them.

"Luckily, you don't have to wait," I flirt. "Because I'm not going anywhere."

Maxime laughs softly, and I do, too.

"I do have a question," Maxime says, his voice turning serious.

"Yes?" I say, wrinkling my brow.

"What the hell was on your pajama bottoms?"

I burst out laughing. "Even in the throes of sexual passion, you noticed?"

"Nothing about you escapes me," he says. "Including bizarre pajama bottoms."

I giggle. "Those were from the Rudolph movie I was telling you about. They had the Abominable Snowman on them."

"That is the creature who makes the noise like your stomach?"

"Yes."

Maxime reaches for his wine and takes a sip. "You're endlessly fascinating."

"I know. I'm going to change your life, Maxime Laurent."

"You already have," Maxime says, his eyes flickering with intensity.

He places his wine glass back on the table and lowers his mouth to mine, and as I kiss him back, I know he's not the only one whose life has changed.

Maxime has changed mine, in the most wonderful of ways. I'm full of love, confident in what we are building and of where it will end up. He's my best friend. My support system. My partner. My love.

He is my forever.

With that thought dancing happily through my heart, I begin to make love with him again.

———

I FEEL MAXIME DRIFT OFF TO SLEEP, HIS ARM DRAPED around my waist. We moved upstairs to his bedroom, and now it's the early morning hours of the next day. I listen to his rhythmic breathing and feel the weight of the dogs on the end of the bed. Amè and Henri seemed to be happy that I was part of the bedtime routine.

If only Natasha and Boris were here. Then it would truly feel like home.

While the dogs and Maxime sleep, I think about the past, of how I was so sure I knew what true love was when I fell for Tom. The world came crashing down when I discovered my feelings were one-sided. But if I didn't go through that, if I didn't know that pain, I wouldn't have what I have with Maxime now. I wouldn't have known what it is like to be with a man who genuinely listens to what I say and who is happy for my successes and wants me to follow my career dreams. Now I have a man who fought for me when I thought about walking away.

That's it, I think, my brain whirling. *Other women need to hear this story.*

They need to hear about how I found everything beautiful about love when I found Maxime. I want them to know men like this exist, and not only in movies and in books but in real life. The right guy might not appear when you expect it, but if you can put aside your fears and take a chance, the most amazing things can happen.

I need to write this, I think, excitement taking over. *The love I feel now is the biggest part of my story, and I want to share it.*

I carefully remove Maxime's arm. He murmurs for a moment, and I lay still until he resettles into sleep. Both Amè and Henri lift their heads as I quietly swing my legs over the side of his bed, but they resettle just like their dad did. I smile as I see the three of them sleeping, knowing this is my forever.

I find my pajama bottoms on the floor and slip them on. Then I put on my cami and cozy cardigan. I creep down the stairs to the living room and retrieve my phone out of my purse. I grab one of the thick throw blankets and curl up on the sofa, opening a notepad app.

Of course, I know Maxime is a private person. He might not want any of this shared, but I'm going to write it, let him read it, and then edit out things he thinks are too personal. If I explain to him *why* I'm doing it, he might be more open to the idea.

The final call will be his, even though this story is mine, too. I love him too much to make him uncomfortable.

So, with love as my guide, I begin to write.

———

"Skye?"

I blink my eyes open, confused. I look around, finding myself on Maxime's sofa. Shit. I must have fallen asleep while writing.

"Skye, where are you?" Maxime calls out.

I hear the dogs come down the stairs, followed by Maxime's footsteps. I push myself up to a seated position just as Maxime enters the room.

"What are you doing down here, *mon chérie?*" he asks.

I don't answer for a moment. His sweat pants and lumberjack shirt are back on, and his waves are a sexy mess on his head.

"I was inspired to write some stuff for my book," I say as he takes a seat next to me.

"You're working so hard," Maxime says, his eyes reflecting concern for me. "I worry about you."

I grin. "This coming from a man who just came off a grueling eleven-day road trip."

"Yes, but I have one job: to play hockey. You— you're a TV reporter, you're a blogger, you're active on social media, and you're writing a book. I don't want you to burn out."

"I'm not going to lie; it's a lot to handle," I say, moving my hand to his silken locks and re-arranging them on his head. "But I can do it."

Maxime nods. "Okay. Make sure you take time to relax, though. It's important."

I'm lucky to have someone who cares so much, I think.

"I promise," I say.

"What are you doing for *Boulder Live* this week?"

"Well, I have my reality roundup segment on Wednesday. Oh, and I will be giving Aly a heads-up that she will not, under any circumstances, discuss that cheesy tabloid article that came out on Friday."

"You mean the one about our wedding?" Maxime asks, flashing me a grin.

I gasp. "You said you wouldn't read them!"

"Skye, the captions on the photos were so cheesy, I *had* to read it," Maxime explains. "Besides, the guys are already giving me shit about it. I was going to know regardless."

A heat-filled shame comes to my cheeks. "I'm sorry, Maxime. I know it's embarrassing, and I know even if you don't say it, you hate this."

Maxime is quiet for a moment. "It's an insignificant price to pay to be with you, Skye. I'll handle this a thousand times over to be with you."

He leans in and kisses me as if to punctuate his point.

I break the kiss and frame his face in my hands. "I'm lucky. So, so lucky to have another chance with you. I can't imagine not being with you now that I am."

"I feel the same way," Maxime says seriously. Then he clears his throat. "I don't have practice today. Coach is feeling generous after that road trip."

"Ooh, does that mean a lazy Sunday for us?"

"No. First, I'm going to make us a huge breakfast," Maxime says, threading his fingers through mine. "Brioche and sprinkles, oatmeal, eggs, fruit, bacon, and coffee."

"You had me at sprinkles," I tease.

A beautiful smile lights up his face. "You're easy to please."

"Okay, so big, huge breakfast. Then what?"

"We need to run to the pet store. I think we need some cat things around here."

261

My heart holds still. "Do you want the babies to come over?"

"They are a part of your family," he says. "They should be here when you're here. We need to get them used to the dogs and to traveling in the car."

I love this man so much.

"I'd like that," I say, keeping the love card silent for now.

Maxime smiles at me. "Good. Then I have one more thing to do."

"Lots of sex?"

An adorable blush sweeps across his cheeks.

"Well, yes, that is definitely going to happen, but if we are to have a fire, I need to cut some more wood," Maxime says.

Hello, my fantasy is going to happen, I think with a wicked grin.

"Ooh, I get to see you go all lumberjack."

"Funny. Most women like the fighting hockey player, but you like a man who can cut wood."

"Oh, speaking of that," I say, removing my hand from his and lightly sweeping it over the cut on his face, "you don't have to be Gavin, you know. Fighting isn't your style. Your teammates know you have their backs. They aren't expecting you to be Gavin. They are expecting you to be *you*, Maxime."

He's silent for a moment. "Gavin is a good captain," Maxime says, choosing his words as if this has been weighing on him. "I wanted to show them I could give them that same leadership in his absence. His injury has left a huge hole on the ice, Skye."

"But the team knows you aren't Gavin," I counter. "You were selected as alternate for all the reasons you are different from Gavin."

"I don't want to let the team down," he says. "I don't know if I'm enough."

For the first time, I hear the ghost of his past creep into his hockey game. He fears being himself isn't enough.

"You are *more* than enough," I assert. "Your coach believes it. Gavin believes it. You need to believe it, too."

"How did I get so lucky that you picked Brussels on a map?" Maxime asks, staring at me in wonder. "And that I met you again? That you moved to Boulder and here we are?"

"It was meant to happen," I say. "We were meant to happen, Maxime."

As his mouth finds mine for a kiss, I know it's true.

This is my destiny. This life, here with Maxime.

He hasn't said he loves me, but I know he does. I can see it in his eyes. I can feel it in his touch.

Which is all I need.

CHAPTER TWENTY-FOUR

Celebrate Life with Sprinkles—The Blog
Re-evaluating the Situation

I'M WALKING DOWN THE HALL WITH A TERRIBLE CUP OF coffee at the *Boulder Live* studio. It's Monday morning, and I'm blissfully happy as I get ready to attend the morning production meeting.

Amazing what real love can do for you, I think with a smile.

I spent all day yesterday with Maxime, and then he came over to my place to bond with the kittens. Much to my absolute delight, Boris came out and flopped on his side, letting both of us pet him. I was so moved by his utter trust, to put himself in that vulnerable position, that tears came to my eyes.

I understood what was in his tiny heart as I felt the same thing when I put my trust in Maxime.

Despite my fear of being vulnerable and my vow not to blindly trust fate, I embraced this new relationship.

I have never made a better decision in my life.

My fears of him not being able to handle my life have evaporated. I *know* he can now. I think I might have misjudged him in the beginning, based on my fears of his private nature. Maxime doesn't seem to be bothered at all by what is written in the tabloids. I love that we were laughing about the most recent article this weekend. I know they all won't be gushy like that, but at least I know he believes they don't say anything of value.

I'm glad he's home all week. Maxime has a game tonight, which I'm going to, of course, as well as one on Wednesday and Saturday. It couldn't have come at a better time, as we've taken a huge step in our relationship by sleeping together.

Many, many times, I think with a wicked grin, as flashbacks of our sexy weekend play in my head.

As they do, I hit pause on the one of him going out into the snow to cut wood, showing me how to do it with his old-school ax. He had a knit, navy cap covering his glorious brown-blond locks, and he wore a navy and camel flannel shirt. He split wood with ease with his strong arms.

Maxime looked oh-so-manly doing it, all rugged outdoorsman.

And oh-so-sexy.

We need another blast of winter weather, I think mischievously.

I turn to enter the conference room, and Aly is already sitting in her chair.

I keep a smile on my face. While everything with Maxime is sorted out, things with Aly are not.

"Good morning," I say, taking a seat several chairs down from her.

"Good morning," she says, flipping a page in her planner.

Silence fills the room.

If it were anybody else, I'd ask if they had a good weekend, share my thoughts on the wintry weather, and ask if they are ready for this week.

Aly, however, makes typical office small talk impossible, as she answers me in one-word sentences as if she's put out having to speak with the reality show castoff.

I absently scroll through my phone as a distraction, hoping someone else will walk into the conference room so this awkwardness can end.

"You seem to be making a fresh round in the tabloids," Aly says, breaking the silence.

Ugh. I'd rather go back to awkwardly not talking.

"It's temporary. They're only interested because he's the first man since Tom," I answer.

"Very convenient."

"What's that supposed to mean?"

Aly shoots me an innocent look. "Well, going from one famous person to another certainly keeps your Q Score up," she says, referring to the rating system that measures celebrity appeal.

"You think I'm dating Maxime because he's an athlete?" I ask, appalled. "Are you implying I have motives for dating him?"

"I didn't say that at all. But dating a professional

athlete would keep your publicity machine rolling. That's a *fact.*"

Anger rips through me. I'm not putting up with this. We might have to work together, but she will not speak to me like this.

It's ending right now.

"You don't have to like me, Aly. That's fine. You don't have to respect me, either. We can work together effectively regardless of how you feel about me, for the good of the show. I can't change what you think about me, but I don't have to listen to it. I'd appreciate it if you would keep your comments about my personal life, including Maxime Laurent, to yourself in the future."

Aly's eyes widen. "You're being *way* overdramatic about this. There's no need to get defensive."

"I'm not being defensive. I'm telling you to not bring up my personal life."

"I'm shocked you think I'm attacking you," Aly says. "I was making small talk about something that isn't a secret, not when it's screaming at me from the checkout line at the store, Skye."

"No, it's not a secret, but that does not mean I want to talk about it."

Aly snorts. "Ha-ha. Funny, coming from the woman who dated, fell in love, and wanted to get a ring on-air. I find it a bit of a stretch to think talking about it would be an issue for you, but whatever. We don't have to talk at all, which I would find preferable, actually."

I sigh in exasperation. "Aly, it doesn't have to be this way. I wish we could work together as two young women supporting each other in a tough business, encouraging

267

each other and having each other's backs. We would both gain more by helping each other."

Aly glares at me. "I'm not your cheerleader, Skye. This isn't the *Is It Love?* mansion, and we're not going to sit around and braid each other's hair and sip wine and cry over some guy we had oh, maybe four dates with? I'm not interested. I take broadcasting seriously. I *have* to work with you, and I will, but I won't be your in-house praise team."

She clicks her pen and goes back to her planner.

I sit still in my chair, the wind knocked out of me from her blunt attack. I've heard all these things before online and in tabloids. Strangers said them. Trolls said them.

But never from someone sitting in the same room as me.

Despite my strong words, I find my confidence shaken by her view of me. How many other people at the station think I'm an idiot? A stupid, young girl who made out with a guy on TV and has no skills or talents to offer?

I'll continue to show them with my work, I think, vowing to take on more assignments. *I'll work harder than anyone here. I'll work my way up to filling Aly's seat when she's out. Then nobody can accuse me of not deserving to be here.*

Then Maxime enters my thoughts, and I bite down on my lip as I think of him. How many of Maxime's teammates think this? Are they saying things behind his back? What about his friends back home in Belgium? His *family?*

I didn't want to drag him through the tabloids, but

what am I dragging him through *without* the media? Do they think I'm seeking to continue my fame by dating him? Do they think I'm after his money? Do they secretly wonder if I'm good enough for their friend, their teammate, their brother? Do they see me as the girl from TV, and not the woman I have become based on that experience?

People start filing into the room, and a box of donuts is placed next to me on the table. My co-workers begin discussing their weekends while I remain locked in my own tortured thoughts.

Maxime might be able to handle the tabloids, but can he handle what his friends and family will say to him based on the little they've seen of me on social media and TV? Maxime hasn't told me if he's mentioned me to his family. Do they know about me? What would they think? Would they want their son with the girl who made out with a man on TV and claimed it was true love?

I need people to understand that the show doesn't define me as a whole. I'm smart and ambitious and have my own career dreams to fulfill. The Skye who was on *Is It Love?* is not the same woman who has fallen in love with Maxime.

It's more important than ever that I prove myself beyond the *Is It Love?* tag. Not only for my professional career, but for the man I love.

My entire future depends on it.

CHAPTER TWENTY-FIVE

Celebrate Life with Sprinkles—The Blog
Priorities

"Honey, I have to say, we're all worried about
you," my mom says.

After lugging groceries up to my apartment, I take a
moment to set them on my countertop with one hand as
I keep my cell against my ear with the other. I spend so
much time at Maxime's now that I rarely have to stock
my kitchen. Since he's going to be gone for the next six
days, playing games in New York, New Jersey, and
Philadelphia, I thought it would be a good time to come
to my place and try to catch up.

Catch up.

With overwhelming despair, I realize that's all I do
anymore.

It's been four weeks since my conference room vow
to prove to everyone I'm worthy of both my career and
the man I love. I've been running nonstop, and I'm so

freaking tired that some nights I can't keep my eyes open. I bounce from the studio to the field, doing interviews and getting footage. I'm hands-on with editing, working closely with the editors for *Boulder Live* and recording voice-overs in the tiny, closet-like sound room. I've even volunteered for community work for the network, appearing at career days at schools and reading to kids during library time.

When I'm not doing stuff for the network, I'm writing my book, blogging, uploading pictures to Instagram and Connectivity, and scheduling my tweets. I've also signed on to emcee a charity gala, shot a public service announcement for a no-kill animal shelter in town, and signed autographs and posed for pictures at some of their adoption events.

I'm shuttling Boris and Natasha between homes, and they seem to have adapted to this crazy life better than I have. After the temporary freak out that occurred when introducing them to Maxime's dogs, they now co-exist nicely. Boris has taken a shine to the dogs, and Natasha has decided she likes Maxime better than anyone else, including me.

Juggling all of this is stressful, and I've lost some weight. My skin is also freaking out again.

I'm tired, I think. *I'm so incredibly tired.*

I shift my thoughts, as Mom would not be happy to hear just how exhausted I am, and attempt to reassure her I'm doing the right thing.

"Mom, you work in this industry," I say, placing my re-useable canvas shopping bags on the counter. "You know how entertainment is. You must take every opportunity presented to you to build your presence and open more doors."

"I understand that, but every time I call or text you, or your sisters do, or your father does, you are in the middle of something. Your social media is full of one event after another. You can't keep going at this pace."

I place a package of whole-wheat spaghetti on the countertop. To my surprise, tears fill my eyes.

"I don't have a choice," I say softly.

"Of course, you do. Honey, you don't have to do everything. How are you finding time to relax? How do you find time for *Maxime?*"

I'm still trying to squeeze in all his home games, but by the time we get home, I'm so exhausted I'm falling asleep on his shoulder. Once, I nearly fell asleep in the car with him and missed a whole chunk of things he was saying to me because of my exhaustion.

"This is for me, but also for us," I say, my voice breaking. I'm about to lose it.

"I don't see how being too exhausted to have quality time for your boyfriend is good for the relationship."

That comment rips straight to my heart. Maxime has been patient and understanding, but he, too, seems concerned that I'm working so hard. I keep telling him it's the industry, but I see the skepticism in his beautiful eyes. I've asked him to trust me, and I've told him this will be good for me in the long run, as I'm building myself as a professional career woman. Maxime said he wants me to achieve everything my heart wants, but having me happy and healthy has to be a priority, too.

I couldn't bear to tell him he is half of the reason I'm pushing myself so hard.

"Sweetheart," Mom says gently, "Maxime deserves you at your best. You're building a relationship with him now; this is important. You know I'm a career woman. I know what you're facing. But I always made your dad a priority, and if that meant saying no to something, I did."

But you didn't have to worry about Dad's friends and family thinking you are nothing more than a stupid contestant on a reality dating show.

I keep that humiliating thought to myself and clear my throat.

"It will be okay, Mom. I promise."

She sighs heavily. "I hate that you are so stubborn."

I manage a smile. "I learned it from the best," I say.

Mom groans. "My own traits come back to haunt me."

"I love you for loving me so much, Mom."

"That I do," she says gently. "I'll always be honest with you because I do. So, I'm asking you to think carefully on my words. Take care of yourself, Skye. Nurture yourself and your relationship with Maxime. Before it's too late."

I say goodbye and hang up, her words hanging in my head. She has no idea I'm doing all of this to *help* my relationship with Maxime.

I finish putting away the groceries, grab a bottle of water, and take a deep swig. I flop down on the couch and think on her words. Maxime's parents and siblings do know about me, but I cringe when I think of what

273

would happen if they Googled me. I'm hoping my present self, the Skye after the show, is what they are thinking of when they picture us together. I can't assume that is the case, though. I have to keep working and showing everyone how I've grown up. The book will be a huge part of this, which is another reason I'm writing nearly every night.

I haven't told Maxime about my favorite section yet, which is the one I'm the proudest of so far. It's about how he came into my life and taught me that women deserve to be treated like this, to have a man like Maxime as a partner, supporter, who helps you be your best you. It's the one section I find myself going back and adding to, as he continually surprises me with the depths of his feelings for me.

He told me, after Juliette, he was very careful about saying the word love, but I know he feels it the same way I do.

I grab the remote and flip to the channel for Maxime's game.

I watch the pre-game show open, and then they cut to the ice, recapping what happened in the previous game in New York. They talk about Westley's recent great saves and how he's coming into his own as a goaltender. They shift to Paul, the other alternate captain, who had great defensive plays to help secure last night's win.

Then they show Maxime warming up on the ice in New Jersey, but I don't hear what they are saying about him because my attention goes straight to a bright, neon green poster two fans are holding up against the glass behind Maxime. My stomach goes queasy when I see it:

IS IT LOVE? LAURENT OR IS IT LUST WITH SKYE?

Then I spot another one, this time, with a picture of us kissing that has been blown up from *Dishing Weekly* that says:

HEY, MAXIME, YOU'RE BETTER AT TONSIL HOCKEY THAN ICE HOCKEY

I wince when I see them, a wave of humiliation washing over me. My love for Maxime is now fodder for fans to use against him. If this were Gavin, he'd think it was hysterical and laugh his head off. Cade and Jude would ignore it as they do with anything the opposing fans do.

But Maxime isn't like that.

Now his dating life is being paraded around opposing arenas, and fans are mocking him for being with me.

I simply hope with all my heart he can continue to fight the attention and stay with me despite it.

———

I KISS MAXIME GENTLY ON HIS FOREHEAD, OVER BOTH closed eyes, the bridge of his nose.

"I love day games," I murmur before kissing his lips.

I can feel him smile against my mouth.

It's Saturday night, and after playing his last game on the road earlier this afternoon, Maxime is finally home.

The first thing we did was fall into bed together to make love.

Being with Maxime is exactly what I needed. In his arms, I feel safe. Revered. Loved. None of the things that had been bothering me matter now. Nothing matters except for this love I feel for Maxime.

This is what will get me through the next few months, I think, feeling sustained again. This love will get me through deadlines and appearances. Once the social media starts kicking in on the book project, rebuilding me as the woman I am now, I can scale back. My love for Maxime will get me through this grueling pace. I know it can.

"I'm glad to be home," he whispers before kissing me sweetly. "With you."

Mmm.

He runs his hand over my waist, pausing at my hip.

"Have you lost weight?" he asks softly.

"Just a few pounds," I say.

Maxime falls silent, and I know he's worrying.

"It will be fine. I'm just so busy right now that I don't take time to eat lunch some days."

I sit up so I can look at him, and I see concern on his face. He reaches up to touch my hair, and as he strokes it, some strands come out in his hand.

Maxime gasps in horror and bolts upright, holding my long blonde locks in his hand.

"My God," he says, his voice filled with alarm. "Skye, this isn't normal. You need to see a doctor. I'm calling the team doctor. Something is wrong."

I close my hand over his, and the lock of my hair he's holding. "No, it's stress."

"Stress or unhappiness?"

"What?" I ask.

"I remember now. You told me your hair started falling out after the show ended, when you were upset about Tom."

"I don't understand what you are implying," I say, a nervous feeling forming in the pit of my stomach.

Maxime shifts his gaze away from me.

"Maxime, talk to me. What are you thinking?" I plead.

He turns back to me, his eyes searching mine for answers.

"Are you happy with me, Skye?" he asks, his voice a whisper.

"Maxime," I gasp, horrified that he would think this. "of course, I am! You are the best thing that has ever happened to me. Please don't take any of this upon yourself."

I lift my hand from his and press my palm against his face. "It's not you. I swear it has nothing to do with you."

"Please tell me if it is me, if you aren't happy. I need to know. I *deserve* to know."

"You deserve to know you make me the happiest I have ever been in my life," I say, my voice choking up.

"You've been distracted when we've been together,"

Maxime says. "You drift off when I'm talking. Sometimes I wonder if you're bored."

I remove my hand from his face.

"You're trying to compare me with Juliette," I say, hurt.

"No, I—"

"You are trying to tie my behavior to hers, and that isn't fair," I say, my voice wobbling as I pull away from him. "I'm *not* Juliette. I happen to be a woman who is working very hard to build a career, and I get tired and exhausted, and sometimes I get distracted, but that doesn't mean I'm bored with you. It means I am a *human being.* You should know how I feel about you. Especially after I've just made love to you in the way I did."

I reach for the silky cotton sheet and pull it up around my body, holding it to me, hating the fact that he has placed Juliette in this room between us.

Maxime swallows hard. "Skye, I'm sorry."

I don't say anything.

He reaches for my hand, and I let him have it. Maxime entwines his fingers with mine.

"You're right. It's not fair for me to put the past into our present. I shouldn't project that on to you. On to us. I don't want you to ever be unhappy because of me, and the person I am."

His words hit me. Maxime is feeling the same things I am.

"I don't want you to be unhappy because of who I am, either," I admit softly.

A confused expression passes over his face.

"What?"

I feel heat rise in my cheeks. "I saw the signs in New Jersey. At the arena."

Maxime grimaces, which makes my heart flinch. "Idiots."

"I know you must hate it," I say, fear gnawing at my stomach. "If you were with someone else, you wouldn't have to deal with that commentary on your personal life."

"Hey," Maxime says, sliding his hand up to my face. "I choose to be with you. I can deal with signs. Besides, if they didn't say that, they'd say I suck. The idiots never change, but what they put on signs does."

A smile plays at his lips, and with relief, I smile back.

"I'm sorry," he repeats.

I decide to tease him. "I might forgive you if you order me a pizza."

"I'm all about you putting some weight back on, so I'll not only order you a pizza but get you one with extra cheese."

We get dressed and head downstairs. Maxime picks up his phone and sinks down on the couch, and I go into the kitchen to get a bottle of water. There, I find the most amazing sight.

Boris is nestled next to Amè, both asleep under the kitchen table.

I watch them for a moment, realizing how much Boris has grown up these past few weeks. He's overcome huge fears to get to this point, and I'm proud of him.

I retrieve my water and take a seat next to Maxime on his couch. He has a huge sectional sofa, yet we always choose to sit right next to each other, which I absolutely love.

"Boris is sleeping with Amè," I say, twisting the cap off the bottle.

I watch as a smile lights up his features. "I think she is getting her mothering in with Boris."

"So, what are we ordering?" I ask. "I'm starving."

Right on cue, my stomach unleashes a loud growl.

"Apparently, I'm ordering large pizzas for an appetizer," Maxime quips.

"Oh, shut up," I say, laughing.

My phone starts ringing from the other side of Maxime, but I don't make a move to get it.

"Don't you want to answer?" Maxime asks.

"No, tonight is dedicated to you."

A smile lights up his face. "While I appreciate that, I'm ordering pizza, so you can at least see who it is."

"Tell me who it is. I can call them back tomorrow."

Maxime reaches for my phone and glances down at it. When he sees the name, his face falls.

"Maxime?" I ask.

He stares at my screen, his face going pale.

"Maxime, what's wrong? Who is it?"

"A ghost," Maxime says flatly, handing me the phone.

Confused, I take it from him and glance down at my cell.

The person calling me is Tom Broaden.

CHAPTER TWENTY-SIX

I STARE AT THE PHONE IN COMPLETE SHOCK. CONFUSION swirls within me. *No*, I think, my mind racing. *It can't be.*

It doesn't make sense, but there's no mistaking the name on my screen.

Tom.

After all this time, he's calling me. There was a time after the show when I prayed for this. I was desperate to get the so-called love of my life back, for him to say he made a mistake and should have picked me.

But now?

I see his name and feel nothing but confusion as to why he's reappeared in my life.

"I don't understand why Wanker Tom is calling me," I say aloud. "I should have deleted his number from my contacts. I'm not taking it."

"Maybe you should. There's got to be a reason why he's calling after so long," Maxime says.

I nod. Maybe there is some bizarre reason he's calling. I answer the call but put him on speaker.

"Hello?"

"Hey, Skye, this is Tom. Tom Broaden," he says, and I swear I detect anxiousness in his familiar voice. "I bet you never expected to hear from me again, did you?"

"No," I say simply. "I did not. Which begs the question, why are you calling me?"

"Can you take me off speaker?"

I feel Maxime's hand flinch next to mine. I give it a reassuring squeeze and stare straight at him while I talk to Tom.

"No. I'm sitting here with my boyfriend, Maxime, and anything you can say to me you can say to him."

Silence.

"Um. Okay. Well, um, this isn't how I wanted to talk to you."

"I don't care how you wanted to talk to me, Tom. You talk to me with Maxime here or not at all."

More silence.

Tom clears his throat. "All right. I, uh, just wanted to give you a heads-up on something."

I furrow my brow. This doesn't sound good.

"On what?"

"I, uh, did an exclusive with *Dishing Weekly*," Tom says slowly.

I feel the air deflate from my lungs. I can't breathe, and I can't respond.

Panic takes over.

"It's my look back on what happened on the show," Tom says, filling the silence. "There, um, some bombshells in it."

I want to cry. Why now? I'm working hard to

overcome this part of my life, and now he's bringing it front and center for the world all over again.

"What kind of bombshells?" I ask, my voice shaking.

Maxime puts his arm around my shoulder, and I think of what a good man he is to put up with this shit when he can easily have a woman with zero baggage.

"Oh, I think you'll be surprised, but we'll need to talk after you see it. The cover should go up Thursday on their website. Online subscribers will be able to read the story then, and the magazine hits newsstands on Friday."

"What kind of bombshells, Tom? I need to know," I snap, anger filling me. "You owe me this much."

"I can't talk about that now, but I will talk to you next week."

"No, you will not," I say, my voice shaking with rage. "I will *never* talk to you again."

"Spoken like a woman who still has feelings. If you felt nothing, you wouldn't be so upset," Tom says, a knowing, smug tone entering his voice.

I hate him. I really hate him.

"No, spoken like a woman who doesn't want you to interfere in my life."

"You might change your mind when you read the article."

"What?" I gasp, confused. "What are you talking about?"

Maxime releases me, and for a moment, I'm terrified he's about to walk away. What if he thinks my reaction is because I have feelings for Tom? When, in reality, I'm worried about what this will do to Maxime.

To my surprise, Maxime takes my phone. "You're done playing games with her," he says, his deep voice low with anger. "Do not call her. Skye deserves better than this, especially considering how gracefully she handled what a jerk you were to her during the show with the media. So, either tell her what is said or get off the damn phone."

The phone goes silent, and Tom ends the call.

I burst into tears.

"Why?" I ask, sobbing. "Why now?"

Maxime's face blurs in front of my eyes, and all I can think is that this bombshell will be the final straw for him. It will drive him away. It's going to be awful; I can feel it with every fiber of my being.

Maxime is silent. He buries his head in his hands.

"Do ... do you still have feelings for him?" he asks, not looking at me.

"What?" I cry. "No, no, absolutely not!"

I drop down to the floor in front of him, pulling his hands away from his fear-ridden face.

Fear that Tom's reappearance has jumbled up everything in my heart.

I wrap my hands around his and squeeze them tightly. I want to tell him I love him. I'm desperate to say those words, but if I do, he'll think it's a reaction to Tom instead of something that has already been in my heart.

"I'm upset because of what this will do to *you*," I say, tears streaming down my face. "I don't want to embarrass you, Maxime."

"Is that why you're crying?" he asks, searching my

eyes as if he's afraid it's a cover for what I'm truly feeling.

"You're the only one who matters," I say. "I don't want to lose you over this. I can't bear the thought of that."

I drop my head on his knees and bawl, my tears falling onto his jeans and my shoulders shaking.

"Skye, stop, please stop," Maxime says, lifting me back up. He frames my face in his strong hands. "That is *not* going to happen, do you hear me? I lost the chance to meet you in Brussels. I found you again in Denver and didn't do anything. I finally got it right the third time, and no matter what that article says, I'm not letting you go."

I see fire in his eyes, along with a determined look, and gratitude for this man overwhelms me.

"Okay," I say, the tears subsiding.

Maxime draws me up, and I sit down on his lap, feeling secure as his strong arms wrap around me.

"I'm sorry I come with all this baggage," I whisper as I bury my face in his neck.

"Don't say that. We all come with baggage," he says.

I wince, because I know that's not true. My baggage is all over the place, for all his family and friends to unpack on social media and the internet. Worse, they can pick what bags to open and discard the rest. They could easily never read things I've written on my blog or said on TV, choosing to read the gossipy, untrue things instead, and never seek out a counterpoint.

Maxime brushes his lips against the top of my head. I swallow hard, desperate to believe him.

Regardless of what side is right, there is nothing I can do now.

Except wait for the bomb to be dropped on Thursday night.

———

Celebrate Life with Sprinkles—The Blog
Dealing with Things You Can't Control

"SKYE, PLEASE EAT SOMETHING," JOJO IMPLORES. "I can't bear to watch you push around your food."

I put my fork down. It's Thursday night, and *Dishing Weekly* will be dropping tomorrow's cover any minute now. I'm with Sierra and JoJo at a wine bar, grabbing a bite to eat before heading over to the arena to watch the Mountain Lions play Miami. We're getting down to the last few games of the season, and Denver is in a fight with Seattle for the remaining playoff spot in the Western Conference. Every game matters, and Maxime has been focused this week because of it.

Or maybe he's waiting to see what bomb is going to go off in his face thanks to me, and wondering if I'm worth living in this circus.

"I can't," I say, fighting back tears. "I can't think about anything else but *Dishing Weekly.*"

I've had emergency group conversations with Sierra and JoJo this week. We talked at Tuesday's game, and they have tried their best to get me to put this aside, but that has proved impossible. A sense of dread has hung over me like a dark, dangerous cloud. Each day brings me closer to the storm that has the potential to sweep away everything I hold dear. It's taken everything inside me to act bright and cheerful on camera and engage in fun banter when inside, I am living with a gnawing fear that grows worse with each day.

What if the people on *Boulder Live* decide I'm not the image they want for their show after this article breaks? Aly could convince them of that if Tom says awful stuff that gets a lot of publicity. The publishing company would probably demand a juicy tell-all rather than the personal development story I'm penning now.

I reach for my hair and twist the ends. Losing my career growth would be a disaster. It would nearly destroy me, but I could survive it.

But *Dishing Weekly* could take away the thing that matters most to me.

I could lose Maxime.

Sierra puts her hand on my arm. "Don't give them this power over you. Do not. It doesn't matter what Tom says. You are you, and a lot of people love you for who you are, including Maxime."

I reach for my water and take another sip. I'm barely eating, so I can't even think about having a cocktail with my friends like I normally do.

"What if this article is too much for him?" I say, as my brain refuses to let go of my deepest fear.

"It won't be," JoJo says firmly. "Maxime is exactly where he wants to be, and that's with you. No tabloid bombshell, no matter what it is, will change that."

A shaky breath escapes my lips. I pick up my fork and twirl some of the house-made tagliatelle with black truffle cream sauce around my fork and make myself take a bite.

"Okay, *now* we're getting somewhere," JoJo says, smiling triumphantly. "No one should ever waste fresh pasta."

"Says the Italian," Sierra teases as she takes a sip of her chardonnay.

"Nonna says that is a sin," JoJo declares as she cuts into her lobster ravioli and takes a bite. "Oh my, another sin is this brandy cream sauce. Worth every. Single. Calorie."

"You can burn those off with Cade later," Sierra teases, raising her eyebrows at JoJo.

"Cheers to *that!*" JoJo laughs.

I manage to eat a few bites of my decadent pasta, but the knot in my stomach makes anything more than that impossible.

I try to keep focused on the conversation, and my friends continually engage me as a distraction. I appreciate their efforts and remind myself of the many positives in my life, like good friends.

As the server brings the check, my phone buzzes on the table.

I watch as it vibrates, and my heart falls into my stomach.

It's usually around this time that *Dishing Weekly* releases their cover and the online magazine.

My chest squeezes tight as I pick it up.

Sierra and JoJo fall silent as I flip it over.

There is a notification from *Dishing Weekly:*

IS IT LOVE? NO! ENGAGEMENT OFF AS TOM DUMPS MILEY BECAUSE HE STILL LOVES SKYE!

Tom Broaden gives exclusive interview to *Dishing Weekly:* "I want her back!" he proclaims.

We have the details straight from Tom, with the following bombshells:

- The producers suggested Miley was a better fit even though he loved Skye.
- Tom reveals how a heartbroken Skye told him she would "always love him" and "prayed he would change his mind" when the cameras were off.
- Is Skye truly happy with Maxime Laurent, the sexy Belgian hockey star? Insiders say the romance is not love and on the rocks!

Below that headline, there's a picture of me walking alone in Boulder, looking exhausted and thin, with dark circles under my eyes. Nobody knows that was from working too hard. It looks like I'm brokenhearted again!

A chill runs through me as I realize how this appears.

It sounds like I'm not over Tom.

I drop my phone, sending it crashing onto the tabletop. I fight for air. I can't bring myself to read the article. I'll fall apart in public if I try.

I take a quick glance around to see if anyone is

filming me. So far the coast is clear, but I need to pull it together fast.

"Skye? Skye?" Sierra says, her face blurring through my tears.

The headlines tell me this article is going to be full of my past, waved in Maxime's face as if he doesn't exist. It will also claim to know my life with Maxime, which is crap. Who *are* these inside sources, anyway? Aly? Made up people? Or people who claim they know me but don't?

It will be hurtful garbage, a hack job of Tom's version of reality, not mine.

A blurred reality, I think with anguish.

Except for my pathetic begging for Tom to take me back, which is all too painfully real. Tom will no doubt explain my heartbroken spiel word-for-word in the article.

I try to blink my tears away. Maxime is already fragile as far as Tom is concerned; he revealed his vulnerability to me this week. What will this article do to him? Will he believe that I'm over Tom? Will he decide he doesn't need to be a part of this circus anymore?

I remind myself to breathe. I'll go to the WAGS lounge and read the article. I need to get to Maxime after the game, to talk about this, to tell him this doesn't change anything between us. I don't want Tom, no matter what he says. I'll apologize for the media that will no doubt intensify, during the most critical time of the season.

The last distraction Maxime needs, when he's already carrying this team on his back for Gavin, is the press following him and shouting questions at him, trying to illicit a reaction. No, no, this is not the life he wanted.

But this is the life I'll give him, if he stays with me.

If.

I must pour out my heart to Maxime, and hope the feelings in his heart are strong enough to get past this.

I pray it is.

Because I don't want to know a life without him.

CHAPTER TWENTY-SEVEN

I wait until I'm in the sanctuary of the WAGS lounge before daring to tap open the article from *Dishing Weekly*. Sierra and JoJo sit down on either side of me on the leather sofa, giving me their support.

With a shaking hand, I tap on the link to the article. As soon as it pops up, I want to vomit. It's my whole past on *Is It Love?*, thrown back in my face. There's a two-page spread of pictures: me gazing adoringly at Tom; snuggling in a hammock in a bikini with Tom, kissing him; standing before him in a sparkling blush evening gown, waiting for a proposal that would never come. Then there is the look of heartbreak on my face when he told me it wasn't love for him.

To anyone reading this, you would think Tom was the only man I could ever love.

Panic builds within me as my eyes dart to the photos of the present: Tom and Miley with the jagged rip placed down the photo to show they are broken up; me appearing stressed out and sad leaving the station last week. Then there's a new picture of Maxime that causes me to pause.

I haven't seen this picture before. It's Maxime, leaving the practice facility on Monday carrying the lunch provided by the team. He's scowling at the camera, looking miserable while the photographer takes his picture.

My heart drops to the bottom of my stomach. How long has he felt like this and not told me? I know he said there were photographers sometimes, but is this how they make him feel every day? Terrible? Pissed off?

I'm doing this to him, I think, biting down hard on my lip. *This is what I've made his life into: a circus that he never wanted to be a part of.*

I force down the nausea and read the article. Tom declares he broke up with Miley because when he saw pictures of me with Maxime, it made him realize he had never gotten over me. He regretted letting me go but felt "obligated" to Miley because he chose her.

Oh my God, he's such a wanker, I think. I continue to read:

DW: So, when did the doubts creep in, that you chose the wrong woman?

TB: The second Skye walked away. That's when I knew I made a mistake, but there was no way out. I couldn't call her back and tell the producers I changed my mind.

Vomit. He could have. The producers weren't

holding him hostage against his will.

He's such an idiot, I think. I say a prayer of thanks for it, though, because otherwise, I'd never have found Maxime.

I go back the article:

DW: How did Miley take the news that you were still in love with Skye?

TB: Miley and I tried to make things work, but in the end, my feelings for Skye were just undeniable. We've mutually ended the relationship, and I have nothing but the utmost respect for Miley.

DW: Skye is now linked with professional hockey player Maxime Laurent of the Denver Mountain Lions. Have you talked to her about your feelings?

TB: I know Skye is dating Maxime, but there's no way she can have the same feelings for him that she had for me. What we had was special, a once in a lifetime love. Skye said that. She told me, the night before the finale, that I was her first love and her only love, that she couldn't imagine a life without me. When she left, she told me she could never give her heart to another man in the way she gave it to me. That was off-camera. So, no, I don't believe she can love Maxime the way she loves me. I can only hope that she will give me a chance to make things right with her and give her the love she's always wanted.

It's all I can do not to throw my phone against the wall in a rage after I'm done.

"How dare he," I say, my voice low and shaking with anger. "How *dare* he say he's my only love."

I hand my phone to Sierra, who reads the article. When I hear her gasp aloud, it confirms it reads just as bad as I thought.

"He's a total wanker," she says angrily.

She passes the phone to JoJo. "Wait, he's saying he had no choice but to let you walk away?"

"Keep reading; it gets better," Sierra says.

JoJo gasps and curses and then hands me back the phone. "I can't believe this jerk is doing this now."

"He only wants what he can't have," Sierra says.

"Or publicity," JoJo says. "He landed himself a cover with this piece of fiction."

"None of that matters," I say, getting up and beginning to pace. Some WAGS come over to say hi, and if they've read the article, they are kind enough to act oblivious about it. After they move on to grab food at the buffet, I stop and face Sierra and JoJo. "What does matter is what this is going to do to Maxime. How is he going to interpret this? What will this do to us?"

My voice cracks as I say the word "us."

Sierra leaps up and puts her hands on my shoulders. "Hey. Maxime knows you. He knows this is your past, and it has nothing to do with your future."

295

I shake my head. "You can't deny how miserable he seems in that picture, Sierra."

"Everyone has a bad day," JoJo says firmly, standing up and huddling around me so we can talk more quietly. "Don't make this snowball into something it isn't."

"This isn't the life he wanted. Don't you see that?" I cry softly. "Do you think he wants his love life dissected in the tabloids? Do you? You know Maxime. You know how protective he is of his privacy, and now it's gone. From taunts from fans and opposing players to photographers waiting for him after practice to people speculating if I still love Tom? I should have ended it before this got out of control," I say, my emotions reeling.

"Wait. You're not going there. We won't let you," JoJo says. "You did that once, and Maxime told you it wasn't going to work; he's not going to let you do that now."

"I'm not going to end it, but I'm certainly going to give him the choice," I say, grabbing my purse and getting up. "I need air. I can't breathe in here."

I flee to the hallway that winds around the ice rink. I'm cold. I'm in tears. I deserve to feel terrible for what I've brought on Maxime.

I don't want to lose him, I think with anguish. But how can I expect him to stay after this?

I need to give him the option to leave. He needs to consider that for his own sake.

Which is exactly what I will do after the game tonight.

————

MAXIME PLAYED A HORRIBLE GAME TONIGHT.

I fight back tears as I wait for him to come into the lounge. The Mountain Lions won 2-1, but I've never seen Maxime play so poorly. I stayed in the WAGS lounge and watched it on TV, feeling sick the entire time. I know he must have read that article before the game, or at least saw the cover. He provoked a fight that landed him with a bloodied nose and a trip to the penalty box. He turned the puck over at a critical time, which led to a Miami goal.

I watched in horror as his game fell apart on the ice, making shots that were wide of the net by a mile and multiple defensive mistakes. This is what I did to him. Guilt ate away at my heart.

Somehow, the rest of the team rallied, and Cade scored the winning goal in the third period. But I know Maxime's poor performance is my fault.

Almost every player has come into the lounge, except for Maxime, which scares me.

Does he hate me? Does he not want to see me?

Sierra and Jude, along with Cade and JoJo, have lingered, not wanting to leave me alone.

"You all go ahead," I say. "I'll be okay."

"No, we're not leaving you," Sierra says, shaking her head.

"Whatever happened on the ice," Jude says, squeezing my shoulder, "it's not you. Everyone makes mental mistakes and has bad games."

"Yeah, like Jude, whenever he runs out of Pot

Noodle cups," Cade adds, shooting me a smile. "His game is shit when that happens."

I don't say anything. I know better.

I know the truth.

"Seriously, don't put all this on yourself," Cade says. "Max is responsible for his play on the ice. Not you."

"He's right."

I turn around and see Maxime in the doorway. His eye and nose are both swollen from his fight, and there's no light in his eyes.

The second I see his expression, I know I've lost him.

I begin to shake as Maxime nears us.

I don't hear the small talk that is being made as my friends leave. I wrap my arms around myself as a chill comes over me.

Within minutes, it's just Maxime and me in the lounge.

He stares at me for a long time, not saying a word.

"We need to talk," he finally says, his words strangled.

Those words shatter my heart into a million fragments.

I sink down on the sofa, and he sits next to me. Maxime doesn't reach for my hand or brush his fingertips against my cheek like he always does.

Instead his hands, the warm, strong hands which are always reaching for me, wanting to physically connect with me, remain limp at his sides.

I stare straight ahead, unable to speak.

Maxime exhales loudly. "I read the article."

I don't say anything.

"Do … do you still love him?"

I jerk my head toward him. "Of course not!"

Maxime is silent for a moment. "I'm not sure."

"Maxime, I won't lie to you; I did say those words to Tom because that is how I felt at the time," I say. "That's not how I feel now. I don't love him."

I love you, I think with anguish.

Maxime gets up and begins pacing, pulling at his hair as if he's tortured with what is going on in his head. I stand up and put my hand on his arm to stop him.

"You don't have to stay in this relationship if you don't want to," I say, my voice breaking. "I don't want to keep hurting you like this."

Maxime jerks his arm away from me, and I'm shocked to see anger flicker across his face. "Why are you always shoving me away?"

"What?" I ask, confused.

"You're always doubting if I want to be with you," he blurts out. "You tried to break up with me before over it. Do you not believe what I feel for you? Or do you not believe yourself?"

His words slap across my face, leaving a sting I can't erase.

"I am sorry if I'm worried about you," I explain. "Everything I've said is because I don't want my life to upend yours. I don't want you to resent me for dragging you into the tabloids."

"How many times," Maxime says, his voice shaking with anger, "do I have to tell you I don't freaking care? Or is this your sub-conscious at work? So when you're bored of me, you have an automatic out that makes you feel better about yourself?"

Anger floods me. "That is *your* issue, Maxime. I love the life we have together. I like being at home with you and going out to dinner. Why don't you believe I'm happy with that?"

"You don't look or *act* happy," he snaps. "You've been nothing but miserable since we started having sex. Should I take that as a clue?"

"You did not just say that," I say, furious. "You *know* why I've been miserable. I'm working my ass off to prove I'm more than a reality dating show contestant. Not just for my career but for *you*. For your family and friends, to show them I'm worthy of you. I need to prove I'm more than what they have seen have seen online, which is a reality show loser!"

"*What?* What are you talking about? My family and friends *love* you. And I don't need you to prove *anything* to me!" Maxime yells, and for the first time, I see him losing his tightly wrapped self-control. "I not only accept your past, but I also don't care about it. You are the one who doesn't accept yourself!"

His words slam me in the gut.

He might be right, but I'm too upset and angry to concede anything to him right now. My emotions are a swirl of hurt, and I'm still in fight mode.

"What about you?" I cry, turning the tables on him. "You're obsessed with the fact that I'm suddenly going to resent you for not wanting to go out to nightclubs or bar hop. That was Juliette's issue, not mine. I'm sorry she didn't appreciate you for who you are, but I do. But you choose to ignore that and obsess over the fact that one day I'm going to wake up and decide to leave you for it. Do you not understand? I want the man you *are*. In fact, I've dedicated a whole chunk of my book to writing about you!"

Maxime stares at me in complete shock as soon as I admit I am writing about him. I panic. Oh, shit, shit, that is *not* the way I wanted to tell him about the book.

"What did you just say?" Maxime asks, his voice low. "Are you *writing* about me?"

"It's not what you think," I say, putting my hand out.

"Do you know me *at all?*" Maxime's voice resonates with shock. "You put my life into a *book?* For everyone to read? Without my permission? You know I would *never* agree to that, Skye, so you went around behind my back and put it in? How could you do this to me? Am I just fodder for a sleazy tell-all? Were you going to break up with me after that?"

His accusations shatter my heart. I can't stand here and listen to this, to the man I love say things that are killing me to hear.

I angrily grab my purse, whirling around to face him.

"No. The truth is, Maxime, I was going to have you read the whole section before I ever submitted it, to see if you were okay with *any* of it. I would *never* publish anything about you without your permission. But I fell in love with you, and that love inspired the words to flow from me. I wanted other young women at a relationship crossroads to find what I had with you: a man who would revere them, be a partner to them, and someone who would love them in the way they deserved to be loved.

"That part of my story was the happiest part of all," I continue. "Through all this crap I went through this past year, I found you. That made all this awfulness worthwhile. We discovered something beautiful and special together, or so I thought. What we had wasn't created in the bubble of a TV show. It wasn't manipulated by producers. I found you, and I love you in a way I've never loved anyone before you. This is *real*," I say, my voice catching. "At least it is for me."

Maxime's eyes grow watery the second my voice breaks. I see him searching my eyes; his chest rises and falls rapidly as my words crash over him.

"Skye, I—"

"No, Maxime," I say, cutting him off, "don't say you love me just because I threw this admission on you. I don't think you do love me as much as my heart wants to believe you do. Because if you think I'm capable of writing a sleazy tell-all, you don't *know* me, let alone *love* me."

"Skye," Maxime says, moving toward me and putting his hands on my arms. "I—"

I break free from him. I can't take this anymore. I need to get out of here, away from the pain. I need to breathe. I'm falling apart at the seams.

"No, I can't," I whisper as my vision becomes blurry. "I can't."

I turn and run out of the lounge, ignoring his cries for me to stop, and leave my Maxime—and my heart —behind.

CHAPTER TWENTY-EIGHT

I walk out of the arena, numb. I don't know where I'm going. It doesn't matter. Because no matter where I am, I'm going to have a shattered heart.

As I stand outside the glittering glass structure, I try to wrap my head around what just happened.

I broke up with Maxime.

My legs start to buckle. Tears stream down my face, and I make no move to stop them. If people want to take pictures of me like this, they can.

This is reality.

Maxime and I are over.

I drop down on the curb, drawing my knees to my chest, and let myself fall apart. I put my head down and cry for Maxime. Part of myself is with him back in that lounge, a part I don't feel I will ever get back. I cry for the future I saw so clearly with him, the life we could have created together, the adventures and holidays, and maybe even children, that would have followed.

He'll have that life with someone else now.

As I picture my Maxime holding another woman in his arms, smiling at her in the way he did to me, as if she's the only woman in the world, I begin sobbing uncontrollably with grief.

You'll always be my Maxime, I think with anguish. *Always.*

I hear a car approach and glance up. A black SUV stops at the curb, and a door opens. Through my tears, I watch as Gavin gets out of the car on crutches.

"Skye?" he asks, hobbling up to me. "What are you doing out here? Are you okay?"

His blue eyes widen as he gets closer and sees I'm anything but okay.

I shake my head. "M-Maxime. We b-b-broke up."

A fresh round of tears breaks free. Gavin stares down at me in shock.

"*What?*" he asks. "God, what happened?"

"Just go, Gavin," I say. "I know Maxime is your teammate and your friend."

"Wrong. I consider *both* of you my friends. I'm not leaving you here, not like this. You're coming with me."

I shake my head. "No, I can't let you do that."

"Skye, I'm not leaving you in a deserted parking lot downtown. Please get in the car."

"I'll get an Uber ride."

Gavin lets out an exasperated sigh. "You're not getting an Uber. I have a driver due to my leg; he can drive us to Boulder as easily as he can back to my place. We'll talk on the way back, okay?"

Gavin's face reflects genuine concern.

The captain is not going to take no for an answer.

"Okay," I say, sniffling.

I get in on one side, and Gavin gets in on the other. He places his crutches between us in the back seat of the Cadillac SUV, and the driver comes around to shut the doors.

"Dave, change of plans," Gavin says. "We need to take Ms. Reeve back to Boulder before heading back to my place."

"Yes, sir," Dave says.

Once Dave is back in the driver's seat, he asks for my address and then raises the privacy glass between us. He heads out of the parking lot, onto the streets of downtown Denver, illuminated by the glittering lights of the skyscrapers at night.

"Tell me what happened," Gavin says gently.

The city blurs in my vision as we drive. "We had a horrible fight," I say, my voice sounding strangled as I try to say the words. "Maxime and I argued after this gossipy article came out in *Dishing Weekly*. My ex said a bunch of stupid stuff, things that made Maxime wonder if I still had feelings for him. Which I don't. I felt terrible about dragging Maxime through all this garbage that is my life, and I told him I'd understand if he didn't want to stay with me. That's when he blew up. It all escalated from there."

I find the courage to glance at Gavin, who is studying me carefully.

"Of course he blew up. He loves you, and the last

thing he wants is to leave you. Maxime envisions a future with you; don't you see that?"

My heart stops beating. "Did he say that to you?"

"Yes. I went through that shit with Veronica, and Maxime told me when I find the right woman, like he did, it will be crystal clear. I will want to marry her, and I'll have no doubts. I will see my future with her, just like he did with you."

A strangled cry escapes my throat.

Maxime saw the same future I did.

A future we both threw away.

Tears begin to stream down my face. "How did we let this happen to us, Gavin?"

"Hey," Gavin says, reaching for my shoulder, "when you care about someone, when you love someone as much as he loves you, things can escalate because of the emotions involved. The fear of losing what you have."

Gavin's words hit my heart.

Fear.

He's right.

This whole time I've been with Maxime, I've worried that I wasn't good enough. I thought my reality show past was going to always be hanging around in the background, and he would eventually leave me for someone without embarrassing TV footage attached to her life.

But Maxime never had a problem with it.

I was the one who did.

Instead of embracing the doors it opened for me, I tried to distance myself from who I was. I worked hard, too hard, trying to prove to everyone, from my co-workers to the public to Maxime, that I was worthy of the jobs I had. Of the man I loved.

When the truth is, the only person I need to prove my worth to is myself.

I am worthy of the things I have, I realize. I don't have to be anything more than the person I am at this moment. The woman I am now earned these opportunities. They weren't given to me just because I was on a TV show. The past is a part of me, and if I didn't go through that, I wouldn't be where I am.

I never would have met Maxime.

The woman I am now is the one Maxime fell for. He might not like the tabloid articles and the media presence, but what matters to him is the woman I am when we are together. He accepts that because he wants what we have together.

I have to embrace my *Is It Love?* past to have the present.

To have the future with the man I love.

I continue to sort through my thoughts with newfound clarity. Maxime must face his own fears for us to work. He needs to believe that history isn't doomed to repeat itself. I love him for all the reasons Juliette didn't. I would never write a tell-all book; my words came from a place of happiness and love. Maxime's accusation still hurts, but I know it was said out of shock and anger, not from his heart.

I turn to Gavin, who is texting on his phone.

"Thank you," I say to him. "You're right. About all of this."

"Good, so you won't be mad at me for what I just

did," he says, slipping his phone back into his coat pocket.

I wrinkle my brow. "What's that?"

"I texted Maxime and said I was taking you home. He said that's not where you're going."

My heart stops beating.

"Check your phone, Skye. Your answer determines where we go tonight."

I nervously retrieve my phone out of my purse. I have been ignoring it since our fight because I didn't want to talk to anyone while I dealt with my heartbreak. There are messages from friends and family about the article, from JoJo and Sierra, and two from Maxime. My stomach clenches as I open the first one, sent minutes after our fight:

I love you, too. You have no idea how long I've loved you. I hate myself for not telling you first. I never should have doubted you. I wish I could take it all back. I love you and I'm sorry. God, I'm sorry. Please call me. Please.

Tears of relief fill my eyes.

Maxime loves me.

We can work this out; I know we can. Before I answer, I read the next text from him.

Come back to our home tonight. Where you belong. Please give me a chance to make this right.

I turn to Gavin, who is waiting for my answer.

"Take me home," I say softly. "Take me home to Maxime."

———

THE SECOND THE SUV STOPS IN FRONT OF MAXIME'S house, I want to bolt from the car and run up to the door. I'm desperate to see Maxime. I need to tell him I love him in the way I want to. Not from a place of ending, but from a place of beginning.

But before I do, I need to take care of something first.

I turn to Gavin. "Thank you for being my friend tonight."

"You were there for me when I needed someone. I'll always be there for you, Skye. That's what friends do, and I consider you one of my best friends."

I choose my next words carefully.

"I know you aren't ready now, but someday, you're going to make some woman very happy. You are a great guy, Gavin. The woman who will love you in the way you deserve is out there. Don't shut the door on meeting her, okay?"

Gavin scowls. "Not only is that door shut, but it's freaking *nailed*. I'll let Maxime live the love story. I'll star in the bad boy, athlete, player one."

I lean over and give him a peck on the cheek. "You aren't fooling me for one second, my friend. But I'll let you believe this piece of fiction. *For now.*"

Gavin chuckles. "Shut up and go get your man, okay?"

I grin as Dave comes around and opens the passenger door for me. I slip out of the car as Maxime jerks open the front door, as if he was waiting for me.

The SUV pulls out of the circular drive and back down the winding road. My heart slams against my ribs. I only have eyes for Maxime, who is staring back at me with a mixture of anguish and longing on his gorgeous face.

Before I can take a step, Maxime rushes toward me. I drop my purse and run to him, collapsing against his pale blue dress shirt and bursting into tears. I hear his heart pounding against my ear and feel his arms hold me as tightly as he can, as if he's never going to let me go again.

And I know he won't.

"I love you, I love you, I love you," Maxime murmurs as he bends down and presses his cheek to mine. "I'm so sorry. Please forgive me."

"I do forgive you," I say, my voice breaking. "I love you so much. You're The One, Maxime. The *only* one."

Maxime's mouth finds mine, kissing me desperately, fiercely claiming me with everything he has. I kiss him back the same way, passionately telling him my words are true. My lips move rapidly against his, my tongue matching his frantic movements, knowing I'll never kiss another man in my life.

Maxime breaks the kiss, and I gaze up at him. His watery eyes are rimmed with red. I put my hands on his face, and he wraps his hands over mine.

"I want forever," he says, his voice growing thick. "I wanted it so badly I was afraid I couldn't have it. You were right, Skye. I was getting mired in the past. If you didn't like the life we have, you wouldn't be here with me."

"I do love it," I say, stroking his face in a reassuring way. "I'm exactly where I *want* to be, Maxime. All your qualities that are different are what draw me to you. You bring me balance. You make me happy in a way I've never known, all because of the man you are. Exactly the way you are."

He nods. "I promise I won't doubt that ever again. As long as you promise to not doubt that I'm here because I want to be, too. I don't love being in tabloids, or having photographers shout inappropriate questions to me about you, but I know it will slow down and fade. And even if it didn't, it wouldn't matter. I will take all of that if it means I get to love you."

"You were right about that," I admit. "I was so busy trying to be worthy of everyone that I lost sight of the fact that I already was. I need to believe it for myself first."

"You do. Skye, you're talented. You have *earned* every success," Maxime says firmly. "The woman I love doesn't need to prove anything to me, or worry about what my friends and family think. They see what I see, Skye. You are a bright, ambitious, intelligent, good person. That's *all* we see."

Love for Maxime fills my heart.

But we still have one big issue to address.

I clear my throat. "We need to talk about the book."

Maxime looks anguished, and I see deep regret in his eyes.

"I never should have accused you of writing a tell-all," he says. "I'm sorry I said that. I was blindsided and angry; as soon as it came out, I wanted to take it back. I know you wouldn't write anything to hurt me. Everything was out of control at that point. I thought I was losing you, and I lashed out because it seemed like something you should have asked me about first."

Regret surges through me. "You're right about that. I *should* have asked you first. I was afraid you'd say no, and I thought if you could see it first, you'd understand why I was writing it. If I could do that over again, I would. My actions were guided out of wanting to share how amazing you are and how every woman should strive to have a man like you. It was driven by wanting to show *real love*, unlike the love I thought I had with Tom."

I brush my fingertips across his strong cheekbones. "I'll delete the whole file. Our story doesn't have to belong to the world."

Maxime wraps his fingers around mine and brings my hand to his heart. "I trust you. If you want to share it, you can share it."

I smile up at him. "You can read it, and together, we'll decide what will go in the book."

"That's how we're doing this from now on. *Together.* We'll talk about things that are bothering us. It all goes on the table; no more hiding how we feel, no matter how stupid it might seem."

"I agree," I say, nodding.

"What about your workload?" Maxime asks, squeezing my hand against his heart. "I'm worried about your health, sweetheart."

"I'm cutting back," I say with determination. "I'm tired of running when I don't have to prove anything to anyone but myself. I'll reduce my public relations appearances for the station. I'll tell Charlotte the book draft might take longer. Instead of a daily blog, I might post twice a week. I want balance in my life. I want to enjoy walks with the dogs and binge watch *Law & Order* in my pajamas all day on a Sunday. Most of all, I want our time together to be good, Maxime. You deserve the best of me."

"I already have the best of you," Maxime says, drawing my hand to his lips and kissing it gently. "I see forever with you, *mon chérie.* It might have taken me three chances and one fight to get it right, but I have it now. I'm never letting you go again."

Joy runs through me. "I'm not letting you go, either. I love you, Maxime."

"I love you, too," he murmurs, kissing me again.

I lose myself in his arms, thinking of the journey we had to take to be here. We both had to fall in love with other people and have our hearts broken. Fate put us together not once, not twice, but three times before we took a chance on each other.

On true love.

At some points in my life, my reality has been blurred. I thought I found love on TV, but I didn't. That was an illusion of a TV bubble and a man seeking fame. It wasn't *real* love.

But right now?
Reality has never been more crystal clear.
This is love.
Maxime is *The One*.
And it's forever.

EPILOGUE

July
Brussels, Belgium

"I *LOVE* THIS CITY," I DECLARE. "I COULD STAY HERE
forever, Maxime!"

I stop on the cobblestone streets of the Grand Place,
the central square of Brussels. I gaze up at the Town
Hall, a magnificent medieval building, and take another
picture of the gothic tower climbing up in the brilliant
blue sky of this sunny summer day. I'm spellbound by
the architecture and history of this cultural city. This
building was built in the 1400s. I think of how it has
withstood the test of time, remaining a centerpiece of a
vibrant European city to this day.

"That's good, since we are staying here for a week,"
Maxime says, interrupting my thoughts.

We arrived in Brussels yesterday after spending a few
days in England, for Sierra and Jude's wedding, which
took place outdoors at the beautiful Rowton Castle. We

took a day to explore London with Cade and JoJo before heading to Brussels to spend the next ten days with Maxime's family.

Last night, we had a big family dinner, and it was incredible. It's funny to think I used to be worried about what they would think of me, because I was welcomed with nothing but warmth and love. Maxime's mom made his beloved *vol-au-vent* and promised to teach me how to do it while we are here. I feel at home with them already.

I gaze up at him and find he's smiling down at me. I move closer so I can wind my arms around his waist.

"It was a year ago that I was first here," I say, "but I feel like I'm seeing Brussels for the first time. That's because of you, Maxime."

The first time I was here, I was heartbroken and lost. I was drowning. *Is It Love?* had nearly destroyed me. My self-respect was in shambles. I played up the cupcake baker storyline and didn't stay true to myself. Every moment I was on TV was dissected and analyzed, and I cracked under the pressure. Nothing can prepare you for that, even if you think you are going into it with your head on your shoulders.

Of course, I didn't plan to fall in love, either. After Tom broke my heart, I was left doubting everything I thought was true. I didn't trust myself to make *any* decisions after proving myself capable of making so many disastrous ones. My reality had been blurred, and I vowed to never make that same mistake again.

Little did I know that half a year later, everything would become crystal clear.

"Come on, I want to show you something," Maxime says.

"But I'm not done here!" I protest.

Maxime flashes me a gorgeous smile. "I promise we'll come back here afterward, but I want to do something this afternoon. Trust me?"

I press my lips briefly to his, detecting a hint of powdered sugar from the street waffles we ate earlier.

"I do," I murmur against his lips.

Maxime takes my hand in his, and as we begin to walk, I reflect on how we got to this moment.

Since March, our lives have blended perfectly. My lease ended in June, and I moved in with Maxime. Our brood, including the kittens and the dogs, is a big and happy one. Maxime built a screened-in porch so Boris and Natasha could get closer to the outdoors, and my heart might have melted when I saw him constructing it.

While the Mountain Lions fell short of their playoff goal, with Seattle edging them out by one game, I'm incredibly proud of how the team played without Gavin. They have already made some moves to strengthen the weaknesses that showed during the season, including obtaining a super-star scorer, Pierre Gaudet, a French player from the Chicago Buffaloes. Gavin is back in Toronto rehabbing his leg, and to the surprise of no one, he's well ahead of schedule in his recovery.

I cut back on my off-air appearances, and despite Charlotte's protests, I revised the deadline for the first draft of my self-discovery book. Maxime read the section dedicated to him, and he was moved to tears after he finished it. To my surprise, he didn't have me change a word. Instead, he told me he was the luckiest man alive to have a woman who loved him as much as I did, and he didn't care who knew it.

I'm now blogging twice a week and doing well at the station. I have a new segment called *Try That Hat*, where I make a fool of myself trying different jobs for a day. I love the feature; it's pure silliness and making fun of myself. Viewers have responded well, and suggestions are pouring in for new jobs to try.

Aly is still Aly. She hates me, but we co-exist on set, and unless you know the story between us, you'd think we were the best of friends. One lesson I've learned is that you can't make everyone like you, or even respect you, and in this case, it's Aly. And you know what? As long as she stays out of my business, which she has, I'm fine with it.

The tabloids still feature Maxime and me from time to time but not on any regular basis now. After the whole Tom-bomb dropped, and I released only one comment, that while I wished Tom the best in life, I was in a new relationship with Maxime and very much in love, it died off. Tom called me, of course, but I never returned it and then blocked his number. Within a week of his confession, he was snapped making out with a girl from a different season of *Is It Love?* in a famous L.A. sushi bar.

So much for me being the love of his life, I think, laughing aloud at what a Grade A wanker he is.

I must thank both Charlotte and Tom for the life I have now. If I hadn't been pushed to go on *Is It Love?* by

Charlotte, I wouldn't have met Tom. If Tom hadn't broken my heart, I wouldn't have fled to Europe.

And I never would have been at the café where Maxime first saw me.

As we continue walking, I begin to get a feeling that I've been here before.

"This feels familiar," I say to Maxime.

"Yeah?" Maxime asks.

Then I see it.

My heart swoons as I realize where we are going.

We are going back to the same café where he noticed me for the first time.

"Maxime," I gasp excitedly, "it's our café!"

"It is. I thought this time we should have a cup of coffee together, don't you think?" he asks.

I smile. "Absolutely."

We enter the café, and Maxime leads me to the same terrace, filled with leafy green trees and flowers in abundant bloom.

I stop walking when I spot a table with a small white cake, covered with sprinkles in various shades of pink, two glasses of champagne, rimmed with the same pink sprinkles, and a bouquet of vibrant red poppies on the tabletop.

My hand flies up to my mouth.

"Maxime!" I cry, delighted beyond words. "Oh my God, look at this!"

He turns to face me and drops a sweet kiss on my lips. "Happy anniversary."

"Oh, Maxime," I gasp, emotion filling me. "I love you."

"I love you, too," he says, leading me to the table and pulling out a chair for me.

I sink down into it, staring at the beautiful cake he arranged for us to share today.

"It's perfect," I say, moved by his sweetness. "Look at all the *sprinkles!*"

A smile lights up his face. "Today had to have sprinkles and poppies."

He sits down across from me, taking my hand in his. "I can't believe it was a year ago that I sat at the table right behind you, thinking you were the most beautiful woman I had ever seen. I wanted to get up and take your sadness away. When you left, and I watched you walk away, I had this feeling I had let someone slip away. I don't know how I knew it. We didn't even exchange a word, but I knew you were special."

I grow emotional. "We were meant to share that moment. Fate knew the right time to bring us back together."

"I believe that, too," Maxime says. "I thought I'd never believe in love again. I realize now that was all part of the plan. We had to have our first loves to find our *real* love. We had to be broken, we had to heal, and we had to grow to have the love we have now."

He stands up.

"Maxime?" I ask.

He moves around next to me. I watch as he retrieves a ring box from his jacket pocket and lowers himself to one knee.

"Oh my God!" I gasp, as I realize this isn't an anniversary celebration anymore.

The love of my life is about to propose to me.

"Skye," Maxime says, his voice strong and unwavering, "you are the woman I was meant to love for the rest of my life. I love your strength and your desire to make people realize their value. You entertain people and bring lightness to their lives. You support me. Believe in me. You make me laugh and, God, you make me happy. You make me a better man. There is no one I want to share my life with other than you."

I'm shaking as he opens the box, revealing a breathtaking, *pink*, cushion-cut diamond ring.

"Skye Amelia Reeve," he says, "will you marry me?"

I begin nodding frantically.

"Yes. Yes. Yes! I will marry you, Maxime Philippe Laurent!"

The café erupts in applause as I lean down and joyfully kiss Maxime. My private love proposed in public, which makes my heart sing. He knew this place was the beginning for us, even if we didn't know it at the time, and this was the only place for us to start our forever story.

We've come full circle now, I think, overwhelmed with happiness.

I lift my head and see pure happiness in Maxime's blue-green eyes, the eyes that I will look into for the rest of my life.

"I can't wait to marry you!" I cry happily. I put my hands on his face and kiss him again. I break the kiss, and happy tears fill my eyes. "I love you, I love you, I love you so much. I would go through everything again if it meant finding you, my love. You are my everything."

"I love you, Skye," Maxime says. Then he flashes me a grin. "Now may I put this ring on your finger?"

"Oh my God, the ring!" I gasp. "Yes!"

Maxime's smile broadens as he takes my hand in his. He carefully slips the gorgeous pink diamond on it, one I know he picked because it reminded him of my love of pink sprinkles. I stare down at the breathtaking ring on my hand, the one the man of my dreams carefully selected for me.

Maxime rises and takes my hand in his. My private man, who loves his quiet life in the rugged mountains of Colorado, is going to be my husband. We'll always be a team, no matter what life throws at us. We'll love each other and support each other and continue to build a life filled with love and happiness.

I kiss him and smile against his lips.

Our life will also be filled with lots of sprinkles, I think happily, *which will be sweeter because I will be sharing them with my Maxime.*

What a delicious and beautiful life indeed.

THE END

Will Gavin get his happy ending, too ? Find out in *Outscored,* the next book in the Rinkside in the Rockies series, coming in the fall of 2019. To keep up with release information, sign up for my newsletter or follow me on BookBub.

Made in the USA
Middletown, DE
10 October 2020